FINDING
MS. WRIGHT

FINDING MS. WRIGHT

A Jo Jacuzzo Mystery

ANNE SEALE

alyson books
los angeles

Celebrating Twenty-Five Years

MANUFACTURED IN THE UNITED STATES OF AMERICA.

THIS TRADE PAPERBACK ORIGINAL IS PUBLISHED BY ALYSON BOOKS,
P.O. BOX 4371, LOS ANGELES, CALIFORNIA 90078-4371.
DISTRIBUTION IN THE UNITED KINGDOM BY TURNAROUND PUBLISHER SERVICES LTD.,
UNIT 3, OLYMPIA TRADING ESTATE, COBURG ROAD, WOOD GREEN,
LONDON N22 6TZ ENGLAND.

FIRST EDITION: APRIL 2005

05 06 07 08 09 **a** 10 9 8 7 6 5 4 3 2 1

ISBN 1-55583-902-9
ISBN-13 978-1-55583-902-4

LIBRARY OF CONGRESS CATALOGING-IN-PUBLICATION DATA
  SEALE, ANNE.
    FINDING MS. WRIGHT : A JO JACUZZO MYSTERY / ANNE SEALE.—1ST ED.
    ISBN 1-55583-902-9; ISBN-13 978-1-55583-902-4
    1. WOMEN PRIVATE INVESTIGATORS—OKLAHOMA—FICTION. 2. MISSING
PERSONS—FICTION. 3. OKLAHOMA—FICTION. 4. LESBIANS—FICTION. I. TITLE.
PS3619.E255F56 2005
813'.6—DC22   2004063788

CREDITS
COVER PHOTOGRAPHY BY CHARLES KREBS/BOTANICA COLLECTION/GETTY IMAGES.
COVER DESIGN BY MATT SAMS.

for Ms. King and my kids

1

I was well into the drenched innards of Oklahoma when I hit a detour that sent me off on a narrow side road. *No problem,* I told myself. *It'll rejoin the main highway in a couple of miles.* But it didn't. Like the Energizer Bunny, the detour kept going and going. There were no campgrounds on it, no motels.

The night was one of the blackest I'd ever seen, and the raindrops splattering on my windshield were easily the biggest. I considered writing to the editors of *Guinness World Records* so they could add an entry:

Blackest Night and Biggest Raindrop Combination:
Unknown detour in northeastern Oklahoma, April 2003.
Contributed by Jo Jacuzzo of Buffalo, New York

The road had no shoulder to speak of, just a few inches of gravel along the edge. I watched for a wide spot where I could pull my little motor home off the blacktop to wait out the storm, but none materialized, so I soldiered on. "Soldier on" was one of Great-aunt Concetta's favorite phrases. She'd used it every time I threatened to quit high school—not that I called and told her. *Somebody* did, however, because soon the phone would ring and I'd be blasted with, "Soldier on, Jo-girl. You won't regret it."

I never did quit school, but I did regret it. I regretted it every night when I didn't finish my homework until 3 A.M. I couldn't do it any earlier because I had to deliver pizza in order to make the payments on my pre-owned 1984 Dodge Power Ram with a 318 V8 2-barrel carb. Now, *there* was a truck.

So I soldiered on down the narrow road in the heavy rain, pondering Great-aunt Concetta in general and my 29th birthday party last Saturday night in particular. I'd rather have had a quiet celebration at home with Mom and her lover, Rose, but in our family it was a tradition to celebrate birthdays with a potluck at Great-aunt Concetta's house with every relative who lived within a half-day's drive and couldn't come up with a prior commitment.

My birthday was actually Friday, but Great-aunt Concetta called in a dither a few days before. "We can't have your celebration on Good Friday," she said. "Everyone will be fasting!" It was a bum excuse because she had an age dispensation, and everybody else in the family had left the church, a fact that she knew well and brought up often.

The real reason for the postponement, I found out later from my cousin Kimmy who heard it from her mother, was that Great-aunt Concetta's VCR was acting up and she didn't want to take a chance on missing *JAG*. In any case, we celebrated my birthday on Saturday, April 19.

Mom and Rose brought cheese polenta and creamy coleslaw,

my two favorite foods in the world. They were excellent, as was every other dish on the table except the chocolate cake Kimmy baked. Her new boyfriend was allergic to wheat so she'd substituted soybean flour. Somewhere in the cake-making process the flour reverted back to bean—I broke two tines off a plastic fork trying to hack a piece off.

Seeing that, Great-aunt Concetta put down her fork, picked up her slice of cake, and bit into it. Her eyes got big, and when she removed it from her mouth there was a big yellow tooth sticking out. We all shrieked, and that was pretty much the end of the party.

The answering machine was blinking insistently when Mom, Rose, and I walked into our kitchen that night. It was my buddy Weezie saying she needed my help: Her ex was missing.

But Mom wouldn't leave until Great-aunt Concetta was in bed asleep, her broken dentures in a glass by her bed next to a note from Kimmy promising to pay for the repair.

A missing ex didn't seem like a problem to me. It's been my experience that the problems begin when the ex shows up. But bright and early the next morning, I drove over to Marlo's Diner, where Weezie was day manager. She waved from the depths of the kitchen and sent out an orange juice. I carried it to a booth that looked out over busy Elmwood Avenue—great for people-watching. I was sure if I sat there for a week, every lesbian in greater Buffalo would pass by at least once.

It wasn't long before Weezie slid into the other side of the booth and handed me a small box labeled GRAND CENTRAL STATIONERS. In a toneless rasp, she sang, "Happy birthday to Jo, happy birthday to Jo, happy birthday to Jo-oh, happy birthday to Jo."

"Geez, thanks, Weezie," I said, ripping the lid off. Inside was a little leather-bound notebook with a ballpoint pen stuck in a slot in the spine. I opened the book, flipped through the blank pages, closed it, turned it over, and opened it again. I didn't know what to say. I truly didn't. Usually, Weezie got me really cool gifts, like baseball caps or DVDs: things I could use.

"Do you like it?" she asked.

"Sure! Sure I do." I took the pen from the slot and made loops on the first page. "It works," I said.

"I thought it might come in handy sometimes, you know, like when you're off traveling in your…whatsisname."

My whatsisname was Dan'l, the motor home I designed and built with help from a guy in town who makes custom RVs. I called the motor home Dan'l for two reasons. The first was that guys often name their vehicles and watercraft after women and refer to them as "her," so I thought I'd like to have a "him" to cart *me* around. Tit for tat, as Rose always says.

The second reason had to do with a large, unexpected inheritance last year, which gave me both the money to pay for him and the precious leisure to take him exploring. Dan'l was truly a *boon*.

I put the notebook back in its box. "So was the message about the missing ex a ruse to get me over here so you could shower me with gifts?" I asked.

"I wish it was." Weezie slumped against the back of the seat. "I sure wish it was."

"Who *is* your ex?" I asked. Weezie and I had been best friends for five years, and I'd never known her to date anyone more than twice.

"Her name's Honey Lou."

"Honey Lou?" I said. "What kind of a name is that?"

She frowned. "It's a perfectly good name. As good as Weezie or Jo."

"Well, sure it is. You just don't hear it too often. What's her last name?"

"Wright." She spat it out.

"You like the name Honey Lou, but not the name Wright?"

"Jo, this is serious," she said.

"I'm sorry." I tossed down the last drop of juice. "Hey, that was good. Do you squeeze it here?"

"You're kidding, right?" She called to the counterperson to bring me a refill.

"So how long has Honey Lou Wright been missing?" I asked.

"Her mother hasn't heard from her for almost two weeks, and she's scared stiff something's happened to her."

"Did she notify the police?"

"Sure, but all they told her was Honey Lou was probably off drinking or doing drugs and would turn up pretty soon."

"She has a drug and alcohol problem?" I asked.

"That's what her mother says. She didn't when I knew her."

"When did you know her?"

"Back in high school."

"High school!" I threw out my arms in astonishment and knocked a plastic glass of juice out of the approaching waiter's hand. Some splashed on me and some on him, but most went on the floor. He rolled his eyes and went for the mop.

I winced. "Sorry."

"Don't worry, the floor can use a cleaning," Weezie said. "And, actually, so can he."

I dabbed at my sleeve with a paper napkin. "So was Honey Lou your high school sweetheart?"

"Yes," she said, "and I should've never let her go."

"Why did you?"

"She got married."

"To a man?" I screeched, careful to keep my elbows in.

"Yeah, it was right after we graduated." Weezie let her head fall so low, I got a bird's-eye view of her D.A. We both watched her finger spread a drop of orange juice into a wide circle.

"But, Weezie, didn't you go to high school in Oklahoma?" I asked.

"Yeah."

"Where's Honey Lou missing from?"

"Oklahoma."

"So what do you want *me* to do?"

She gripped the edge of the table with both hands. Her massive shoulders shook, and a tear splashed into the circle of juice. "Go f-find her," she gasped.

If it hadn't been for the birthday gift, the spilled juice, and the tear, I would have told her I needed time to think about it. Instead, I heard myself say "OK."

After leaving the diner, I drove out to Uncle Greg's to fetch Dan'l. Greg and his wife Nola had moved to the suburb of Hamburg years ago so they could be near the horse track. I kept my motor home in their garage addition because there was no room at the house in south Buffalo where I lived with Mom and Rose—their two sub-compacts took up the whole driveway. I had to park my Ford Ranger on the street in front...unless, of course, the neighbors got there first.

Uncle Greg had built the garage addition to house a big boat he no longer owned. When I asked him if I could keep Dan'l in it, he said no because he didn't want to move out all the furniture he'd stored in there the last time his wife redecorated. But when I offered him a hundred dollars a month, he said he'd been meaning to get rid of all that old junk anyway. I could see trifecta odds flashing in his eyes.

It looked as if nobody was home this morning, which was fine with me, since Greg and Nola had been at my birthday potluck last night and would want to rehash the tooth incident.

I shoved their garage door up and stood gazing at Dan'l, marveling that I owned such a mechanical wonder. He'd started out life as a GM cargo van with a heavy-duty engine, then I'd had all kinds of storage tanks installed in his gut, along with a sink, refrigerator, microwave, a tiny bathroom, a bed that doubled as a sofa, and, finally, a 14-inch flat-screen TV/DVD combo. I'd decided against adding a built-in computer too, only because I knew if I did I'd never venture outside.

Dan'l was only four months old. The farthest I'd taken him was to South Carolina for two weeks in January to tie up a business deal. I'd been thinking of going to the Dakotas this summer, and maybe even taking him on the car ferry from Washington to Vancouver Island.

Going to the state of Oklahoma had never crossed my mind.

2

Weezie called the next morning. "Are you leaving today?"

"I can't leave today," I told her. "I have a ton of stuff to do, including laundry. You don't want me meeting Honey Lou's mother in a smelly old T-shirt, do you?"

"It's Monday. I'm off. I'll come wash your clothes so you can do the other stuff."

"Absolutely not!" I said. What if one of Mom's Maidenform Body Hugs had landed in my basket by mistake? Weezie would never look at me the same way again. "No, Weezie, I'll do my own laundry, and I promise I'll take off tomorrow morning. OK?"

She came over anyway, late in the afternoon while I was stocking Dan'l's pantry with bread, peanut butter, and Mom's homemade jelly from the grapes in our backyard arbor.

"Did you pack the notebook I gave you?" she asked.

"It's in the glove compartment."

"Good. Keep it handy. It's for clues and stuff." She followed me up to my room and sat on the bed, chatting about plans she'd made for my trip while I rolled up clothes so they'd fit in Dan'l's compact drawers. "My friend Rube says you can park at her boat repair and plug into her electricity," she told me. "Is that all right?"

"Sure," I said. Weezie had insisted on reimbursing me for all my expenses, so I figured she didn't want me staying in fancy RV parks. "Hopefully I won't be there too long, anyway," I said. "Who knows, by the time I get to her mother's house, Honey Lou may have shown up."

"I suppose that's a possibility," she said. "I talked to her mother an hour ago and she told me Honey Lou's husband beat her up bad before she disappeared. She could be somewhere hiding out from him."

"Geez!" I said.

"If you find her and that's the case, bring her to me, and I'll protect her."

Since I'd seen Weezie strong-arm unruly patrons to the door of the diner without breaking a sweat, I didn't doubt it. "So have you been e-mailing with Honey Lou or something?" I asked. "How do you know she wants to come here?"

"I haven't seen or talked to her since graduation day. That's the day she told me she was getting married." Weezie looked so sad, it could have happened yesterday.

"Honey Lou left you for a man, what, 10 years ago, and you'd still take her back?" I asked.

She didn't hesitate a second. "Yes. I've never stopped loving her. There's not a day goes by that I don't think about her and want her with me."

Wow, who knew Weezie was so deep? I figured this explained why she never dated anyone more than twice.

While I was trying to decide which of my cutoffs was still wearable in polite company, she took a scrap of paper from her pocket and asked, "Can I use your phone? It's long-distance."

"Use this." I tossed her my cell phone. Signing the contract for it had been one of the great mistakes of my life. To use up the national minutes I was paying for, I found myself calling out-of-town people I didn't really want to talk to, like former classmates from my certified nurse's assistant courses. One woman hadn't remembered me, even after I described myself and a torrid night we'd spent together. When she in turn described herself, I realized she wasn't the person I'd thought she was. If color traveled across cell towers, her phone would have turned bright red.

"Is that you, Mrs. Lemming?" Weezie said into the mouthpiece. "This is Weezie again. I'm at my friend Jo's house now—she's the one I'm sending to Oklahoma to help you find Honey Lou. Hold on a minute—I'm going to put her on."

What? If there was anything I hated, it was being forced to talk on the phone to somebody I'd never met. I shook my head and whispered, "Weezie, no."

She put her palm over the mouthpiece. "Come on, Jo. It's Honey Lou's mother."

"I'll talk to her when I get there."

She made sad eyes. "Please?"

I glared at her and took the phone. "Hello?" At least we were using up prepaid airtime.

"Is this Weezie's friend Jo?" It was spoken in a slow drawl. The high pitch of her voice was almost childlike.

"Yes, ma'am."

"You're coming here to find my Honey Lou?"

"I'm going to try."

"I didn't want to ask Weezie, sweetie, but are you one of those private eyes? Are you going to be sending me a bill?"

"No. I'm just a regular person with a bunch of time on my hands."

"Well, that's OK, then. Will you be staying with us?"

"No, I guess Weezie's made other arrangements," I said, wondering how I could work around to "Goodbye."

Weezie saved me the trouble. "Jo, don't hang up," she said. "I want to talk to her again."

I told Mrs. Lemming I'd be seeing her soon and handed Weezie the phone, into which she said a lot of things about me that were so nice I'd be embarrassed to repeat them anywhere but on a résumé. After hanging up, Mrs. Lemming probably knelt down and gave thanks for the Jo Jacuzzos of the world.

Then Weezie handed me a map of Oklahoma with my route from Interstate 40 to Mrs. Lemming's town, Worthing, highlighted in hot pink. She said she was sending me on a series of back roads—that way I'd be able to see how beautiful her home state was. She'd also marked big X's on every spot I might want to check out, including the Oil City Grill in Tulsa that she said "serves up the best chicken-fried steak in the state."

"What's the difference between chicken-fried steak and steak-fried steak?" I asked.

"It's thickly breaded, and the gravy is to die for. Be sure to get some deep-fried okra on the side."

I made a face. Anything called *okra* couldn't be very tasty.

"No, really, it's good," she said. "Promise me you'll try it. If you do, you'll thank me for sending you to Oklahoma, even in tornado season."

"Even in what?"

"It's tornado season in all the plains states right now," Weezie said. "Didn't they teach you about Tornado Alley in school?"

"I don't think so." I got a flash of the Wicked Witch cackling as she pedaled an airborne bike round and round with a terrified Toto in the basket.

"Maybe they don't bother 'less you live in it. Tornado Alley runs across the middle of the country."

"I could wait a few days to leave," I said. "When is the season over?"

"It's just starting. But don't worry, Jo, you'll never see a real twister. All the time I lived there, we only went in the storm cellar twice, and both times it missed us by miles."

"What's a storm cellar? Like a basement?"

"Ours was a big hole in the ground out away from the house, with a thick wood trapdoor. Ma made us climb down the ladder while Pa fetched the family valuables, and when he finally came down, he pulled the door tight, shutting out all the light. It was cold and damp, and there were spiderwebs all over. My sisters and I huddled against the dirt wall and just shook."

"Geez, Weezie," I said.

"Yeah, but don't worry. Nothing like that's going to happen when you're there. Wish I could go."

"Why don't you?!" I said. "I'll buy you a plane ticket."

"Remember, Jo? I used up all my vacation days at Christmastime."

I did remember. She'd spent the holidays in St. Louis visiting her sister, brother-in-law, and new baby niece. I'd served as her airport taxi, and I hit severe snowstorms coming and going. And now she was sending me to a place called Tornado Alley? What price buddyship?

"Enjoy Oklahoma, and find my Honey Lou, OK?" She gave me a bear hug and left.

When Mom and Rose came home, I told them, "Weezie says it's tornado season in Oklahoma right now."

"Well, that's kind of scary, isn't it?" Mom said.

"Yeah, kind of. Does Buffalo ever get tornadoes?"

After thinking a minute, she said, "Not that I can remember. Seems I read about one in the southern counties some years ago. I don't think there was much damage."

Rose said, "But Delia, don't you remember the tornado over near Batavia that pushed a semi off the road and killed the driver?" Then she saw Mom's subtle shake of the head and added, "Of course, you know what crazy drivers those guys are."

"Do you know what to do in case you run into one?" Mom asked me.

"No." I knew what was coming. I said it in unison with her: "Why don't you go look it up?"

In my room, I logged on and Googled "tornado." One site said to crouch under a stairwell or in an interior hallway if a tornado was about to hit. *Yeah, sure, Dan'l has lots of those.* And to be sure to stay away from windows. Wait, Dan'l *did* have lots of those.

But it didn't matter what Dan'l had or didn't have, because they went on to say that if you happened to be in a vehicle of any kind you'd need to get out immediately and lie facedown on the ground away from trees.

Later, when I was in bed hugging my pillow and picturing myself frantically pressing my body into the dirt while a howling wind tried to suck me into the ether, Mom and Rose passed my door on their way to bed. "Sleep well," they called.

Yeah, sure.

3

When I came downstairs in the morning, Mom and Rose were in the kitchen cooking a dozen eggs: Rose was scrambling six for our breakfast while Mom boiled the rest for me to take on the road. I ate quickly and went out to start up Dan'l's engine. Then I had to come in again because I'd forgotten to brush my teeth. I could have done it in Dan'l, but one of the goals in RVing is to use your waste tanks as seldom as possible because emptying them is no picnic in the park.

It was still an hour before they had to leave for Mary Talbert High School where Rose taught Spanish and Mom was secretary to the principal, so they came outside in their robes and slippers to wave and call, "Drive safe" and "We love you." Mr. Wing next door appeared on his porch and shouted, "Watch out for the other guy." One of the college students in an upstairs apartment opened a window and yelled something that translated loosely to "Isn't it a little early to be making all that noise?"

A block later, as I turned the corner onto the street that would eventually spit me out on Interstate 90, I could see Mom and Rose still waving. I hoped I hadn't forgotten anything, because after a send-off like that there was no way I could go back.

Despite Weezie's thoughtful map, I'd plotted my own route, careful to steer clear of cities where I had relatives. If they found out I'd been in the area and didn't stop in, I'd never hear the end of it. "Jo couldn't even spare a minute for a cup of coffee?" they'd complain to Mom.

This meant I couldn't go near Pittsburgh, Cleveland, Cincinnati, or Minot, North Dakota. Minot would be easy to avoid, but the other three were right in the way.

At Ashtabula, I dropped south, wending my way to Charleston, West Virginia. From there I went west and south again to Nashville, where I picked up Interstate 40 and stayed on it to Fort Smith, Arkansas. Not exactly what you'd call "as the crow flies"—unless the crow had been eating fermented cherries.

At Fort Smith, I gassed up and started following Weezie's map. Her highlighted line took me south on 540 and spat me out on a two-lane in Oklahoma. Weezie had penned above this road ENJOY THE SCENERY—not knowing, of course, that it would be pitch-dark and storming like crazy. And that's when I hit the detour from hell.

Everything was pitch-black except for my headlights on the driving rain and the eerie green of the digital clock; 11:11, it said, looking like the highway I'd been staring at for two long days.

The wind grew steadily stronger. Dan'l lurched into the other lane every time a gust hit. Flashes of lightning lit the dancing treetops like strobes, and dismembered branches scudded across the road. Every once in a while a car would pull up behind us, honk impatiently, and zoom around. "See, Dan'l," I'd say, "that car is on his way somewhere. If we keep going, we'll get there too…won't we?" He didn't bother answering.

I slowed to a crawl and scanned the shoulder for a wide spot. When I spied a graveled entrance to a field, I pulled onto it, flicked off the headlights, and sat in the darkness, rocking with the gusts. Then it occurred to me that I'd better check the bubble in Dan'l to see if he was sitting level. Parking at a slant wasn't good for his refrigerator—the coolant might jam up. The level told me I needed to go out and put boards under the right-hand tires. Bummer.

Whirling dirt peppered my face as I fetched the boards from an outside storage bin. After positioning them in front of the tires, I went back inside and drove up on them, setting the liquid sloshing in Dan'l's tanks. It reminded me I'd had to pee for miles, so I swung into the tiny bathroom. It was quiet inside, a gently swaying womb complete with the gurgle of amniotic fluid. I considered staying in there to wait out the storm, but the seat was too hard and I was too jumpy.

After packing the aisle until I became dizzy from constantly pivoting, I perched on the edge of the sofa/bed, nibbling my fingernails and listening to the wind. It would die down for a while, giving me hope the storm was over, Then, without warning, a gust would hit like a wrecking ball, lifting Dan'l's weight off one side and slamming it back down. I'd never heard of a motor home being blown over in a storm, but there were lots of things I'd never heard of.

Some of the gusts were accompanied by cracking noises. I jumped to the window, but whatever had hit Dan'l's side was gone with the wind.

I wondered if this was the way tornadoes started. Maybe I

should get out right now, run into the field, and lie facedown in the dirt. *All right,* I thought. *I'll give it 10 more minutes.*

Craving information, I cranked up the antenna and played around with the TV until I got a grainy version of the *Tonight Show*. A ribbon was running across Jay Leno's chin with the names of counties where a tornado watch was in effect. The problem was, I had no way of knowing what county I was in—I didn't even know what road I was on.

I turned off the TV, opened the side door, and scanned the sky for funnels. Seeing nothing but blackness, I pulled my head back in before it could get conked by whatever had been cracking Dan'l's side.

Not one car had passed in either direction since I'd pulled over. I could have been the last person in Oklahoma.

So, Matt, what do the experts think happened to all the people who used to live in that great state?

Well, Katie, satellite photos are showing a giant funnel cloud heading toward Jupiter, with arms and legs sticking out. It's probably them.

But, Matt, why do they think the funnel cloud went off in that direction?

It's still speculation, Katie, but NASA thinks it may have been following a detour.

A little after 2, things got very quiet. Either the big blow was over or I was in the twister's eye. I switched the TV back on. They were airing a *Seinfeld* rerun, the one where Kramer gets a hot tub. The tornado-watch ribbon was gone.

It looked like I'd live to see another day, although if they were all like this I wasn't sure that was a wonderful thing.

I lowered the antenna, retrieved my leveling boards, and pulled back onto the road. Within a few miles the detour joined up with my original highway, and I drove into a little town. I didn't see a WELCOME TO sign, but the name of the town must have been Everly. In the yellow light of three streetlamps I could make out signs for the Everly Food Center, the Everly Branch of the Sooner State Bank, and the Holy Palace of Our Sovereign Monarch Church of Everly.

To my right was a boarded-up gas station with the letters S, I, N, C, and L mounted above a bay door. I figured a tornado must have taken the final A, I, and R. I pulled in and turned off the engine, hoping no one would care if I spent the night. If they did, too bad. I was so tired that if they towed me away, I probably wouldn't have noticed.

When I woke, sunlight was filtering through the pleated blinds next to my bed. I raised the nearest one an eye-width. On the other side of the street, several cars were parked at the Everly Food Center, and the clock on the bank read 2:30. *2:30!* I checked Dan'l's clock and my sports watch. Both said 9:15. *Better.* Then I remembered I'd gained an hour on the road, so it was actually 10:15 in Buffalo. I could hear Weezie fretting, "Are you going to sleep all day, Jo? This is the last time I'm sending *you* to find one of my exes." I jumped behind the wheel and headed out of town.

After an hour, I pulled over and checked Weezie's map. I was only about 20 miles from Worthing, where Honey Lou's mother, Mrs. Lemming, lived. Between here and there, however, was a big pink X with a circle around it. Next to it Weezie had written MOTEL—CHECK FOR HONEY LOU. It made sense—if she was hiding from an abusive husband, she might pick a place that was near her mother's house. In any case, motel rooms had showers, and I badly needed one.

The Très Magnifique Motel was V-shaped, with five units to a side and an office in the crotch. Next to the driveway was an eight-foot Eiffel Tower holding a green neon VACANCY sign. It blinked bleakly in the morning sun. I pulled in, parked, and did a walk-around check of Dan'l, looking for dents and scratches from last night's windstorm. Miraculously, there weren't any.

No one was in the motel office, so I hit the chrome bell on the counter a couple of times. There was a flush and a muffled "Hold on!" Soon a woman came out of a bathroom, patting her hairdo as if whatever she'd done in there might have mussed it. "*Bon jour*," she said with a Midwestern twang.

"Hi there," I said. "I'm looking for a woman named Honey Lou Wright. Would you check to see if she might be staying here?"

"*Non*," she said.

"You won't check?"

"I don't have to check, *chérie. Non ici.*"

Thanks to a year of high school French and my Lucie Blue Tremblay CD, I understood her. "Ms. Wright may be using a different name," I said.

"Like what?"

"I have no idea."

"Well, what does she look like?" she asked.

"She's about my age, but otherwise I don't know."

"Then how are you going to know when you find her?"

She had a point, but I wasn't going to admit it. "Do you have any female guests who are about 29?" I asked.

"I have only one female guest right now, and that's her right there." She pointed out the window at a woman and a man who were coming out of a motel room. The woman looked older than 29, but who knew what drugs and alcohol might do to a person? They started down the sidewalk, then stopped abruptly and exchanged words. The man grabbed the woman's arm and started pulling her toward a black Buick Regal. I ran outside, calling, "Honey? Honey Lou?"

The man let go. The woman immediately raised her fist and smacked him on the side of the face. "Bastard!" she said. He stood by the car rubbing his cheekbone while she flounced over, high heels clacking on the cement. "What was that you just called my boyfriend?" she demanded.

"Not him, *you*," I said. "I mean, I'm looking for a woman named Honey Lou. I thought you might be her."

She surveyed me, from my short hair to my sneakers, and said, "No, I'm not her. My name's Wanda. What's yours?'

"Uh…Jo."

She lowered her voice. "Well, Jo, why don't you come by this afternoon about 2? Room 7. *He'll* be gone."

"Are you OK, then?" I asked.

"Of course I am," she said and clacked back to the Buick. The engine gunned, and they were gone.

Turning to go back in the office, I almost ran into the clerk standing in the doorway. "Was that your *friend*?" she said as if she hadn't been listening the whole time.

"No," I said, and headed for Dan'l. I did need a shower, but no way was I going to give this person any business—I didn't like her. *Je ne sais quoi.*

4

Mrs. Lemming's house was on a narrow, busy street. In order not to block a lane, I had to park with two wheels on her grass. I'd have much preferred to pull into her long double driveway, but it was already chock-full of vehicles: I counted six cars and two pickups. Was she having a party? On a Thursday morning?

Not finding a doorbell, I rapped on the narrow edge of the aluminum screen door. There was a good-size hole in the middle of the screen, and when no one answered, I reached through the hole and knocked on the actual door.

A face appeared in the middle of three descending glass panes next to the jamb. The door opened and I was blasted by cold air and a screaming TV.

"Whatever you're selling, I can't talk to you now," drawled a woman wearing a humongous red-flowered muumuu.

"We're in the middle of watching *The View,* you see." She slammed the door.

The View? *Are they having a* The View *party?* I checked my sports watch: 10:50. With any luck, the show would be over at 11. I sat on the concrete stoop watching cars zoom past, wincing whenever one zoomed too close to Dan'l.

I mused about how the TV schedule was controlling my life lately. My birthday party had been postponed because of *JAG,* and now my investigation into Honey Lou's appearance was being held up by *The View*. It reminded me that I wanted to be settled tonight in time to catch *CSI*.

At 11:05, I rose and knocked again. When the face appeared in the window, I hollered, "I'm not selling anything. It's Jo Jacuzzo. Weezie LaDuca sent me!"

The door flew open. The woman in the muumuu said, "Well, Jo, why didn't you say so? Come on in. I didn't think you'd be here until…well, I don't know when I thought you'd be here."

The TV had stopped its blasting. "Is *The View* over?" I asked.

"Oh, my, yes. Are you a fan? Joy did a fantasy wedding—it was great! I'm sorry you missed it."

"That's OK," I said. "You must be Mrs. Lemming."

She nodded. "Call me Sylvie. Come in the kitchen, Jo. We're making lunch." I followed the muumuu through a living room into a frigid kitchen.

Another muumuued woman who could have been Sylvie's much older twin was sitting at a table peeling potatoes. "This is my mother, Flo," Sylvie drawled. "Ma, this is Jo, Weezie's friend."

"Who?" Flo asked.

"Ma doesn't hear too well," Sylvie told me. "She's supposed to be wearing a hearing aid, but she keeps losing it—it's around here somewhere." She scoped the cluttered room as if the hearing aid might pop out from between the canisters and piles of dishes and cookbooks. When it didn't, she yelled in her mother's direction, "Where's your hearing aid?"

"Don't know, don't care. Who'd you say this is?" Sylvie's mom had the same drawl but an octave lower.

"You remember Weezie?" Sylvie asked her.

Flo stared at me. "Weezie? Dear Lord, what happened? You used to have meat on your bones. Look, Sylvie, she's so skinny, she's shivering."

"Ma," Sylvie hollered, "this isn't Weezie. This is Weezie's *friend.*"

"My name's Jo," I yelled. "I'm very glad to meet you."

"Haven't seen *you* in a long time neither," Flo said. "Where in tarnation you been keeping yourself, Weezie?"

Sylvie heaved a great sigh. "Ignore her, Jo. But she's right, you *are* shivering. How about a cup of coffee to warm you up?" She picked up a mug from the counter, turned it upside-down, and shook it.

"No, thanks. I'll be fine," I said, perching on a gingham-padded stool. "Any news of your daughter?"

Another great sigh. "I just can't imagine what happened to that girl. What's today? Thursday? She's been gone 16 days now." She took a package of hamburger from the refrigerator and started forming patties.

"When's the last time you saw her?" I asked.

"She was here for dinner the Sunday before she disappeared—I remember because we had some of that tough venison Chuck killed last year. Then she went to work that Monday and Tuesday, and nobody's seen her since."

I didn't want to ask, but I had to. "Weezie tells me Honey Lou has a problem with drinking. And maybe drugs?"

"Drinking. Drugs. Men. She has a problem with all of them. Wish I knew where I went wrong raising her. Why couldn't she settle down and have children like a normal person. You have children, Jo?"

"No," I said.

"You neither, huh? I sure would like some grandkids." She washed her hands and opened the freezer door. With loud bangs, three cans of orange juice fell on the floor and rolled in three directions.

"Holy Toledo, Sylvie!" her mother yelped. "I almost peeled my finger."

"Sorry, Ma. That's probably enough potatoes, anyway. You can quit now."

I rounded up the cans and Sylvie put them back in. As she dug out a bag of corn, I said, "Weezie said Honey Lou got married soon after graduating from high school."

"Indeed, she did," Sylvie said. "It was a lovely wedding. I wore mauve."

"Weezie also told me her husband is abusive."

"He is, but we're talking apples and oranges here, Jo. Honey Lou's first husband was a pretty nice guy. Unfortunately, they got divorced after a few years and she got married again. This latest one, Baxter Wright, is a mean sucker. If she's dead, he's the one that done it."

"You think she's dead?"

"Bite your tongue, Jo!"

"I'm sorry."

"It's easy to give up," Sylvie said, "but we gotta keep hoping. We gotta look on the bright side. Every cloud—you know what I mean? On the other hand, if she's not dead, why doesn't she call? Honey Lou never went more than two days in her whole life without calling. Why doesn't she *call*, Jo?" She raised the bag of corn like she was going to throw it at me.

Instinctively ducking, I said, "I don't know."

She slammed the corn on the table and smacked it with her fist, breaking the kernels apart. "In any case," she said, "her car's been here at our place since the end of March. When the cops told me she might've just went off for a while, I asked them, 'How could she go off without her car? That's what *I'd* like to know!' "

"Why is Honey Lou's car here?"

"Needs fixing. Chuck fixes cars for people on his days off. He's a little behind right now." She looked over at her mother. "I said that's enough potatoes, Ma. You can stop peeling." Flo picked up another potato and started in on it.

"So are the police out looking for Honey Lou?" I asked.

"I don't think so. I called them last week. They said it's still an open case, but they've run out of leads."

"Do you think I should talk to them?"

"I can't imagine they'd tell you anything they aren't telling me," she said, pouring the corn in a microwave dish.

"You've got a point," I said happily. I'd done my share of dealing with authorities, and it wasn't my favorite thing.

"Sylvie," Flo said, "Look at the girl. She's turning blue."

Sylvie looked my way. "Good grief, she is." She took a striped dish towel from a drawer and draped it across my shoulders. I started to protest, but it actually felt good.

"Does Honey Lou's husband—what's his name, Baxter— have a car?" I asked.

"If you can call an old junker like that a car, yes, he does. The cops asked me that very same thing, insinuating she might have gone off with him. I told them Honey Lou wouldn't go anywhere with Baxter now—not after he sent her to the woman's shelter, she wouldn't."

"She was in a woman's shelter?"

"Sure. Just before she disappeared. He knocked one of her

teeth out. She had him arrested, but they couldn't keep him. So I think maybe she's hiding out from him somewhere. But if she was, she'd still call *me*, wouldn't she? You staying for lunch, Jo?"

"If you don't mind."

"Great. You can meet Chuck. He works for the town, mowing and such, so he's never too far to come home for lunch." She pushed the hamburger patties back into a lump and started forming smaller ones.

"Is Chuck your husband?" I asked.

Her mother threw a potato into a bowl and snorted. She was hearing more than Sylvie gave her credit for.

"Not exactly," Sylvie said.

"He lives with you?"

"*We* live with *him*," she said loudly in her mother's direction. "And, Ma, I told you that's enough potatoes, hear?"

Flo reached in the sack and pulled out another potato. Sylvie grabbed it out of her hand and threw it back in. Grinning slyly, Flo got out a big pot and set the peeled ones to cooking.

Chuck turned out to be a puzzling kind of guy. He came in the kitchen door saying, "Who owns that dinosaur out there on my lawn? Don't they know it rained last night? Gonna need me a steamroller to get the ruts out." Then he smiled at me and winked.

I hadn't noticed any ruts, but I told him I was sorry.

"Well, you should be." He winked again like it was all a big joke.

"Chuck, Jo. Jo, Chuck," Sylvie said, kissing his cheek. "'Member, sweetie? I told you Jo was coming from New York to help us find Honey Lou."

"You never told me anything of the sort," he said with another wink. "Why's she wearing a dishtowel?"

I took my keys from my pocket. "I'll go move my motor home. Where do you want me to park?"

"Harm's done," he said. "No use moving it now." Sylvie was wearing a big grin, and she knew him better than I did, so I decided not to worry about it.

While Chuck was off washing up, Sylvie put the corn in the microwave and gave me the job of frying the patties. I bent over the pan, basking in the beef-scented heat. While Sylvie set the table, Flo mashed the potatoes. By the time Chuck got back, the meal was on the table.

I dug in, hoping to finish before the food turned cold. Between mouthfuls, I asked how long Honey Lou and Baxter had been married. At the word "Baxter," Flo looked up from her mountain of mashed potatoes and said, "He ain't coming over, is he?"

"No, Ma, never again," Sylvie told her, stabbing her patty with a fork.

"Easy on that plate, babe," Chuck said. "It's an antique."

Flo humphed and said, "Being old don't make things antique."

"You should know," Chuck told her, winking merrily.

"'Nuff, you two," Sylvie said, and turned to me. "To answer your question, Jo, Honey Lou and Baxter celebrated their third anniversary the day before he sent her to the woman's shelter. I couldn't believe it, my own daughter in one of those places! It wasn't so bad, though—they let her go to work, and she called me every evening to let me know she was back safe. I'd 'ave rather had her stay here with us, of course, but it's a good thing she didn't. Baxter showed up drunk one day looking for her, mad as hell. When I wouldn't unlock the screen door, he put his fist right through it. I told him if he came around again, I'd sic Chuck on him."

"I'll castrate the prick with a hacksaw," said Chuck. There was no wink for Baxter.

"The funny thing is," Sylvie said, "Baxter's disappeared now too. I drove over to their house a few days ago—in case Honey Lou had shown up, you know. His car was gone, and a neighbor told me he hadn't been around for quite a while." She spooned the last of her corn into her mouth and took her plate to the sink.

"More mashed potatoes, Weezie?" Flo asked me.

"No, thanks," I said. She scooped the rest of them onto her plate. I turned to Sylvie. "So if Honey Lou's car is here waiting to get fixed, how did she get to work every day?"

"She pools with a woman at work. She must owe that woman an awful lot of rides by now. Chuck, sweetie, you just *got* to get around to fixing that car. Honey Lou will need it when she comes back."

"Tough titty," he said. Treating me to one last wink, he patted Sylvie's backside and left.

When the table was cleared, I returned Sylvie's towel and told her I needed Honey Lou's home address and the name of the place where she worked. "Sure," she said, looking around for something to write on. Finally, she took a utility bill out of its envelope. "She and Baxter rent a house over in New Scotia, about 40 miles from here, and her workplace is there too. She's suing her boss, you know," she said, writing on the back of the envelope.

"Why?"

"Discrimination. He promoted a guy who had less seniority."

"What kind of company is it?"

"It's a meatpacking plant. Honey Lou's a butcher."

"No kidding," I said, impressed. "Where does her husband work?"

"I can't remember the last time Baxter worked. Honey Lou supported them both."

"He'd be pretty dumb to get rid of her then, wouldn't he?" I asked.

"Did I say he wasn't dumb?"

"Do you know the address of the woman's shelter?" I asked her. "I ought to go talk to them. Honey Lou might have told them where she was going."

"I know it's somewhere in New Scotia, but she wasn't allowed to tell anybody where it is, including even me."

"How about places she likes to hang out?"

"I can't think of anywhere but some bars in New Scotia where she called me from at one time or another. I had to go get her because she was, you know, too snookered to drive."

"You drove all the way to New Scotia to pick up Honey Lou at a bar?" I said.

"Of course. Wouldn't your mother do the same for you?"

I tried to imagine the situation and decided she might do it *once*. What I couldn't imagine was being "snookered" enough to ask her. "Do you remember where those bars are?" I asked. "I'd like to check them out."

"Yes. I wrote them all in my address book. Now where did I put it?" She pawed through a purse and several piles on the counter. "Have you seen my address book?" she said in her mother's ear.

"624 Duncan Street," Flo said.

"I *know* where we live, Ma—oh, wait, I remember." She opened a tea canister and removed a red-bound book. After copying several addresses from it to the envelope, she handed it to me, saying, "Jo, I don't know how I'm ever going to thank Weezie for sending you to us. By the way, how did you happen to meet her?"

"It was at a picnic a few years ago."

"A church picnic, no doubt. Like her ma and pa, Weezie's always been a devout Baptist."

I tried to keep from looking amazed. "No, it was a… nonchurch kind. We were both working security."

"Security? What sort of picnics do you go to? But then, you *do* live in New York, don't you?"

"*Western* New York," I said. "Anyway, Weezie and I hit it off right away, and we've been friends ever since."

She nodded. "Weezie was the kindest, most easygoing kid I ever knew. She and Honey Lou were so close. Every weekend of their high school years, they'd sleep over at one or another of our houses."

I'm sure. "So is that why you called Weezie in Buffalo?" I asked. "Did you think Honey Lou might have gone there to be with her?"

"Dear, no. I didn't even know Weezie *was* in Buffalo. No, it was her folks I called. We used to be neighbors, you know. They still live in New Scotia in the same house, so I thought Honey Lou might have showed up there, asking to stay for a while—she always got along good with Weezie's ma. That's when I found out Weezie'd moved to New York. I didn't think any more about it until Weezie called last week and said her ma told her the news, and she was sending you to us. I'm so glad you're here, Jo. Thank you so much."

"You're welcome, but all I'm going to be doing is nosing around. I can't promise I'll find anything."

"Do whatever you can, and be sure to call me if you need more information, although I can't think what I haven't told you already."

"There is one more thing I need," I said. "Do you have a recent picture of Honey Lou?"

"Why, sure I do. Here, come in the spare bedroom." I followed her down a hall and into a room that was more sewing room than bedroom. Bolts and lengths of fabric in bright colors and prints were spread across the bed and dressers, and stacked on and around an electric sewing machine. Draped over an ironing board was a purple paisley muumuu that looked finished except for the hem. "Did you make this?" I asked.

"Yes. It's a little business I have. All the ladies in town wear my creations. You should come to a women's social over at the church—you'd swear you were at a luau. Would you like me to make a muumuu for you, Jo?"

"Geez, no thanks. I mean…"

"That's OK, dearie, not everyone can wear them." Pushing the spread aside, she dragged a big box of photos from under the bed. "I mean to sort these into albums one of these days, but you know how it goes. Here, this one on top is the newest one. It's from Christmas."

She handed me a photo of a smiling young woman in a fuzzy red sweater holding a pair of gold hoops to her ears.

"I gave her those earrings," Sylvie said with a break in her voice.

I studied the photo so I'd be able to identify Honey Lou when I saw her, although it might be tough if she wasn't wearing a fuzzy red sweater and holding gold hoops to her ears. I never understood how cops on TV, after looking at a mug shot once, could identify a guy who had let his hair grow, put on weight, and was running away from them at night. My guess is that they couldn't if it wasn't written in the script.

"Isn't she lovely?" Sylvie said with a catch in her voice.

"She sure is. She hasn't changed her hair since this was taken, has she?"

"No. She's worn it long since fifth grade."

I could see why. She had tons of deep red waves that tumbled around her shoulders. Her dark eyes sparkled above full, rosy cheeks. Honey Lou Wright was a knockout.

"You can take that print with you," Sylvie told me. "If it gets lost, I still got the negative."

I said thanks and gave her my cell phone number, telling her to call if she heard anything. Before leaving, I poked my head in the kitchen to say goodbye to Flo. She waved a pot lid and said, "Now don't be a stranger, Weezie."

When I got to Dan'l, I checked the ground around his tires. It wasn't rutted; it was hardly even dented. I peeled out, hoping to kill some grass. *Tough titty, Chuck. Wink, wink.*

It was 20 miles before I warmed up enough to open the air vents.

5

On a map, Lake Eudora looks like a startled dragon blowing a strand of blue smoke to the west. The tiny town of Shoreville, the home of Rube's boat repair shop, sits in one of the dragon's armpits.

Rube had been Weezie's best buddy when they were growing up, and they still kept in touch. Weezie had told me Rube was the greatest person in the world, present company excluded.

When I was within a few miles of Rube's, the road started following the lakeshore. Since the shore was full of curves, so was the road. It seemed I wasn't taking the curves fast enough as a tan pickup hugged my rear so tight, it could have been in tow.

When I hit a straightaway, I slowed down, hoping the car would pass. But it didn't. Instead, the driver started honking. When I spotted the sign RUBE'S SMALL ENGINE REPAIR AND BOAT STORAGE, I pulled into the driveway with relief. To my surprise, the tan pickup followed. Was the guy looking for a fight?

I glanced around for a weapon. The heaviest thing in reach was my blue plastic flashlight. Grabbing it, I threw open my door, jumped out, and was immediately enveloped in a big hug. "Jo! I knew it was you," the hugger said in my ear. "I saw the New York plate, and Weezie told me what your thing here looks like."

"Rube? Was that *you* in the pickup?" I pulled back and checked her out. For some reason, I'd expected her to look like Weezie, all big and burly. Instead, she was more like me: slight, wiry, and butchy to the max. The hair sticking out around her baseball cap was the same nondescript brown as mine.

Her ragged sweatshirt and jeans were spotted with grease. I glanced down at my clothes to see if the spots had transferred during the hug, but I didn't see any. What I did see was the blue flashlight in my hand. Rube was looking at it too. "Are you still on New York time, Jo?" she asked. "It don't get dark in Oklahoma till later."

"Oh, I, well…" I stuttered

"You thought I was some guy gonna hassle you, didn't you?" she said.

"Maybe." I tossed the flashlight on to the driver's seat.

"You're right to be cautious," she said. "Some of these ol' boys can get mighty cantankerous." In addition to the regional drawl, Rube's voice had a high-pitched twang that might get irritating over the long haul. But I wasn't here to marry her, was I?

"Come in, come in," she said, leading the way to a corrugated metal building. "I had to go pick up a part for a rush job. Jenny's working over at the marina today, and I was afraid you'd get here and find it all locked up." She turned a key in the door, and I followed her in. "Want a root beer?" she asked. "Weezie told me it's your drink, so I stocked a few."

"Sure, thanks." I said. "Who's Jenny?"

"She's my lone employee, part-time. Wish I could afford her full-time." She opened a grimy refrigerator and tossed me a can. I popped the top and looked around. Two trailered boats with dismantled motors took up half the room. Other motors were clamped to workbenches, their innards spread around them. A wall was lined with red tool chests.

"Here, Jo, sit," she said, clearing a stack of catalogs from a chair. "Now, tell me, how's Weezie coping with Honey Lou being lost? She sounded awful when she called."

"She's really upset."

"I don't see why."

"I guess she still cares for her," I said.

"That's nuts! I don't think Weezie's seen her for years. Probably not since Honey Lou got married."

"Have you?"

"Have I what?" she asked.

"Seen Honey Lou."

She leaned against a workbench and studied her shoes. "Well, yeah, actually. She came over here, in fact."

"She was here? When?"

"It was two weeks ago Tuesday in the evening.

"It was? That's the day she disappeared. Did you tell Weezie?"

"I didn't tell anyone. Honey Lou asked me not to because her husband was stalking her. But now Weezie told me she's missing, I'm rethinking the whole thing."

"How did she get here? Her car's at her mother's," I said.

"Rita brought her, and she picked her up the next day too."

"Who's Rita?"

"She's the fourth Little Dutch Girl."

"Little Dutch Girl?"

"Didn't Weezie tell you? That's what her and me and Honey

Lou and Rita called ourselves in high school. The 'Four Little Dutch Girls'—get it?"

"No."

"Remember the story about Hans Brinker, Jo? Finger in the dike? We thought it was real clever, but we were kids, weren't we? Anyway, Rita—"

"Wait," I said. I was learning too many names way too fast. It was like the alphabet game Mom and I used to play on long car trips. *I went to the store and bought an apple, some bacon, cottage cheese...* I usually lost it somewhere around *popcorn.*

I searched my pockets for Weezie's notebook so I could start a list, then remembered it was still in Dan'l's glove compartment. *Dan'l!* He needed to be leveled. Rube's driveway was a slanting fridge-killer. I took out my keys.

"Something wrong?" Rube asked.

"Weezie said you had space here to park my motor home?"

"There's plenty of room out back. Would you like to move it now?"

"Yes, please," I said.

"Come on, then. I'll show you where to put it." We went down a hall and through a door emerging on a backyard right on the water. A gravel ramp sloped gently to a long metal dock. Tied to the far end of the dock was a gently rocking inboard. Rube led me to a grassy area near the ramp. "How about here?"

"Great!" I said. I'd assumed I was going to be parked in the middle of a boatyard. This, however, was a prime waterfront site. "Is that your boat?" I asked.

"Yeah." She gave it the look of melting pride most people reserve for their firstborn. "It's a '96 19-footer. I got it free after a guy crashed it into a dock and his insurance company declared it totaled. Took me three winters to get it back in the water, so I named it the *Big Fix.* Would you like to take it for a run sometime? I'll show you where I keep the key."

"We'll see," I said noncommittally. The truth was, I had no idea how to take it for a run. I'd never driven a boat and had no wish to.

After showing me where to plug in Dan'l's electric cord, Rube went back to the shop, saying she had to install the part she'd gone out for.

When Dan'l was in place and hooked up, I propped open his double doors and sat on the floor between them, my feet on the grass. Wrenching my gaze from the stunning lake view, I opened Weezie's notebook. The first page had my practice loops on it, so I tore it out. On the new first page, I drew two lines that sort of looked like the trunk of a tree. Inside the trunk, I lettered HONEY LOU WRIGHT. Then I gave it a branch named SYLVIE LEMMING (MOTHER) and angled twigs off it labeled FLO (GRANDMA) and CHUCK (THE WINKMAN).

On another branch—I drew it crooked on purpose—I wrote BAXTER WRIGHT (HUSBAND). A third branch I called THE OTHER THREE LITTLE DUTCH GIRLS. The twigs were RUBE, RITA, and WEEZIE.

I named a fourth branch WORKPLACE and optimistically added a couple of blank twigs.

Then I turned to the next page and titled it CLUES. Clue number one was H. L.'S HUSBAND BAXTER IS ABUSIVE, which was followed by RITA PICKED UP H.L. FROM RUBE'S PLACE WEDNESDAY MORNING. I closed the book, stuck it in my pocket, and took out my cell phone.

First, I called home and left a message that I was safe and sound in Oklahoma. I didn't mention last night's terrible wind storm because Mom and Rose wouldn't want to know about that. They thought they would, but they wouldn't. Then I called Marlo's Diner and asked for Weezie. "She's out id the back checking a delibery," said a girl whose nose was so stuffed up I wouldn't want her cooking *my* burger.

"Tell her Jo called and I'll call again later."

"The Jo that used to work here and left to hab a baby? This is Ashley, Jo."

"No, Ashley, it's another Jo. Just tell Weezie I called."

"Oh, OK….Wait, she's cubbing id." There was a confusion of voices and some cracks and thuds, and finally Weezie's voice said, "Jo? Jacuzzo?"

"Yes. Not the Jo who had the baby."

"She didn't have it yet. It's a week overdue, and she's miserable. Every evening she makes her husband drive her back and forth across the railroad tracks. So did you find Honey Lou?"

"Well, *no*, Weezie, I just got here. I met Mrs. Lemming, though, and now I'm at Rube's. You're right, she's great."

"Ain't she, though? She'd give you the shirt off her back."

"I don't want the greasy one she's wearing today," I told her.

"You know what I mean. How do you like Oklahoma? Hold on a sec." She spoke sharply to someone and then she was back. "Now, what was I saying?"

"You asked how I liked Oklahoma."

"Yeah, well?" she asked.

"I like it fine now that it stopped trying to blow me back to New York."

"Did you hit a storm?"

"A storm and a half," I said. "There were tornado warnings on the TV."

"Well, that's Oklahoma. How's Mrs. Lemming holding up?"

"Not too bad, but she's worried about her daughter, of course. Weezie, did you ever meet Mrs. Lemming's boyfriend, Chuck?

"No. Why?"

"I wanted your take on him. He's a weird guy. By the way, Mrs. Lemming tells me you're a devout Baptist."

She snorted. "In my mother's dreams. Look, Jo, I'm in the middle of a mess here. Call when you know something, OK?"

I was going to ask about the Four Little Dutch Girls and tell her that Honey Lou had been at Rube's, but I decided it all could wait. "Later then," I said.

I was rapt in the patterns of intersecting speedboat wakes when Rube emerged with fresh sodas and a bag of potato chips. "Snack time," she said, fetching a pair of webbed lawn chairs from a shed. I grabbed one, unfolded it, and sat.

"Sorry I interrupted you in there," I said, taking a handful of chips. "You were telling me about Rita."

"Ah, yes, Rita," she said. "She was my lover in high school, and Honey Lou was Weezie's lover. Rita and Honey Lou were the femmes, although we didn't know the concept back then. They dated guys too—Weezie and I couldn't take them to the prom, could we? After graduation, they decided there was a heap of stuff we couldn't do for them. Honey Lou got hitched that summer, and a year later, Rita did."

"That had to hurt," I said.

"You bet. But I was enrolled in the vocational school where there was a bunch of lesbians to hang with, so I got over it. I tried to get Weezie to enroll, but she wouldn't—Honey Lou was in the meat-cutting program, and she was afraid of running into her. Finally, Weezie just up and left town."

"Is that why she came to Buffalo? She never told me. I was starting to think it might have been because her folks were so religious."

Rube laughed. "If that was a reason for leaving, we'd *all* be out of here. My folks were over at the church so much, us kids called them the Freakin' Deacons. No, the reason Weezie left was because she needed to be far, far away from Honey Lou."

"But you kept in touch with Rita and Honey Lou?"

She shook her head vigorously. "No way. I hadn't seen Rita or Honey Lou for ages....No, wait, Rita came here all by herself for my grand opening three years ago—I could have dropped my teeth. I was so busy, though, I didn't have time to do more than say hi and accept her congratulations. Then I didn't see her again until she popped up with Honey Lou in tow—what'd I say it was, two weeks ago?"

"Why did they come here?"

"Like I said, Honey Lou's husband was stalking her. She asked if she could stay with me."

"Where do you live?"

"Right here. I've carved out a living space." She pointed to a door and window near the corner of the building. "It's small, but it suits me."

"I'd like to see it sometime," I said. Since designing Dan'l, I'd become fascinated with compact living spaces. One of my favorite ways of killing time was to visit RV Web sites and pore over floor plans. "Do you have a shower in there?" I asked.

"Sure. Do you want to use it?"

"That would be great. I thought about jumping in the lake, but I didn't want to pollute it."

"On behalf of the fishies, I thank you," Rube said. "As soon as you finish your root beer, I'll show you where it is."

"Super!" I took a big gulp. "So Rita brought her here that night, and you agreed to let Honey Lou stay with you?"

"I didn't want to. What if her husband got wind of it? I don't need that kind of trouble. But Jenny and I were in the middle of an overhaul and I didn't have time to argue. I told her she could stay one night and one night only. The next morning Rita came and picked her up."

"Did they say where they were going?"

"I didn't talk with them—I wasn't here. But Jenny was working in the shop and saw the car out the window. It was yellow, so it had to be Rita's. When she drove in Tuesday evening, I remember wondering how she'd found a car the exact shade of her hair. It actually looked more natural on the car."

"I should have a talk with Rita," I said. "Do you know where she lives?"

"It's probably in the New Scotia phone book. Her husband's name is Ken Kane. It's burned in my brain from reading the announcement of her engagement in the newspaper. That was Rita's way of breaking up with me."

"Whoa!" I said.

"Tell me about it."

"You didn't know she was dating him?"

"I'd never even heard of him. He moved here from out of state and swept Rita off her size nines. But that's ancient history, isn't it? Come on, I'll show you my little home," she said, and ushered me in. It was very much like a studio apartment—an all-purpose room plus a bathroom. In the kitchen area, a round table with four captain's chairs sat in front of a big uncurtained window that looked over the lake. The nearest wall was studded with appliances. Farther in, there was a small sofa and a compact entertainment center holding a TV and VCR. A twin-size bed was shoved in a corner. The place was neat and uncluttered. When I told her I loved it, she beamed and left me to take my shower.

When I finished, it was still only the middle of the afternoon. I went in the shop and told Rube, "Maybe I'll drive to New Scotia. I want to talk with the people at the meatpacking plant where Honey Lou works."

"Yeah, she was telling me about having a job there. She said they pay well."

"Did she mention she was suing her boss?"

"No, she didn't say anything about that. Will you be back for supper?"

"Geez, Rube," I said, "you don't have to feed me."

"I wasn't planning to. There's a decent hash house down the road. I was hoping you'd join me for a burger."

"Sure. What time?"

"It'll be at least 6:30 before I finish up here."

"I hope to be back by then. It'll be a little while before I even get going. I shouldn't have hooked Dan'l up."

"Who?"

I gave her a quick explanation of Dan'l's name. She thought it was pretty cool. "I'd let you use my pickup truck," she said, "but I never know when I'll need to run out for something. Hey, maybe I should give a guy's name to my pickup," she said. "How about Elvis?"

"Presley or Costello?"

"Irish setter. I had to have him put down last fall. About killed me."

I patted her shoulder and left.

6

The meatpacking plant was a sprawling brick building near a cattle stockyard. As soon as I got within a few blocks, I knew what Mom meant when she used to come in my messy room and say, "It smells like a stockyard in here!"

When I went in a door marked OFFICE, a woman wearing shoulder pads big enough for Jim Kelly was busy at a computer. She waved a finger at me and kept typing.

Taking a chair, I sorted through some periodicals on a coffee table. Luckily the shoulder-padded woman came to a stopping place before I had to make a choice between *Modern Feedlot* and *Beef Oklahoma*. "Hello," she said. "What are you selling?"

I crossed to her desk. "I'm not selling anything. My name's Jo Jacuzzo. This plant has an employee named Honey Lou Wright—"

She interrupted. "Ms. Wright's not in today."

Duh. "OK, but when she is in, do you happen to know who she carpools with?"

"Why?"

"Ms. Wright seems to be missing, and her mother, Mrs. Lemming, has asked me to help find her. You can call to check on that, if you like."

She thought about it and decided it was too much trouble. "You'll have to talk to Mr. Proudflesh, but he's not in today either."

"Mr. Proudflesh is Honey Lou's boss?"

"He's everybody's boss. He'll be in tomorrow." She started typing furiously. That was all the information I was going to get out of her.

I looked at her computer like I'd never seen one before. "This is a nice piece of equipment. I'm thinking of buying one, but I don't know what kind I should get."

The typing slowed. "You mean, like, should you get a PC or a laptop?"

"I guess," I said.

"Well, you'll have to decide what features you want and how much you want to spend. This is a PC." She stopped typing and gestured palm up at her computer tower like she was a model on *The Price Is Right.* "Laptops are littler, but they're more expensive."

"Why?"

"It don't make sense to me neither. Anyway, I'd recommend a PC. The keyboard's bigger."

"Thanks. I'll take that into consideration," I said. "Do you happen to have a phone book?"

"Of course." She pulled one from a drawer. I leafed to the *K*'s and found the address of the Kenneth Kane. When I asked Shoulder-Pad Woman if she knew how to get to their street, she opened the drawer again, took out a city map, and carefully wrote the route on a piece of notepaper decorated with tiny cows wearing bonnets.

She even softened enough to suggest I should try to catch Mr. Proudflesh before noon tomorrow. "Otherwise, he's out in the plant or wherever." She sighed deeply to let me know how tough it was to keep track of Mr. Proudflesh.

Ken and Rita Kane's street wasn't very wide, so I parked Dan'l in the lot of a nearby office building and walked the half-mile to their house, a rambling ranch with a three-car garage. The doorbell chimed with that mournful echo doorbells get when nobody's home. I rang it again for the heck of it and was turning to leave when the middle garage door stuttered up and a yellow Honda sedan pulled in. Through the open doorway, I could see that the third stall held a big white boat on a trailer. The Kanes were doing all right for themselves.

I waited outside while a woman wearing a classy navy suit and beige heels unfolded herself from the driver's seat. Rube was right: Rita's hair was the exact same yellow as the Honda.

"May I help you?" she asked.

"My name's Jo Jacuzzo," I said. "Honey Lou Wright's mother asked me to look into her disappearance."

"Her disappearance? Honey Lou's disappeared? When?" She opened the Honda's back door and freed a sleeping baby from a car seat. Slinging a diaper bag big enough to hold two more babies over her shoulder, she opened the door to the house and went in. I followed her into a large kitchen.

"Nobody's seen her since a week ago Wednesday," I said, "That was the day you picked her up from Rube's repair shop. Where did you take her?"

She laid the baby in a small crib in the corner, stuck a pacifier in its mouth, and eyed me warily. "What makes you think I picked up Honey Lou from Rube's?"

"She was seen getting into your car."

"Well, that's impossible because I didn't pick her up. Who said they saw me? Rube? Figures. Well, it wasn't me. It wasn't my car. Now, excuse me, I have to make dinner. My husband will be home soon." She led me through an elegant living room, opened the front door, and waited for me to exit.

My brain was churning. This was a development I hadn't expected. Is it possible that it hadn't been Rita's yellow Honda that Honey Lou got into? How many friends with yellow cars did Honey Lou have? Rita could be lying, of course. For all she knew, I'd been sent there to grill her by Honey Lou's low-down husband, Baxter. How could I set her mind at ease? "You and I have a mutual friend," I told her.

"If you're talking about Rube, forget it."

"I'm talking about Weezie LaDuca."

"You know Weezie? How is she?"

"She's fine, but she's very upset about Honey Lou being missing."

"Well, I am too, of course," Rita said. "Look, I really do have to make dinner." She closed the door and I followed her back to the kitchen.

Rita's way of making dinner was to take a package of Stouffers Oven Sensations from the freezer and stick it in the microwave. Then she leaned against the counter and said, "Tell me about Weezie. Where's she living now?"

I caught her up on Weezie's life in Buffalo, which didn't take long. "I always liked Weezie," she said when I'd finished. "I haven't seen her since high school."

"When you were members of the Four Little Dutch Girls?" I asked.

She gasped and looked at the door to the garage. "Please don't ever say that in this house. Ken is born-again, you know. He hates the fact that I was ever a...a..." She couldn't say it.

"So he knows?"

"I told him before we got married. I didn't want him finding out some other way and leaving me with a dozen kids."

"You have a dozen kids?"

"I *wanted* a dozen. We tried and tried and when we finally gave up, *she* came along." She tossed her head at the baby in the crib. "I can't tell you how much damage she has done to my career. I mean, I love her and everything, but...do you have kids?"

"No."

"Ah." Taking a bottle of red wine from a low cupboard, she half-filled a plastic tumbler and said, "Would you like some?"

"No, thanks. What *is* your career, Rita?"

"Do you know anything about banking?"

"Not much."

"Then let's just say I'm working my way up from the bottom. It's been a hard road without a college degree. What do you do, Jo?"

"I'm a certified nurse's assistant, but I'm not working at the present time."

We heard a garage door grind up. In one motion, Rita drained the cup, threw it in the dishwasher, and stuck the wine bottle in the cupboard. "Look, can you come back tomorrow night? Ken's leaving at 6 for a weekend fishing trip. I want to know more about Honey Lou being missing, and I'd like to know more about you too."

"I think I can," I said. "I'm planning to nose around some of Honey Lou's favorite bars to see if anyone has seen her. I could stop here first."

"You're going to bars? If you don't mind, I'll get a sitter and go with you. I could sure use an evening out."

That actually sounded great—I'd been dreading doing it alone. "Could we take your car?" I asked.

"What's wrong with yours?"

It's hard to park and sticks out like a sore thumb. "It's going to be in the shop for a few days. Oil leak."

"Oh. Then how are you going to get here?"

"I'll catch a ride. Shall I come about 8?"

"Make it 7, and I'll give you dinner."

The door to the garage opened and a man with a fat black briefcase and a stiff brown mustache walked in. He wire-brushed Rita's cheek and gave me the once-over. "Jo, this is my husband, Ken," Rita said. We nodded warily at each other.

"I was just leaving," I said. Neither of them protested.

Rita followed me to the door. "I'm going to tell him you're selling something," she whispered.

As I walked away, I considered that I might want to actually find a product to sell while I was in the area. Maybe Sylvie Lemming needed a muumuu representative.

7

Rube's "decent hash house" didn't look like much from the outside. There were no windows, and the only sign I could see was a flickering EAT over the door. But inside it was bright and clean, and they had a four-page menu. I looked through it for hash, but it wasn't there. Chicken-fried steak was, though. I was tempted to order it, but since I'd had Sylvie's hamburger patty for lunch, I decided to unclog my arteries with a fish sandwich. "It's local. You'll like it," the waitress told me.

While we waited for our food, Rube asked about my trip from New York. When I got to the part about weathering the storm last night, she said, "That storm was nothing. You should have been here Saturday. A guy over in Crowder lost his fence and part of his barn. And up in Dewey—"

"Don't believe a word of it," laughed a tall woman who

appeared out of nowhere. She had such a deep tan, her white shirt seemed to glow. A sun-bleached ponytail cascaded out of the rear opening of a green baseball cap.

"Jenny!" Rube said with real pleasure. "I didn't think you could make it tonight. Hi there, Gus. How you doing?"

Jenny was so spectacular, I hadn't noticed the man behind her. He stepped forward and said, "Things are good with me, Rube. Thanks." He and Jenny looked to be about the same age: middle 30s, maybe.

Jenny slid into Rube's side of the booth, shoving Rube over with her butt, and gave me a blinding smile. "You must be the Yankee private eye."

"That she is," Rube said. "Jo Jacuzzo, I'd like you to meet my temporary employee, Jenny Nye. And this is Gus Peevey. He works with Jenny at the Lake Eudora Marina."

I said hello and slid over so Gus could sit. He was a slight guy, a little round-shouldered, but not bad-looking for a man. He nodded his thanks and turned his attention to the menu the waitress handed him.

Jenny took her menu and smacked Rube over the head with it. "Just a minute, missy," she said. "What was that you called me, a *temporary* employee? You meant part-time, didn't you?"

"I meant temporary. You're still on your 50-year probation."

"In that case, I resign effective 51 years from today."

Rube threw a sugar packet at her, and they laughed like it was the best joke ever. Gus and I exchanged amused glances. I wondered if he and Jenny were friends or more. "You and Jenny eat here a lot?" I asked, by way of finding out.

"Jenny does. I mostly eat at home with my family," he said. "But they ate early tonight so they could go to Molly's graduation rehearsal." I smelled the sharp-sweet scent of beer on his breath.

Rube stared at him. "Molly's a baby. What's she graduating from?"

"Third year of day care. I know it's silly, but try to tell my wife that. They got little caps and gowns and everything. I'm planning to work late on graduation night."

"Watch out, you'll become a workaholic like Jenny," Rube said.

Jenny shrugged. "I guess you could accuse me of worse things."

"You're right, I could," Rube said, and they exploded in laughter again.

After the waitress took the second round of orders, Jenny turned to me and said, "Rube tells me you're here to find that friend of hers that's gone missing."

"Yes. I'm helping her family look for her," I said.

"Well, good luck. This is the second friend of Rube's who's disappeared, and they never did find the first one."

"No kidding?" I looked at Rube.

"That was a long time ago," she said, "and anyway, Beth lived over in El Reno. That couldn't have had anything to do with Honey Lou."

"Maybe not," Jenny said. "But, Jo, you might not want to get too close to Rube, or who knows what may happen." She hummed the eerie tones from *Close Encounters of the Third Kind*.

"Jenny, stop," Rube said. "Honey Lou's disappearance is serious stuff. Her husband's been stalking her. She's in real danger."

Jenny frowned and smoothed some blond wisps under the cap. "Sorry, darlin', " she said.

"So, Jo," Gus said, "how do you like Oklahoma?"

"Well…" I started.

Rube interrupted. "She don't like it much so far. She got caught in that storm last night."

"Storm?" Jenny said. "That wasn't a storm, that was a little bitty blow. Why, up in Dewey the other day…"

Rube's and my food came at that moment, so I never did hear what happened up in Dewey the other day. Gus's and Jenny's bowls of chili weren't far behind. Jenny must have been a regular at the restaurant, because the waitress said, "I sprinkled some raw onion on top. That's the way you like it, isn't it?"

"You *know* how I like it, babe," Jenny said with a sly grin. The waitress blushed and hurried away.

"Jenny, you're going to get yourself in trouble, flirting like that," Rube told her.

Jenny stirred the onions into her chili before saying coyly, "Jealous?"

"I'm green as Jo's shirt."

I looked down to check. My shirt was deep red. I glanced at Gus to see how he was taking the conversation, but he was emptying cellophane packages of oyster crackers into his bowl and didn't seem to be listening. He must have seen me looking at him, though, because he looked up and asked, "So how's the fish tonight?"

"Great," I said. It was too. It wasn't a filet like I'd expected—it was a whole breaded fish hanging over the sides of the bun with its tail still intact.

Between bites of her burger, Rube asked Jenny what sort of things she'd been working on over at the marina. "That's her main job," she told me. "She helps out at my shop evenings and on one of her days off."

"I'd work for you more often if you paid me," Jenny said.

"I pay you!" Rube said. "But it's not near what they pay you over there. I know that."

Jenny patted Rube's cheek. "Doesn't matter. The pleasure of your company is pay enough. But today I worked on a houseboat so big they needed a semi to get it out of the water. Made my little place look like an orange crate."

"Tell me another one," Rube laughed. Turning to me, she said, "Jenny lives in the coolest little houseboat. She converted it from a pontoon party boat. You know what that is?"

"I'm not sure."

"It's a glorified raft," Jenny said.

"It's an expensive glorified raft," Rube said. "You see them cruising the lake every night in summer, all lit up."

Gus chuckled. "What's lit up, the boat or the people on it?"

Rube laughed. "Both, usually. Anyway, Jo, you really should see it."

"I'd like to," I said.

"Well, bring her on over," Jenny told Rube. She finished her last bit of chili and slid out of the booth. "I have to get going now, but first…" She took a camera out of her brown leather fanny pack.

Gus wiped his mouth and jumped up. "I've got to be going too. Nice meeting you, Jo. See you later, ladies."

"Don't you pay, now," Jenny called to his retreating back. "It's my turn." She backed up a little, aimed her camera at Rube and me, and clicked. "That's good. Thanks." As she put the camera away, she said, "I won't be over tonight, Rube, but I'll see you tomorrow evening, 6:30 or so."

Since I wouldn't be around the next evening, I said, "Jenny, I need to ask you something."

She leaned over me, her strong arms on the table. "What is it, lovey?" she said. A whiff of musk gave me a three-point tingle.

"Rube tells me you saw Honey Lou Wright get into a yellow Honda Wednesday morning, April 9."

"I don't personally know Honey Lou Wright, but yes, I saw a yellow car pull in the driveway, and a redheaded woman got in. It might have been a Honda."

"Did you see who was driving? Was it the same woman who brought her?"

"I don't know who brought her. I didn't meet either one of them."

"Was there a baby in the backseat?"

"I honestly didn't see," she said.

"And you're sure it was Wednesday, April 9?"

"I don't remember the exact date, but it had to be a Wednesday—it's the only day I'm at Rube's in the morning."

"What time was it?"

"Eleven, maybe a little later."

Rube said, "It couldn't have been much later because I was back by noon and you had already left."

"That's right. I had a dentist appointment that day. I left at 11:15. Anything else I can help you with?"

I considered asking for the name of her dentist; I didn't think I'd ever seen such white, even teeth. "That's it for now," I told her. "It was good to meet you."

"You too." She dropped a generous tip on the table and left. Rube and I and every guy in the place watched her glide through the restaurant, pay at the counter, and leave.

I was too full for dessert, but Rube ordered a dish of chocolate ice cream. While she ate, I told her, "I went to Rita's today. She said it wasn't her that picked up Honey Lou that morning."

Her spoon stopped in mid scoop. "Who'd she loan her car to, then?"

"She said it wasn't her car."

"Well, it wouldn't be the first time she's lied. Remember me telling you how she kept me in the dark about Ken until they announced their engagement?"

"Yeah," I said. "But why would she lie about this?"

"She probably promised Honey Lou she wouldn't tell anybody, just like I did. Or more likely, she's covering her own ass."

"You're still really sore at Rita, aren't you, Rube?"

"Sure, I am. She hurt me bad. Did you meet Ken?"

"Briefly. He came in as I was about to leave. Have you met him?"

"No, thank goodness," she said. "Honey Lou told me he's pretty protective of Rita."

"That may be. However, he's going fishing this weekend, so she's going to fix me dinner tomorrow night. Then we're going to visit some of the bars Honey Lou frequented. I was going to ask if you wanted to go along."

"No, thank you very much. And if she's fixing your dinner, you'd better watch her while she does it," she said.

"You think she'd poison me?"

"Why not? Maybe that's how she did away with Honey Lou."

I laughed and made a mental note to check for tiny holes in the packaging of my Stouffers Oven Sensations.

When I was back at Rube's and plugged in, I turned on Dan'l's TV and watched *CSI* and then the news. The weather-person warned that a cold front would be moving in overnight, so I put an extra blanket on the bed. I still woke up shivering at 3:30 and had to turn on Dan'l's furnace. When I couldn't get back to sleep, I lay in the dark playing Game Boy until I finally warmed up and got drowsy. So when at 7 A.M. there was a tap on the door, I didn't feel like answering, but I did. It was Rube with a steaming cup of coffee and the New Scotia newspaper. "Going to be windy and overcast today," she said. "Want to borrow some sweats?"

"I'm all set. Thanks."

"Help yourself to a shower. I've had mine." As she turned to leave, we heard honking from the direction of the lake. Somebody on a boat was waving both arms at us. Rube waved back.

"Is he in trouble?" I asked.

"No. That's Jenny testing a repair she made at the marina."

I waved too, and she took off with a roar. "Where's the marina?" I asked.

"Over on the east side of the lake. It's a huge place with indoor and outdoor storage and a repair shop that makes mine look penny ante. They've got a pretty good restaurant too. We'll go over there this weekend—Saturday, maybe. You can have a look at Jenny's houseboat then."

"That'd be great."

"Good. I'll be in the shop all day today if you need anything."

I unfolded the newspaper. It was mostly a rehash of what I'd seen on TV the night before plus an in-depth story about the March of Dimes Walkathon scheduled for the next day. The *best* news in it was that no red-haired bodies had been found.

I showered and donned a clean pair of Levi's and one of my Buffalo Bills sweatshirts, and I headed for New Scotia.

Shoulder-Pad Woman was on the phone when I walked in the meatpacking plant office. "No, you may *not* have half your sister's chocolate bunny," she was saying. "Well, I can't help it that you already ate yours. Now, stop crying and put your daddy back on." She spotted me and pointed at a door with a nameplate that said JAMES PROUDFLESH, MANAGER. It was ajar, so I pushed it open and went in.

The man behind the desk was bent over. All I could see was the back of his white shirt and several hairs hovering over a bald spot. "Mr. Proudflesh?" I said.

A drawer slammed, and he shot up in his chair. I wondered what he'd been doing down there. Looking at dirty pictures?

"I'm Jo Jacuzzo," I said, sticking out my hand. "One of your employees, Honey Lou Wright, is missing. Her family has asked me to help figure out where she might have gone."

He ignored my hand, which was a relief, since I had my suspicions about where his had been. After clearing his voice, he said, "As I told her mother several days ago, Mrs. Wright hasn't been in since Tuesday, April…"—he consulted his calendar— "…8th. She worked a full shift that day and left at 4 as usual. The following day she didn't come in or call, and we haven't seen her since."

"Had she been having problems on the job?"

"Other than spotty attendance, no."

"So it's happened before that she hasn't shown up for work?"

"On occasion, but she's never been gone this long," he said. "My receptionist tells me you wish to speak with Mrs. Herzog."

"Is that the woman Honey Lou carpools with?"

"Yes, but I've already spoken with her, and she hasn't seen Mrs. Wright since that day."

"I'd like to talk with her myself," I said.

"She's not in." He picked up a pile of papers and shuffled them.

"Thanks," I said, and pretended I was leaving. I hadn't watched all those reruns of *Columbo* for nothing. At the door, I spun around and said, "If Honey Lou wasn't having problems on the job, why was she suing you?"

Mr. Proudflesh was already bending behind his desk to continue whatever I'd interrupted. I heard a drawer open as he said, "My attorney has advised me not to talk about the lawsuit. Now, I'm very busy. Please go."

Since I didn't have Columbo's badge to back me up, I left, but I didn't go far. After driving Dan'l down the road a ways, I parked at a strip mall and walked back to the plant. Avoiding windows, I skulked to the rear of the building, where I'd noticed a couple of picnic tables. Three men and two women were huddled next to a gray metal door, smoking and drinking from steaming Styrofoam cups. They all wore bloodied white aprons. I decided if I were a butcher, I'd wear a red apron.

I walked up to them and said, "Excuse me, do you know if this plant is hiring?"

One of the men said, "Depends. What do you do?"

"I'm a butcher."

"What kind of experience do you have?" he asked.

"I used to work in Chicago. You know, hog butcher for the world?"

He snickered. "'Scuse me, lady, but you're not big enough to lift a hog."

Before he had time for another snicker, I was behind him, lifting him completely off the ground. "Yes, I am," I said, putting him back down.

Ignoring the others' giggles, the guy pointed toward the front of the building and said, "You're going to have to go to the office if you want a job, but you might not want to work here *now*." He threw his cigarette in the dirt and ground it with his heel. Yanking the door open, he stomped inside. The rest of them followed, except one woman, who paused for a last drag.

"Should I be scared of that guy?" I asked her.

She shrugged. "Maybe."

"Do you happen to know a Mrs. Herzog who works here?"

"Naomi?" she said. "Sure. Do you?"

"No, but a mutual friend told me to look her up. She said maybe she'd vouch for me."

"Baby, you don't want to work here, believe me, and not just because of that bozo."

"Really? My friend told me the pay is good."

"Who's your friend?"

"Honey Lou Wright."

"Honey Lou?" she said. "Whatever happened to her?"

"That's what I'm trying to find out. I wish Mrs. Herzog was working today."

"What are you talking about? She's working. I just saw her."

"You did?"

"Sure. I'll tell her you're out here." She stubbed her butt in a bucket of sand and hurried inside.

I retreated behind a bank of Dumpsters in case the bozo came back. My back and knees were pretty mad at me for lifting him, so I did a few stretches. I was getting out of shape—back when I was a nurse's assistant at Box Elder Nursing Home, I used to lift patients every day who weighed a lot more than he did. I made a mental note to dust off my weight bench when I got home and start a fitness program.

The Dumpsters reeked. I hoped Naomi Herzog would emerge before I collapsed from the stench. What was it like here on a *hot* day?

8

In a few minutes the door opened and a woman emerged, folding her arms against the wind. I ran up and said, "Are you Naomi?"

"Yes," she said. "And you are?"

"Jo Jacuzzo. I'm a friend of Honey Lou Wright's family."

"Betty tells me you wanted to talk to me about Honey Lou. Where is she? I've been very worried about her."

"I don't know where she is, but I'm working on it. I wonder if you'd mind answering a couple questions about the last time you saw her."

"Sorry, I don't have time right now—Betty's covering for me, and I don't want to get her in trouble. Can you come back at lunchtime?"

"I promise it won't take more than a minute," I said. "Her mother is frantic, just frantic."

Naomi pulled a cigarette from her pocket and lit it with a Bic. She took a deep pull and said, "Make it quick."

"I will. Did Honey Lou ride with you that last Tuesday she worked?"

Through exhaled smoke, she said, "In the morning, yes. But not in the afternoon."

"Why not?"

"Somebody saw her husband sitting in his car in the rear parking lot, so she went up front and left through the office. I drove around to pick her up, but she was already getting into another car. Turned out it's a good thing she didn't ride with me because Baxter followed me home and demanded to know where she was. I was happy to say I had no idea."

"Whose car was she getting into?"

She lowered her voice. "Don't say I was the one that told you, but it was a silver Porsche, so it had to be Mr. Proudflesh's."

"Mr. Proudflesh, the manager?"

"Yes. Nobody else around here can afford a Porsche. Now I've really got to go."

"Wait," I said. "They tell me Honey Lou was staying at the women's shelter. Do you know where it's located?"

"No. I picked her up at a Citgo station every day while she was staying at the shelter. I have no idea how she got to the station." She pinched the burning ash off her cigarette and, lifting the side of her stained apron, stuck it in her pants pocket. Firmly bidding me good-bye, she opened the door and disappeared down a dark hall.

As soon as the door closed, I marched around the building and back into the office. Shoulder-Pad Woman was nowhere in sight. I looked in Mr. Proudflesh's office, but he was gone too. I couldn't resist. Circling his desk, I opened his bottom drawer, the one he'd been bent over before. In it were a comb and mirror, a bottle of Brut, and a half-full box of condoms.

As I passed through the reception area, the phone on Shoulder-Pad Woman's desk rang once and quit, but the glowing button stayed lit—somebody somewhere had answered it. I carefully lifted the receiver in time to hear Shoulder-Pad's voice say, "Packing Company. How may I...shhh!"—giggle—"hold on now!...help you?"

Had Mr. Proudflesh installed a phone in a broom closet? Were the two of them in there having a condomed good time? I hung up and helped myself to her city map on my way out.

Back in Dan'l, I used the map to locate the street where Honey Lou and Baxter Wright had lived in happier times, if there had been happier times. Then I drove to it, getting lost only once.

The house was a one-story affair with faded aluminum siding that was coming loose in spots. One of the wrought-iron posts supporting the carport had buckled, causing the roof to hang so low on one side that only a convertible with the top down would fit in, and then only maybe. At the moment, however, there wasn't any car in it, convertible or otherwise.

I parked at the curb and got out. A man sitting on a tipped-back chair on the porch next door was watching me with great interest. In spite of the chill in the air, he was wearing nothing but a pair of shorts and an undershirt.

I knocked on the Wright's front door and, after a minute, tried the knob. It wiggled but it wouldn't turn.

"Hey!" It came from the direction of the underdressed neighbor.

I walked over and said, "Yes?"

He pointed at Dan'l. "That one of them mobile crime labs?"

"No. Have you seen the Wrights lately?"

"Like I tole them other cops..." He spat a stream of dark liquid into a jar with a ragged Miracle Whip label and wiped his mouth with his arm.

"I'm not a cop."

"You kin?"

"Excuse me?"

"You know, cousin or somethin'?"

"A friend of the family. Ms. Lemming sent me to check on her daughter."

"Well, they ain't around. I tole Mrs. Lemming that when she was here last week. I tole the cops that too."

"How long have the Wrights been gone?" I asked.

"The missus bin gone a while. I heard she was over to the shelter after Baxter knocked one of her choppers out."

"Did you see that happen?"

"Nah, it was night," he said. "We was asleep."

"How long was Baxter here after that?"

"We-e-ell," he scratched his arm, "don't believe his car's been here since, I don't know, last Thursday?" He spat again. My stomach churned.

"Do you know where he was headed when he left?"

"I din't ask, and he din't say. We din't neighbor much since I stopped drinking." He turned and gave his front door a dirty look. I figured the cause of his stopping was somewhere on the other side.

"Did Baxter hit his wife a lot?" I asked.

"No, just normal 'mount."

He was lifting the jar again, so I told him I needed to have a look around and hurried to the Wrights' backyard.

Honey Lou and Baxter must not have spent much time back there. The weeds were so high, plastic bags were caught in them, and a lop-sided glider had so many boards missing that you couldn't sit without falling through. A charcoal grill next to the kitchen door was turning to rust.

The screen door had a big tear in it—I wondered if it had

been another victim of Baxter's fist. I pulled it open and tried the knob on the solid wood door, but it wouldn't budge. Looking in a nearby window, I could see a chrome dinette set, the corner of a stove, and part of a doorway to the next room.

I considered trying to trip the lock by sliding my credit card between the door and jamb like I'd seen people do on TV, but the thought of Baxter coming home while I was doing it was a real deterrent. An equally frightening prospect was that the credit card might slip through the crack and wind up inside. It never happened on TV, but this was real life.

Just in case Honey Lou was tied up inside, I knocked and put my ear to the door, listening for groans or thumps. I didn't hear a thing.

The neighbor waved as I hurried up the drive on my way to Dan'l, but I kept going. If he were to expectorate in my presence again, I might lose my lunch, even though I hadn't had any.

I spent the next hour exploring New Scotia. A double line on the city map turned out to be a main drag, built up on both sides with malls and big-box stores, car dealers, restaurants, motels, and, hallelujah, a multiscreen cinema. I memorized the location.

Turning right at a stoplight, I found myself on a street lined with small businesses, fast-food places, and gas stations with mini-marts. Seeing a sign for the New Scotia Treatment Center, I turned in, speculating that if Baxter had found Honey Lou and hit her hard enough, she might have ended up here, in a coma, which would account for why she hadn't called her mother.

The parking lot was full except for a few cramped spaces that would have been tough to get Dan'l in and even tougher to get him out of. Backing up in a limited area was a skill I was still working on. I drove out of the lot and parked down the street. It was a bit of trek back, but walking in the brisk air felt good. My new fitness program would definitely include more walking.

A woman at a desk in the treatment center wondered how she could help me.

"Have you by any chance admitted a woman named Honey Lou Wright?" I asked.

"Do you know what she would have been admitted for?

"Not exactly, but her husband is physically abusive."

"Then you should try the county hospital," she said. "Here, we offer drug and alcohol treatment exclusively."

"Oh," I said. "But come to think of it, she could be here for that too. Would you check?"

After consulting a computer, she said, "Sorry, there's no one here by that name. There are other treatment centers around. Would you like a list?"

"Yes, please." The list she handed me was so long, I sighed in discouragement.

She smiled. "I'll call the closest ones for you if you like."

"Would you? We are *so* worried."

The woman not only checked other treatment centers, she called the county hospital and hospitals in Muskogee, Tulsa, and Oklahoma City. Honey Lou wasn't in any of them. I thanked her all over the place, then left.

My stomach had finally recovered from the Spitman episode, so I bought a couple of take-out burgers and drove to a park I'd passed earlier. It was too chilly to sit on a bench so I ate in Dan'l. Next, I acted on my new resolve by taking an after-lunch power walk. The sky was dark with clouds, and sporadic gusts tossed tree limbs. I hoped it wasn't whipping itself up into a storm like the other night, but just in case, I cut my walk short. The stitch in my side had nothing to do with it.

Recovering on Dan'l's sofa, I opened the New Scotia newspaper

Rube had given me that morning and scanned the personal ads in case Honey Lou had sent a cryptic message to her mother. On the other hand, if it was cryptic, how would I recognize it?

What I did find, though, nestled among the ads for lost pets and "adult fun" was this:

> I, Baxter Wright, am not responsible for Honey Lou Wright's bills as of Tuesday, April 8, 2003.

Whoa, does Sylvie know about this? I found her number and punched it into my cell.

"Hello?" It was her mother's voice.

"Is this Flo?" I said loudly. "Can you hear me?"

"'Course I can. Quitcher yelling."

"Sorry." She must have found her hearing aid. "Is your daughter there?"

"No, she's off conducting a fitting. Who's this?"

"It's Jo Jacuzzo," I said, wondering what there was to fit on a muumuu.

"Who?"

"Jo Jacuzzo. I was at your house yesterday." When she didn't say anything, I added, "You were peeling potatoes."

"I peel potatoes every day...except when we bake them, of course."

"OK, thanks. Goodbye." I broke the connection, then called right back.

"Hello?" Flo said.

"Hi. This is Weezie," I said.

"Weezie? When you coming back to see us, Weezie?"

"One of these days. Do you know if Sylvie has seen today's New Scotia newspaper?"

"No. We don't get it. They don't deliver this far out."

"There's something in it she should know about." I read Baxter's ad to her.

"What's that mean?" she asked.

"What it means to me is that he thinks Honey Lou is still alive. If he'd killed her, why would he run an ad saying he wasn't going to pay her future bills?"

Flo snorted. "That deadbeat never paid a bill in his life. Maybe he wants us to *think* he didn't kill her."

"You've got a point there. Anyway, tell Sylvie about it, all right?"

"All right, Weezie."

"One more thing, Flo. Did Mr. Proudflesh tell Sylvie that he gave Honey Lou a ride the day she disappeared?"

"No, he never did."

"Maybe she just didn't tell you about it," I suggested.

"There's something Sylvie didn't tell me about? I should be so lucky."

"OK, thanks," I said. "Goodbye."

"Bye, Weezie," she said. "Don't be a stranger."

When I hung up, I couldn't help wondering if Flo was right. Was Baxter's ad a cover-up? But Sylvie had more than hinted at the fact that Baxter wasn't too bright. Would a less-than-bright man come up with such a cover-up? In any case, it belonged on my page, so I added it:

BAXTER RAN A CLASSIFIED AD IN NEW SCOTIA NEWSPAPER.
THIS COULD MEAN HE'S INNOCENT. OR NOT.

It was only 4:15, and I didn't have to be at Rita's until 7. I wondered what I should do for a couple of hours. Then I remembered: the multi-screen cinema! Making a beeline for the beltline, I quickly found it. I'd already seen all the films on their marquee except *A Man Apart*, which I'd read about and had great hopes for. It just turned out to be so-so. The Gummi Worms were good, though.

When I got to Rita's, she was feeding the baby from two jars of Gerber's. One was pureed squash and the other was applesauce; except for being less lumpy, they looked a lot like the side dishes Great-aunt Concetta served with ham.

The baby was using the opportunity to perfect his spit mechanism. Standing back, I said, "What's his name?"

"Sophie. She's a her. Want a beer?"

"No, thanks."

"Would you mind getting me one?" she asked. I fetched a bottle of Bud from a full six-pack in the refrigerator and helped myself to a glass of water.

The doorbell chimed as Rita was scrubbing Sophie's face and hands and everything within firing range. Pointing to a $20 bill on the counter, she asked if I'd go get the pizza. I didn't *really* think she'd poison me, but I was perfectly happy to be the food handler.

Setting the box on the table, I planted slices on two plates. Rita tore off a crust for Sophie to gnaw on, and we dug in. Between bites, I told her I'd heard her husband wasn't a New Scotia native.

"Where'd you hear that?" she said

"Rube told me."

"Figures. She's so mad at me she'd say anything. I actually swallowed my pride and went to her grand opening, and she practically ignored me."

"So your husband *is* a New Scotia native?"

"Of course not. I just don't like Rube talking to people about us. She's still pissed at me for marrying him. We were kids back then, for crap's sake. I can't help it—I wanted a normal life. I'm not a...a..."

"Lesbian?" I said.

She put her hands over the baby's ears. "Please! Ken would kill me if she ever repeated that word."

"Does she talk?"

"Not *yet*. In any case, Ken's originally from Denver. He came here to take a position with the Muddy River Bank."

"What kind of position?"

"Loan management. That's how I got into the field; he got me a job. We don't work at the same place, though. He's downtown and I'm at one of the branches."

"Yesterday you told me he was born-again. Christian?" I asked.

"Baptist. I'm born-again too—he just takes it more seriously than I do. That's why I told him you were a salesperson. I was sure he was smelling *dyke* on you. I mean, if he thought you were in any way connected with Rube…" She shuddered.

"What would he do?"

"Oh, nothing really. It's just better he doesn't know. I mean, first he saw Honey Lou and now you."

"He saw Honey Lou?"

"That day she came here, that Tuesday afternoon—"

I interrupted. "Do you know who brought her here?"

"I have no idea. They didn't stay to chat. But I remember the car all right. It was a Porsche. Anyway, Honey Lou asked if she could stay here a few days because her husband was stalking her, and I said *no way* but offered to take her to Rube's. That's when Ken walked in."

"He recognized her?"

"He'd never met her, so how could he? I threw the baby at him and drove Honey Lou out to Rube's."

I shook my head. "I still don't understand. If they never met, how did Ken know she was Honey Lou?"

"He didn't. Turns out he heard me say the name Rube, so he thought that's who she was. I keep telling him, 'Honest to God,

Ken it was Honey Lou,' but he won't believe me, so now he thinks
I got something going on with Rube again. He's been sleeping in
the guest bedroom ever since."

"Wow," I said. "So what was I selling?"

"What?"

"You told Ken I was a salesperson. What was I selling?"

"Bibles."

Oh, well, it's a living.

Rita's sitter showed up at 8. She looked the typical grandma,
with graying hair and pink lacy cardigan. Rita told her I was a
fellow church member and the reason we were going out was to
visit the sick.

The baby was already in bed, so while Rita changed clothes,
I made what I hoped sounded like small talk with the sitter.
"Do you sit for Rita and Ken a lot?" I asked.

"Oh, yes. I live down the block, so it's very convenient."

"Do you take care of Sophie while they're at work too?"

"No, dear. Rita takes her to day care."

Damn. I was hoping she could tell me if Sophie was there on the
Wednesday morning when Rita may or may not have taken her
yellow car to Rube's to pick up Honey Lou. I couldn't imagine Rita
would pay for someone to take care of the baby when she wasn't
working. "Do you know which day care center?" I asked. "A friend
of mine is pregnant, and I told her I'd visit some facilities for her."

Grams thought a minute, then said, "I don't think Rita ever
told me the name of the day care. Why don't you ask *her*?"

"Good idea."

"When is your friend due?" she asked.

"Oh, um, May sometime."

"Does she live near here?"

"No. She lives over by the stockyard."

She wrinkled her nose, and I nodded sadly.

Rita came back wearing a low-cut dress in a deep shade of green that she'd accessorized with patent-leather heels and a beaded black shoulder bag. It was a good outfit for sick calls. Just looking at her, I felt better.

9

Sitting shotgun in the yellow Honda, I took the envelope with Sylvie Lemming's list of bars from my back pocket. The first one was the Big Clog. I asked Rita if she'd ever heard of it.

"Oh, sure," she said. "That's where I first met Ken. We were doing the tush push." That was all I wanted to hear about *that*, so I steered the conversation to day care centers. Apparently, Sophie spent her weekdays at the Tot Plot. I etched it in my memory.

The Big Clog turned out to be a warehouse-size room with giant cowboy boots painted on its lofty walls. There were only eight people in the place, including the bartender and three guys doing sound checks on a stage in the corner.

Rita bellied up to the bar and ordered a sloe gin fizz, telling me, "They're like soda pop. I can drink them all night and never feel them." Since she was driving, I hoped that was true.

I followed her to a table by the stage, where one of the musicians was tuning a guitar. As he turned the knobs and picked the strings, he consulted a little black box balanced on his knee. Once in a while he said "Fuck." Then he yelled at an idly picking mandolin player, "Keep it down, fuckhead. You're fuckin' up my tuner."

Figuring that filled my quota of "fucks" for the evening, I went back to the bar. The bartender, a young woman in fringed Western wear, was straining at the lid of an immense jar of maraschino cherries. "What can I get you?" she asked.

"Have you seen this person lately?" I held up Honey Lou's picture.

"Don't think so," she said. "We get so busy, I couldn't tell you who's here when. Anyway, I work at three different bars. How would I remember who I saw where?"

"She's missing a tooth," I said.

She shrugged. Turning the jar upside down, she banged it on a cutting board.

"Would you like me to take a stab at opening that?" I asked.

"No. I'll get it." She carried the jar down the bar to continue her struggle in private.

I showed the photo to the four patrons and the musicians, but they all said they'd never seen Honey Lou, with or without all her teeth. "I guess that's it for this place," I told Rita. "Let's try the next bar on the list,"

She stuck out her lower lip. "The band is going to start playing in 20 minutes. Couldn't we stay for the first set?"

"No, we've got to get going. Maybe the next place will have a band too."

Still pouting, she chugged her drink.

The Tip Top Tap not only didn't have a band, it had nowhere to put one if one stopped by. It was a dingy neighborhood tavern with a dozen stools filled with silent drinkers, all of whom qualified for the senior citizen discount. The only noise was the thunk of darts from a corner, where two younger men played under a bare bulb.

A bartender was watching a muted TV screen on which skateboarders were performing impossible stunts. When I held up Honey Lou's photo, he reluctantly pulled his attention to it. "Nope," he said. "Never seen her."

"She might have come in with a guy named Baxter," I prompted.

"I don't know any Baxter."

"Come on," I said. "Everybody knows at least one Baxter."

He gave me a disgusted look. "So what can I get you?"

"A sloe gin fizz."

"And what for the lady?" he nodded toward the jukebox, where Rita was flipping through the selections.

"That *is* for the lady. I don't suppose you have root beer."

Another disgusted look.

By the time I brought the drink over to Rita, Willie Nelson was moaning "Help me make it through the night," and the dart players had abandoned their game in favor of keeping her company. I showed them the photo. One couldn't peel his eyes off Rita long enough to take a decent look. The other thought he may have seen Honey Lou once but couldn't remember where.

I showed the photo down the bar. A few of the stoolies squinted at it and shook their heads, but most were past the point of identifying anybody. The lone woman said I looked a lot like her grandson, and would I mind buying her a beer?

Back in the car, I told Rita we'd try one more place, and that was it for me. She was sorry to hear it. "Why don't we go back to the Big Clog?" she suggested. "There'll be more a lot more people there by now."

"I think we should go to the next one on the list," I said.

"I *sure* would like to dance," she whined.

I ignored her and read aloud the address of the next bar, Club DVS. Rita had never heard of it or the street it was on, so I had to turn on the dim overhead light and find it on the city map I'd had the foresight to bring. When we got there, I was sure I'd read it wrong, because the address was a carryout fried chicken place in the middle of a bunch of empty storefronts and trash-filled lots. However, there were way too many cars around for a carryout fried-chicken place, so we decided to check it out.

We finally found a parking space four blocks away. As we walked back, we noticed strobes flashing around the edges of the painted-out upstairs windows. Since there wasn't any door other than the one to the fried-chicken place, we went in and asked the guy behind the counter if he knew where Club DVS might be. After looking us over, he jerked his head toward a doorway at the back. Behind it was a set of stairs. Everything in the dark stairwell, including the air, was pulsing to the beat of the bass.

I paused and looked at Rita. "What do you think?"

"I don't know. It's pretty creepy," she said. Just then, two good-looking men pushed past us and ran up the stairs. There was a deafening blast of music as they opened a door at the top long enough to pass through. Rita seized my arm and started climbing. "We owe it to dear Honey Lou, don't we," she said.

The pounding of the bass increased in volume as we ascended. When we opened the upper door, it hit us so hard Rita jumped back against me. I caught the handrail just in time to avoid falling backward.

"Hello, girls," hollered a burly fellow sitting on a stool inside the door. "That'll be $20 each, cover."

"Twenty dollars!" I said, taking a moment to observe the

clientele. At the other bars, they had been mainly men. At this one, they were *all* men, including a few who looked like women but were, to my trained eye, men. Men sitting at tables, standing in groups, dancing. Rita put her mouth to my ear. "I can't believe it," she said. "In New Scotia! Who'd have thought?" She rummaged in her bag, presumably looking for her wallet.

I turned to the guy on the stool. "We're not staying. I just want to see if anybody knows this person." I held up Honey Lou's photo.

"Never saw him before in my life," he said.

"It's a *her*," I told him, but he still shook his head.

Rita held up a MasterCard. "Do you take these?" she asked him.

I turned to the guy. "Please, can't we go in for a minute and ask around? The woman in this picture is a missing person. I've been told she comes here sometimes."

He shouted at a man in a black suit who sauntered over. They whispered, stared at us a while, and whispered again. Finally, the suit nodded. I grabbed Rita and pulled her across the big room to the bar on the other side. It was behind the amps, so the music wasn't quite so loud. I beckoned to a bartender in semi-drag. His nipples, pushed up by a lacy corset, were pierced by little arrows. Over his heart, he had pasted a paper nametag that said his name was Betsy. He took the photo of Honey Lou and cried, "Cool earrings!" Another bartender wearing a black leather vest and chaps came over to check out the excitement. Betsy passed him the photo, saying, "Doesn't she look familiar?"

"Maybe. What's her name?"

"Honey Lou Wright," I told him. "She's missing, and we're trying to find her."

"Who's we?"

I looked around. Rita had disappeared into the crowd. "*I'm trying to find her.*"

Black Leather stoked his Van Dyke. "Yeah, I remember her. She hits Ladies' Night once in a while."

Betsy grabbed the photo and held it up to a Michelob sign. "This picture doesn't do her justice at all. Her hair is this *smoldering* auburn."

"When's Ladies' Night?" I asked.

"Thursdays. Drafts are a dollar each."

"They should be free if you're going to have a $20 cover charge," I said.

They laughed up a storm. Betsy said, "That Geordie! It's supposed to be five bucks—he saw you coming."

"When was the last time you saw her?" I asked, nodding at Honey Lou's photo.

"She hasn't been in for a long time," said Betsy. "Months. I miss her. Good tipper."

"Did she come in alone or with somebody else?"

"Alone," said Black Leather. "I mean, she might have left with some butch once in a while, but never the same one."

Betsy smacked him on a bare cheek. "Don't tell her that. She might be her lover."

"Don't worry, we're not lovers," I said. "Is there anyone here who could give me more information?"

They surveyed the room. Betsy said, "No. Sorry. When you locate her, tell her we miss her."

I said I would and went to find Rita. Shoulder bag bouncing wildly, she was dancing with three guys to "We Are Family." Sloe gin fizz sloshed in all directions. When I told her we were leaving, she almost threw what was left at me.

On the way to the Honda, as I was telling her what I'd found out from the bartenders, she tripped over a crack in the sidewalk. After regaining her balance, she said, "What nightsh are ladiesh' nightsh?" She tripped again, and there wasn't a crack in sight.

"Thursdays, and I'll drive your car if you don't mind."

On the way home, I thought I'd see if the pie-eyed Rita would stick to the sober Rita's story. "So *where* did you say you took Honey Lou after you picked her up at Rube's that Wednesday morning?"

She answered with a gentle snore.

When we got to her house, I pulled in the garage, woke her up, and sent her in. Then I took off on foot, without waiting to see what the baby-sitter thought of her condition.

10

By the time I got up Friday morning, the sun was high in the sky and the air felt a lot warmer. I celebrated by donning a pair of cut-offs and setting one of Rube's folding chairs at the edge of the water, where the ripples reflected the sunlight like a zillion tiny mirrors.

Opening Weezie's notebook to the Honey Lou Tree, I used its little pen to draw a twiglet off the RITA twig, naming it KEN KANE. Then, for fun, I added a tiny one named SOPHIE. I wrote MR. PROUDFLESH, SHOULDER-PAD WOMAN, and NAOMI HERZOG on the empty twigs of the WORKPLACE branch, hoping there wouldn't be any more—I was running out of space on that side.

Finally, I turned to the CLUES page. In the spirit of fairness, after the entry RITA KANE PICKED UP H.L. FROM RUBE'S PLACE WEDNESDAY MORNING, I added ALTHOUGH RITA DENIES IT.

Sticking the pen in its place in the spine, I flipped back to the first page and contemplated the tree. Not counting Honey Lou, there were 12 people on its various branches, and I'd met all of them except Baxter. You'd think by now I'd have at least one solid theory as to what happened to her, but I didn't. It was extremely discouraging.

What was especially worrisome was the length of time it had been since anybody had laid eyes on her. The agents on *Without a Trace* would be shaking their heads and offering the family little hope. Her mother was right—if Honey Lou was alive, she would have called. Whenever I was away from home, I tried not to go more than three days without calling Mom. Well, OK, four. Five? *Whoops.* I ran and got my phone.

Mom answered on the first ring. "Hello, Jo."

"How'd you know it was me? Oh, yeah, that caller I.D. thing."

"I'm so glad we got it. Rose had to talk to her sister Mandy only once this week."

"Why did she have to talk to her at all?"

"Mandy got wise and went over to their mother's house to call. Isn't that nervy?"

"There should be a law," I said.

"Indeed. How are you doing? Did you find Weezie's friend?"

"Not yet. I'm starting to wonder if Honey Lou might be dead."

"Really? Who has the best motive?"

"Motive? I'm not here to look for motives, Mom—that's the job of the police. And even if she is dead, it doesn't mean somebody killed her. She has serious drinking and drug problems. She might have overdosed."

"My goodness! But you're right, leave the dangerous business to the authorities. I want my little girl back in one piece. I *wuv* my little girl."

"Aw, Mom," I said.

"Well, I *do*. However, if Honey Lou is dead, wouldn't they

have found her body?" she said. "I mean, after two weeks, she must be rather smelly."

Yeah, I really want to find her now. "I've got to go, Mom."

"I do too. We're having the annual Trash for Cash sale at the school this weekend, and Rose and I are getting ready to take a load over." Mom and Rose had been teaching at our local elementary school for 20 years. That's where they met. "By the way, I happened to notice your old bench and weights in the basement. You haven't used them in years."

"Don't sell them! I want them!"

There was a muffled "Rose, take those back down," followed by a distant groan. Then she said, "OK, dear, I love you. Call again soon. Goodbye." My "Bye, Mom" trailed off into dead space.

I hit the *end* button, already back to speculating on who did have a motive to kill Honey Lou. Her mean husband, Baxter, had a good motive; she'd had him arrested. But was he mean enough to kill her? Sylvie Lemming thought he was. And like Flo suggested, he might have put the "not responsible" notice in the newspaper to cover his ass.

And what about Honey Lou's boss, Mr. Proudflesh? He couldn't be very happy about her lawsuit. I found it incriminating that he hadn't told Sylvie or me about giving her a ride that afternoon—what else wasn't he telling? Maybe Honey Lou had discovered the phone in the broom closet and was blackmailing him and/or Shoulder-Pad Woman.

Did Rita Kane have a motive to do away with Honey Lou? She seemed relatively harmless to me, but Rube sure didn't think so. And as far as I knew, Rita was the last one to see her alive. Or was she? If somebody wanted to cast suspicion on her, it would be easy enough to find another yellow car.

Thinking of Rita reminded me to call information for the number of Sophie's day care. "In New Scotia, please. Do you have a number for Tot Lot?" I asked. The operator said she didn't see a listing. "Um, what about Tot Spot?" I tried.

With more than a hint of impatience in her voice, she suggested "How about Tot Plot?" and gave me the number.

The human firewall who answered the phone at Tot Plot refused to tell me anything despite a tale I wove about being Rita Kane needing to know if Wednesday April 9 was the exact morning my daughter Sophie had been absent because I'd taken her to the doctor's for a checkup and wanted to deduct the mileage from my income tax. The firewall told me she knew Rita Kane's voice and mine wasn't it, and if I called again, I'd find myself smack in a jail cell. I felt frustrated but was glad Sophie was in such good hands.

Sticking the phone in my pocket, I went to find Rube. She was in her shop working on an Evinrude Ficht outboard motor. This I knew because the motor had EVINRUDE FICHT printed on its side.

"Morning, Jo," Rube said, wiping the grease off a donut-shaped part with a towel. "I see you survived Rita's cooking. Did you have fun on the bar tour?"

"As much fun as chewing tinfoil. But I did discover something interesting."

"What?"

"Honey Lou was still having sex with women."

Rube dropped the part. It rolled across the floor and under a bench. "Shit," she said and went after it. "How'd you find that out?"

"A bartender at this gay club said she used to show up on ladies' night and sometimes left with butches."

"Geez, don't tell Weezie."

"I won't. She's hurting bad enough already. Aren't you surprised to hear there's a gay club in New Scotia? Rita sure was."

"I'd heard there's one. Don't like bars myself. Too smoky. So what's on your agenda today?"

"I don't know. Maybe I'll go do a load of laundry. Is there a laundromat anywhere near?"

"Real near," she said. "There's a wash machine under my kitchen counter. Couldn't fit in a dryer, though. You'll have to hang 'em."

"No problem," I said.

She wiped her hands on a rag. "I'll show you where things are. By the way, don't eat supper. Jenny called; she's bringing it when she comes to work."

We entered her apartment and crossed to the kitchen area. Behind a cabinet door was a sweet little front-loader. When Rube took a bottle of detergent from a nearby closet, I spotted a beat-up guitar case standing inside. "Do you play guitar?" I asked.

"Not really. One of my exes left it. Every once in a while I take it out and fool around. Do you?"

"No, but I'd sure like to try."

"Knock your socks off." She pulled the case out and handed it to me.

"I don't know anything about it."

"There's an instruction book and a video around here some-where," she said. The video turned out to be on the closet shelf, but the book was harder to locate. She finally found it under a pile of boating magazines. "Have fun," she said and went back to her Ficht.

I wasn't interested in doing laundry anymore, but dutifully I went out and got a bagful. After setting it to sloshing, I opened the case and carefully removed the guitar. It was blond and beau-tiful, a little beat-up but not as bad as its case.

I plucked a string lightly. A lovely *ting* hung in the air for a nanosecond and faded away. Opening the instruction book to

the first lesson, I placed my left hand on the strings in the con-
figuration they showed for the C chord and used my right-hand
fingers to strum. Not lovely. The guitar needed tuning.

I leafed through the instruction book, but there was no clue
about how to tune. The guitar player at the Big Clog had been
using a little black box. I looked on the closet shelf, but there was
no little black box. Sticking my head in the shop, I yelled, "Hey,
Rube, how do I tune it?"

"Watch the video," she yelled back.

I stuck the video in her VCR and perched in the middle of the
sofa. The instructor started out by naming parts of the guitar, as
if I was going to have a test later. Then he produced six tones,
directing me to bring my strings into agreement by twisting each
of the guitar's pegs like I'd seen Jamie Anderson do for aeons
between every blasted song. It turned out to be harder than it
looked. I rewound the tape and played the tones over and over so
many times, I was afraid I was going to wear out the video or the
VCR or both.

Finally, I felt confident enough to chance another strum. This
one sounded sweeter, so I let Video Guy go on and teach me a
couple of chords. That accomplished, he said, "You are now
ready to play 'Tom Dooley' with me."

I played it, but took so long to change chords, it came out as:
"Hang down your head, Tom"—long pause—"Dooley"—long
pause—"Hang down your head and…"—*D? Where the hell is
D?…oh, yeah*—"cry." By this time the instructor had finished
two verses of "Tom Dooley" and moved on to "Kumbaya."

Even so, I was pleased with myself. If you didn't count my
xylophone pull-toy, it was the first music I'd ever made with anything but my vocal chords.

In the middle of "You Are My Sunshine," the fingertips on
my left hand started smarting from pressing on the sharp strings.

I never realized how hard Jamie must have been pressing—
she'd made it look so effortless.

I gritted my teeth and pressed on. By the time my laundry
had completed its final spin, I was accompanying myself to such
top-of-the-chart favorites as "Merrily We Roll Along" and "We
Wish You a Merry Christmas." "And a happy"—*A7?...did I learn
A7?*—"new"—*Ringfinger, get your butt over here. You're sore?
Who cares!*—"year."

11

I was in the shop chatting with Rube when a blue pickup pulled in the driveway and Jenny climbed out, holding a cardboard bucket and a fistful of paper napkins. While Rube fetched sodas, I went out back and positioned the two lawn chairs under a tree. "We'll need another chair," I said when they emerged.

"Don't bother," Jenny said, "I'll sit on the ground. Oh, look at the cute rig. Is that yours, Jo?"

I jumped up and gave her a tour of Dan'l's interior, complete with demonstrations. Then I walked her around the outside, explaining every bin and connection port until she said, "That's very interesting, Jo, but I think the ribs may be getting cold."

When we were settled, she pried the lid off the bucket and wrapped one end of a barbecued rib in a napkin. Handing it to me, she said, "Brace yourself for a treat. You ain't got nothing like this baby up yonder in Yankland." The baby was tasty, but we *did* have something like it up yonder in Yankland. In fact, this particular baby was way too spicy. I didn't want to spoil Jenny's day, though, so I kept it to myself.

Jenny sat on the grass leaning against Rube's legs, looking out over the steel-blue water. "Lake's choppy," she said between bites.

"Yeah," Rube said. "Not many boats out for an April Saturday."

"Suits me. I won't go out on busy weekends 'less I got a motor test that won't wait—too many sloshed drivers and beginners out there who haven't read the rules. It's a wonder there aren't more accidents than there are."

"I can see why people want to be on the water. It's beautiful," I said. "I had no idea Oklahoma had a big lake like this."

Jenny looked at me. "Are you kidding? This is only *one* of our big beautiful lakes. There's more shoreline in Oklahoma than the entire eastern seaboard of the U.S. *and* Mexico. I wouldn't live anywhere else."

"Were you raised around here?" I asked.

"Sure was. My folks have a house over on the north end of the lake. I grew up on the water, boating, fishing, exploring. They had to threaten holy damnation to get me to school and church."

"Your folks were religious, like Rube's?"

"Everybody around here is religious, 'cept a few heathens we're working on." She grinned up at Rube.

"Better work a little harder, preacher," Rube said. "It ain't taking root." With her little finger, the only one that wasn't covered in sauce, she tucked an errant hair behind Jenny's ear.

Jenny grabbed Rube's hand and started licking the sauce off her fingers. Rube jerked her hand away and glanced at me. I quickly looked out at the lake and said, "Is the water very deep?"

"The average depth is 23 feet," Jenny said, "but there are lots of spots deeper than that. Do you dive?"

"Not really."

"Too bad. There's a whole town down there from when they dammed up Muddy River and let the water rise. That was in 1963. Wish I could have been here to see it."

"You'd be an old lady by now," Rube said.

Jenny laughed. "Maybe then I'd have enough sense to steer clear of the likes of you."

"Get out of here," Rube said. "You know I'm the best thing you got going for you." She turned to me. "I agree with Jenny, Jo. I don't know why anyone would want to live anywhere but here. It's perfect."

"What about the tornadoes?" I asked, automatically scanning the horizon.

"Don't you get tornadoes up north?"

"Once in a great while, I guess. But you have them a lot, don't you? Every year about this time? That's what Weezie told me, anyway."

"Weezie's right," Rube said, leaning back in her chair. "The winds can get pretty wild. But here's the way I look at it: If a tornado hits, it either kills you or it doesn't. If it doesn't, you get yourself some timber and rebuild."

"Well put, darlin'," Jenny said.

I thought about my first night in Oklahoma—the howling winds and blowing debris. "But it's *scary*!"

"That it is," Rube said, "but there's a heap of things scarier, like…" She stopped to think.

Jenny took over: "Like shoveling snow. Now that's scary! In this part of Oklahoma, it hardly ever snows, and when it does, you make yourself a cup of cocoa and go watch it melt."

"And *crime* is scary," Rube said. "I hear there's places in New York you can't walk without getting mugged."

"If you're talking about Buffalo, that's not true. I walk downtown all the time and I've never been mugged." *But, Jo, I thought, while you were out walking, didn't somebody break into your truck and steal your CD player?* "Of course we do have our share of crime," I added lamely. "What big city doesn't?"

Jenny said, "Speaking of crime, Belle Starr lived around here in the late 1800s. You've heard of her, haven't you, Jo?"

I probed the history-retention section of my brain; it didn't take long. "Was she a sharpshooter in a circus?"

She laughed. "You're thinking of Annie Oakley. Belle Starr was the leader of a bunch of bandits. They hung out in a cave not far from the Eudora Dam. She's buried somewhere around there too. Hey, maybe it's Belle's ghost that's doing away with Rube's friends." She glanced around, shuddering in faux fear.

"Enough, Jenny," Rube said. "We don't know that Honey Lou has been done away with at all, and I doubt if Belle's ghost went all the way to El Reno to 'do away' with Beth."

"Whatever you say, ma'am. But, Jo, you should visit the dam while you're here. I'll take you over there."

"When are you going to do that, Jenny?" Rube said. "You don't even have time to pick your nose."

"I didn't know it needed it. But now that I know…" She stuck a sauce-covered finger in her nostril.

"Look at you!" Rube said, laughing. "Where's those extra napkins?"

"I'm sitting on them. But don't clean me up yet—there's still a couple of ribs left. Who wants one?"

I shook my head.

"They're all yours, Jen," Rube said.

Taking another rib from the bucket, Jenny said, "I'm afraid

Rube's right, Jo—with all this nice weather, it's an awful busy time for me. Everybody wants their boat lake-ready yesterday. How long you planning on staying?"

"I don't know, not too long maybe—I'm running out of people to interview," I said. "What I really want is to talk to somebody at the women's shelter in New Scotia, but nobody knows where it is. You don't know, do you?"

They shook their heads and Rube said, "I suppose they have to keep the location secret or it wouldn't be safe."

"I know how you can find the shelter," Jenny said.

"How?"

"Get somebody to beat you up."

Rube gasped. "Jenny, that is *not* funny."

"Just trying to get a rise out of you, darlin'," Jenny said, rubbing her sauce-covered mouth on Rube's leg.

Rube jumped on Jenny, laying her flat. They wrestled on the grass, giggling like kids. After a minute, Jenny cuffed Rube playfully on the ear and wheeled up. "I win," she said. "And now I'd better get my ass to work or I'll be here all night."

"You wish," Rube said as she scrambled up and followed Jenny into the shop.

I ran around gathering up the blowing napkins, wondering what the deal was between those two. They sure looked like lovers, but if they were, why hadn't Rube said so? More likely, they were soon-to-be-lovers, and what I was witnessing was their pre-sex flirting. Maybe tonight was the night.

Thinking about this made me restless, so I decided to take a drive over to the dam. I was inconveniencing these people enough without making either of them think they had to play tour guide.

They were pulling an inboard when I went in for directions. I waited until they had it free, then told them my plan.

"Hell, Jo, if you don't like my company..." Jenny said in a mock-serious tone.

"It's not that."

"Yeah, yeah. Well, at least let me show you how to get there." She found a piece of paper and drew a crude map.

"Jenny," Rube said, "why don't you let Jo take your truck? No point in her hauling her turtle shell all over creation."

"*My* truck? Why don't you let her use *your* truck?"

"I would, but yours is blocking mine so we'd have to move it anyway."

"I don't know," Jenny said.

Rube folded her arms. "Don't be a royal poophead."

"That's OK," I said. "I can take my RV."

Jenny pulled a set of keys from her pocket, saying, "No, no. Take my truck. I'll save my poop for more important things."

"Are you sure?" I didn't mind driving Dan'l, but it would be a real treat to tool around in a smaller vehicle.

"I'm sure, and by the way, there's couple of biker bars on the way in case you get thirsty," she said.

"As if," I said, grabbing the keys before she could change her mind.

Because of all the coves and inlets, the road to the dam crossed a zillion bridges and causeways. I thought about my cousin Lorena's asthmatic mother-in-law in Rochester who had a bridge phobia. She wouldn't go to a doctor or hospital unless it was located on her side of the Genesee River. If she lived in Oklahoma lake country, she'd have been dead by now.

Since Jenny was substantially taller than me, I had to strain to reach the pedals. After a couple of uncomfortable miles, I pulled to the side of the road and groped for the seat-adjustment lever. When I didn't find it, I opened the door, and a square of paper flew out from behind the seat and fell to the ground. I jumped out and picked it up. It was a head shot of Rube—a young Rube, not more than 21, if that. She was wearing a beige V-neck sweater, and her hair was an inch longer than she wore it now. Handwritten in a corner was "Us 4 Ever." So much for my not-yet-lovers theory. They'd been together quite a while.

I looked behind the seat for a photo album or envelope, but there was nothing there but a jack. I ended up wedging the edge of the photo under a corner of the jack so it wouldn't blow out again. After adjusting the seat to my liking, I continued on my way.

The sun was low when I finally drove across the dam and followed a driveway that descended to the Muddy River. The river lived up to its name—the water was mud-brown and there was barely enough of it to accommodate a fisherman in a small outboard and a wading egret, both of whom may have been targeting the same fish.

The dam was small compared to the one at Niagara Falls, but still impressive. I'd always found it remarkable that a man-made structure could hold back a whole lake when a bucketful of water nearly pulled your shoulder out of its socket.

When I'd had my fill, I drove back to the top of the dam and watched the sun set over the lake. Streaks of gold outlined coral-pink clouds on a bed of deepening teal blue. It was doubly beautiful because the whole drama was reflected in the lake. Rube was right, this place was perfect. Then I remembered the storm and revised my opinion to near-perfect.

She and Jenny were sitting on the lakeshore when I got back. As I handed the keys to Jenny, she said, "Did you find it?"

"Yes, I did," I said. *And I left it behind your seat.*

12

If there was one thing you could say about Rube, it was that she was a hard worker; she didn't even take Sundays off. I was startled awake at 7 sharp by a great roar coming from the direction of her shop.

After throwing on yesterday's Levi's and a clean shirt, I made a pot of coffee and filled two mugs. On the way over, it occurred to me that I'd be a mug short if, as I'd theorized, Jenny had spent the night. If she had, though, she was already gone—Rube was alone. The great roar was from an outboard she was testing in a tank of water. When she saw me, she turned it off. "Hey, thanks, Jo," she said. "I'm ready for some caffeine."

"What's wrong with the motor?" I asked.

She patted it proudly. "Nothing anymore. The owner told me it froze up, so I ran a compression test. But the compression was real good."

"No kidding," I said, like I knew all about compression.

"Then I checked the starter and there wasn't any spark. So I replaced it along with the coils, and that took care of it. The owner is going to be mucho pleased when he gets his bill."

"Great," I said. "That's great."

She pointed her mug at another motor that was lying partly dismantled on a workbench. "Now, that 85-horse over there is another story. It was losing power, so of course I thought it was a hot short in the ignition system, but it's not. So now I've got to start on the carbs, but first I'm going to check for a slipping hub."

Her phone rang, thank goodness. A self-identified butch, I should have been interested in the inner workings of combustion engines, but I wasn't. As she started to give a customer a progress report, I played an air guitar and gestured toward her apartment. She asked the caller to hold. "Sure, go ahead. I've got a couple of deadlines here, so I don't know if I'll be able to take you to the marina today, like I sort of promised."

"Don't worry about it. If I want to go, I can get myself over there," I said.

"If you can hold off till 4 or so, I'll know better how I'm doing by then."

I said OK and went to her apartment. As I took the guitar from the closet, I found myself looking around for signs that Jenny had spent the night. It was none of my business, of course, but it would be good detecting practice—that's how I justified it, anyway. By way of that justification, I pictured a page labeled DID JENNY SPEND THE NIGHT? in Weezie's notebook, and as I nosed around, I mentally wrote in it.

1) ALL THE CLOTHES IN THE CLOSET SCREAM "SHORT BUTCH," WHEREAS THE CLOTHES JENNY WEARS ARE LONG, SOFT, AND FEMININE. *Of course, Jenny could spend the*

night without leaving clothes, couldn't she? CONCLUSION? UNCERTAIN.

2) THE BED IS TOO SMALL FOR TWO PEOPLE AND HAS ONLY ONE PILLOW. *For lovers, however, no bed is too small.* CONCLUSION? UNCERTAIN.

3) SPEAKING OF TOOTHBRUSHES, THERE ARE TWO OF THEM IN THE BATHROOM CABINET, ONE BATTERY-DRIVEN AND ONE MUSCLE-DRIVEN, BUT ONLY THE FORMER IS DAMP. *Once at a music festival I shared a lover's toothbrush because I had forgotten mine.* CONCLUSION? UNCERTAIN.

4) THERE ARE TWO KNIVES IN THE SINK, BUT ONLY ONE CUP, ONE PLATE, ONE BOWL, AND ONE SPOON. *Rube and Jenny might share a knife, plate, and bowl, but a spoon?* CONCLUSION? UNCERTAIN.

I checked the closet again in case I had missed something. I had. In a corner under a pile of sweaters was a shoe box, and in the box was a pair of black sandals that consisted of three thin straps and a silver buckle. Rube would *never* wear sandals like that, but Jenny sure might.

Quietly chortling, I gathered up the guitar and instruction book and took them outside to review the chords I'd learned yesterday. For some reason they didn't sound as good today; instead of lovely musical tones, all I heard were metallic vibrations and thunks. Maybe my fingers, still sore from yesterday, weren't pressing the strings hard enough. Maybe guitars sounded different outside. Maybe my expectations were too high.

Anyway, I soldiered on and learned three new chords, using them to play "Twinkle, Twinkle, Little Star." In the middle, my fingers started screaming bloody murder. Each string felt like the edge of a razor blade. Also, I was realizing that the only strum I knew, a steady downstroke, sounded stupid. I gave up in disgust and was putting the guitar back in its case when Rube came out.

"How's the playing?" she said.

"Not so good. I need some guidance. Would you mind, sometime?"

"Sure. I'll help you first chance I get. What I came to tell you is that Honey Lou's mother called. She's been trying to raise you on your cell with no luck."

"Sorry. I left it in Dan'l. Thought I'd be able to hear it out here."

"No problem. I told her you'd call her," she said.

"Thanks, I will."

I spent a few minutes trying to think of a progress report before calling Sylvie. All I could come up with was, "I know several places where Honey Lou isn't."

Sylvie didn't ask for a report, though. What she told me was that her Aunt Fiona who lives in Oklahoma City had called and said she'd spotted Baxter Wright at a mall there wearing a security guard uniform.

"Did your aunt talk to him?"

"Yes, but he said he wasn't Baxter. He told her his name, but she couldn't remember what it was."

"Is she sure it was him?"

"I guess so. I didn't talk to her—Ma did. The problem is, Fiona's only met Baxter once or twice. I think you ought to go over to that mall, Jo. You could follow him to wherever he's staying and see if Honey Lou is there. If she is, he must have her all tied up so she can't call her mother."

"The problem is, Sylvie, I never met Baxter at all. I don't know what he looks like. Why don't you go?" I asked.

"I can't. I have to finish three muumuus by next Saturday for a wedding. They moved it up when the bride found out she was…well, you know. Won't you go, Jo, please?"

"Oh, all right. Do you have a photo of Baxter I can come get?"

"I used to, but Honey Lou was so mad at him, she went and tore them all up, even her wedding pictures. So I think you ought to take Ma with you."

"Take your mother?" I wasn't eager to go to Oklahoma City at all, much less with Flo in tow.

"Sure. Ma knows what he looks like. She knows the way there too. Do you know the way there?"

"I got a map. I can figure it out." I took my map from the glove compartment and started searching for Oklahoma City.

"No, no, those maps don't know nothing," Sylvie said. "Ma can tell you the best way. And anyway…" She started mumbling.

"I can't hear you, Sylvie," I said.

"I said anyway, I been promising to take her to visit Aunt Fiona. After you identify Baxter and find out if my daughter's with him, you could drop her off."

At that moment, I spotted Oklahoma City on the map. It was in the exact opposite direction from Rube's as Mrs. Lemming's house. Picking up her mother would add 50 miles to the trip. "If I agree to take her," I said, "will you at least bring her as far as Shoreville?"

"I would, dearie, but Chuck's got my car in pieces and I don't know when he'll have it back together—you know *him*. You were going to come over here anyway to pick up a photo, weren't you? I don't see the difference. Didn't Weezie send you to help us out? What else are you doing that's so important?"

She was right. I wasn't doing anything at all important.

By noon the next day, I was on my way to Oklahoma City with Flo firmly buckled in Dan'l's other bucket. She was wearing a green polyester pantsuit, and her head was covered with tiny blue-white coils.

"You got your hair curled since I saw you," I said.

"It's a perm, and I told her not to cut it this short," she said.

"Told who? Sylvie?"

"Are you kidding? I wouldn't let Sylvie near my head with a pair of scissors. She'd probably carve out a muumuu."

I couldn't help notice that Flo was having no trouble hearing me today, even though Dan'l's engine was roaring. "Did you find your hearing aid?" I asked.

"Yup, it's right here." She patted one of her pockets.

"I thought you couldn't hear without it," I said. "The day we met, Sylvie introduced me as Jo, but you kept calling me Weezie."

"No, I didn't."

"You did too."

"I don't know what you're talking about, Jo. You don't look nothing like Weezie. Do *you* think you look like Weezie?"

"No, but... What is this, a game?"

She grinned. "Don't tell Sylvie, OK?"

Oklahoma City was in a north and westerly direction from the Lemming house. I planned to take Interstate 40, but Flo told me that was a lousy way to go. She'd been born and raised here, she said, and she knew the roads like the back of her hand. Since I felt the same way about the Buffalo area, I told her to go ahead and navigate.

"Good. Take a left here," she said, pointing to a road we'd already passed.

"You need to give me a little notice on the turns," I told her. "This is a big vehicle. It doesn't exactly stop on a dime."

"You think I don't know about big vehicles, Jo? I've been driving big vehicles since I was old enough to see over the hood. I think I was 10."

"You were driving alone at 10?"

"Not alone, you think I'm crazy? I always took my sister Fiona along—she was 9. Our milk truck didn't have any brakes to speak of, so when we needed to stop, we both had to throw out our feet and drag 'em." This tale triggered others about life on a dairy farm, all equally unbelievable but highly entertaining. At least they distracted my mind from the unsettling fact that I didn't have the foggiest notion where we were. If it hadn't been for the compass on Dan'l's dash, I wouldn't have even known which direction we were going.

Narrow two-lane roads led to narrower two-lane roads, through woods and farmlands and little towns. Flo had a story about each one. This farm was where her aunt and uncle raised hogs and 12 kids. That town was chock-full of Indians.

"Native Americans?" I gently suggested.

"No, just Indians," she said.

Several times I had to stop so she could roll down the window and take pictures. "Honey Lou gave me this cool camera a couple of Mother's Days ago," she said. "It puts the date on every picture so I don't have to remember when I took it. There's times I don't remember what the picture's of or who the people are, but I always know exactly when I took it. Whoops, turn here!"

After turning, I looked at the compass; it said we were heading back east. I asked Flo how that could be and she said she'd missed the road to a town where she used to live, so we were circling back.

When we finally got to the town, she directed me to drive a mile or so down a gravel road and then had me turn in the dirt driveway of a farmhouse. Five dogs appeared, providing a noisy escort.

As I pulled to a stop by the front porch, she said, "This is my house. I haven't laid eyes on it for 25 years, ever since Sylvie got her divorce and came to fetch me to help raise her kids. Hasn't changed much." She rolled down her window and leaned out. "See those plaid curtains up there? My children were born in that room." The camera went click, and the dogs ran started jumping and snapping. She quickly raised the window.

"How many children do you have, Flo?" I asked

"I had two. My other daughter got killed in a car accident."

"I'm sorry."

"I am too. She was the smart one. *She* would've never shacked up with a bonehead like Chuck."

Someone appeared in the doorway and stood there staring at us. "Who lives here now?" I asked Flo.

"I have no idea. Maybe we'd better get going."

At that moment, a man carrying a shotgun ran around a corner of the house. "Hey!" he hollered, lifting the gun to his shoulder. The dogs went into a barking frenzy.

I did the fastest reverse in RV history, throwing gravel as I backed onto the narrow road. As we sped up toward the town, I said, "I thought you said it was *your* house."

"Well, it was once," she said.

As I drove along the town's main street, she asked me to slow down and look for a place to eat. "All this talk about potatoes has made me hungry," she said.

"When did we talk about potatoes?" I asked.

"Maybe I was talking to myself. What do you think about this place coming up?"

"It's fine, I guess." I pulled over and parked in the middle of two parallel spaces so I'd be able to get out again.

The diner looked as if it could have been around when Flo had lived nearby; the windows were that dirty. When I asked her, she said, "No. This was a funeral home back then." The information didn't improve my appetite, but I thought since Flo was eating, I'd better have a burger. One look at their grease-caked griddle, though, and I changed my mind and ordered a turkey sandwich.

Flo asked for two baskets of French fries with cheddar melted on them. "Yum," she said when they came, "I never get these at home. Sylvie hates cheese, so that means nobody gets it. I always felt bad for the kids when they were little. They never got pizza or grilled cheese or nothin'."

I remembered she'd also referred to Sylvie's *kids* back at the farmhouse. "So does Honey Lou have siblings?" I asked.

"I don't know, but if she does, she caught 'em from Baxter."

"I mean, does she have brothers and sisters?"

She stuck a fry in her mouth and talked around it. "She's got one brother, Ralphie the Third, named after his lazy no-good father, Ralphie Junior, who never bothered to see him or Honey Lou after the divorce. Ralphie Junior's dead now, bless his obnoxious soul."

I was noticing that Flo was harder on men than some lesbian separatists I knew. To give her credit, it seemed like her family had more than its share of bad male apples. I wondered what Mr. Flo had been like, but decided I didn't want to know. What I did want to know was why Sylvie hadn't told me she had a son. "Where does Ralphie the Third live?" I asked. "I should go talk to him. Maybe Honey Lou went to his place to hide out from Baxter."

"Nah," Flo said.

"How do you know? Don't they get along? Couldn't I at least go talk to him?"

"Sure you can, but first you got to file a visitor request form."

"Why? Where is he?"

"Prison. They caught him selling. Again."

"Geez, you mean both of Sylvie's kids *and* her son-in-law are into drugs? How'd that happen? Did they get in with a bad crowd?"

"They *are* a bad crowd," she said. "This is Ralphie the Third's second stretch. He met Baxter during his first one. When they got out, Ralphie brought Baxter home and introduced him to his sister, whose divorce had just come final. Sparks flew, and before you could say boo-boo, she'd up and married him. Of course, when you consider Baxter was a pusher and Honey Lou was a user, it was a match made in heaven."

"You sound like you don't like any of them too much."

"Honey Lou was my darling growing up, and she still is in spite of it all. But Ralphie the Third was hell on wheels from the start. I washed my hands of him long ago. You must think I'm a lousy grandma to talk this way."

"Well, no…"

"What the heck, maybe I am. But Ralphie's got a chip on his shoulder a mile wide. Chuck won't have him in the house."

"How's Chuck feel about Honey Lou?"

"He likes her a little too much, if you know what I mean. Last month I heard Honey Lou tell him to keep his filthy hands off her. I'll bet that's why he's in no hurry to fix her car." She threw the last fry in her mouth and headed for the bathroom.

After paying for our meals, I went out and drew a RALPHIE THE THIRD twig on the Sylvie branch of the Honey Lou Tree, adding PRETTY GOOD ALIBI, THOUGH.

13

It was late afternoon by the time we I drove into the parking lot of Oklahoma City's Great Prophet Mall. When I told Flo I needed to park the motor home in the lot's outskirts to avoid backing up later, she asked me to drop her off by an entrance. "I'll start looking for Baxter," she said. "If I find him, I'll wrassle him to the floor and hold him till you come."

"No, no," I said, "don't even approach him. If he sees you, he'll never lead us to Honey Lou. And don't go too far from the entrance. It's a big mall. I don't know how I'd ever find you."

"Try Foley's," she said, and slid out.

After I'd parked and leveled, I went in and found a mall directory. It took me a while to break the color code, but I finally figured out where Foley's was located. As I walked there, I spotted a uniformed security guard. He was middle-aged and balding, and had a sizable paunch hanging over his gun belt. I didn't see him as being Honey Lou's type, but how would I know what her type was?

I paused in front of a slinky gown in a nearby store window, put my cell phone to my ear, and said loudly. "Honey Lou? I think I've found just the dress for you. What did you say, Honey Lou? Honey Lou, are you still there?"

The security guard didn't even blink, but a woman walked up to me and said loudly, "Them damn phones should be banned. Can't you take it outside?"

I said into the phone. "I can't hear you, Honey Lou. Some woman here is hollering. I'll call you later." I continued on my way.

Foley's turned out to be a big department store. I found Flo in the accessories department trying on scarves. "Come on," I told her. "We'd better start looking."

"I am looking." She draped a striped scarf around her neck. "So what do you think of this one? Too busy?"

"It's OK, I guess."

She held up a green one with white splotches. "This one's a better color for me, don't you think?"

"I don't know. Come on, Flo, let's find Baxter and get out of here."

"OK," she said, putting the scarf on the shelf and walking toward the store's entrance.

"Wait," I said, "you forgot to put the striped scarf back."

"Oh, dear, so I did." She replaced it and we left the store. "Where do you think we should we look first?" she asked.

"I don't know. Yesterday, when you were talking to your sister—"

"Who?"

"Your sister. Isn't Fiona your sister?"

"Why, yes, she is. You know Fiona?"

"No, I don't," I said. "But didn't Fiona tell you she saw Baxter? That's what Sylvie told me."

"Sylvie's right."

"Well, did Fiona say whereabouts in the mall she saw him?"

Flo paused, then said, "Maybe it was over at Sears. Yeah. It was at Sears. In the ladies' plus-size department."

"I don't think so," I said, calling her bluff. "Let's just roam around. If you see him, nudge me."

Three hours and four stops for cold drinks later, we hadn't seen hide nor hair of Baxter. While Flo sat on a bench sipping iced tea, I went over to a sunglass wagon and asked the clerk if the mall had an office. "Sure," she said, "but they'll be closed by now."

"Bummer," I said, and went to tell Flo we'd need to call it a night and come back tomorrow.

As we neared our exit, I saw the paunchy security guard, standing in the exact same place as before. If he hadn't been blinking, I'd have thought he was one of those life-size statues. "That guy's not Baxter, is he?" I asked Flo.

"No," she said, "Baxter's not that good-looking."

"I wish Fiona hadn't forgotten the false name he gave her," I said.

"Who says she forgot?"

"Sylvie."

"Aha! Sylvie got it wrong this time. Fiona told me the name, but it was me that forgot. I remember it now, though. It's Axel."

"Axel?" I couldn't imagine anybody choosing Axel as an alias. Bob or Bill maybe, but Axel? "Did he tell her what his last name was?"

"I don't think so."

"Maybe I should ask this guy here if he knows another guard named Axel."

"Ooh, let me," Flo said. "I'm the one who remembered the name."

"Watch me for technique," I said, "and you can do it next time."

"It's a deal," she said.

The guard pulled his eyes from a miniskirted teenybopper and said, "What can I do you for?"

I laughed politely. "Do you know a mall guard named Axel?"

"Axel, Axel... I think so. Isn't he new?"

"You're right, he is. This here's his grandma from out of town, and she needs to find him. It's a family emergency." Flo helped out by nodding enthusiastically.

"I haven't seen him today. Maybe he had an earlier shift."

"Will he be here tomorrow?" I asked.

"I don't know. I got enough trouble keeping track of my own schedule."

"Well, do you happen to remember his last name?"

"Doesn't his grandma here know his last name?"

"Of course she does. I just wanted to make sure it was the same Axel."

"Yeah," Flo said. "We don't want to get the wrong sumabitch."

I thanked the guy and hurried her out of the mall.

When I'd brought Dan'l around to pick Flo up, I asked, "Which way to your sister's?"

"I don't remember," she said.

I stared at her. "You remembered every little town, road, and farm on the way here, and you can't remember where your sister lives?"

"No, I can't. Where do you sleep in this thing?"

"I take the cushions off the sofa, and it's a bed. Why?

"Do you stay in campgrounds?"

"Sometimes, but tonight I was planning to park in your sister's driveway." I handed her my cell phone. "Here, call her and ask for directions."

"I don't have her number with me, and it's unlisted."

"Then call your daughter and get it."

She punched in some numbers and waited. After a minute she asked, "What's today?"

"Monday."

"Well, that explains it," she said, handing me the cell phone. "On Mondays, Sylvie and Chuck play cards with a bunch of friends. They won't be home till late. Real late."

"Where do they go to play cards? Maybe I can get the number from information."

"It's a different place each time."

"Guess I'll have to take you to a motel then. Didn't we see a Travelodge on the way here?" I asked.

"I can't stay in a motel," she said.

"Why?"

"I just can't. I don't like 'em. I knew this guy once who got shot at a motel."

"He did? Who shot him?"

"His wife. He was coming out of a room with a neighbor lady on his arm. Now, you're probably thinking that couldn't happen to us—"

"Of course, it couldn't." *Or could it?* "You don't have a boyfriend, do you, Flo?"

"Sure, I do. How old do you think I am?"

I pulled over, fetched my campground directory, and found the numbers of a couple of RV parks in the area. Choosing one at random, I called for directions and drove there.

"Oh, thank you, thank you," Flo gushed. "I always wanted to go camping, but my family never had a nice motor home like this—hell, we never even had a pup tent. I'll sleep anywhere you want me to, Jo—on the ground even."

She didn't sleep on the ground. She slept on my bed, and I

arranged the cushions on the floor for myself. That was after we'd eaten the subs I'd bought on the way, and she'd dragged me over to the campfire next door, where two older couples were singing songs about trains and rivers and moons, most of which I'd never heard before. One of the men accompanied them on a guitar.

I munched happily on blackened marshmallows and watched the guitarist's expert hands. I considered asking him for a few tips but couldn't get up the nerve.

The next morning Flo and I grabbed showers and went back to the mall. This time we went directly to the office. Flo nudged me on the way in and hissed, "This one's mine."

"OK," I said, standing aside.

She approached the young woman behind the counter, whose streaked ash-blond hair was arranged in a manner that defied gravity. After squinting at the woman's identification badge, she burst into tears. "Oh, Charlene," she blubbered, "thank God for angels like you!"

" 'Scuse me?" Charlene said.

"Without you, I don't know how we'd ever find my grandson, Axel. Do you happen to have a Kleenex, Charlene?"

"I don't understand," Charlene said, reaching under the counter and bringing up a box of tissues. "Is your little grandson lost somewhere in the mall? I'd better call a security guard."

Flo took a tissue and wiped her eyes "No, no, angel. He *is* a security guard. All I need is his home address, so I can go sweep him into my arms and make up for all the years we've missed."

"I'm sorry, ma'am," Charlene said. "I'm not at liberty to divulge information about our employees."

"But you haven't heard the whole story," Flo said, her eyes leaking again, "Axel's little sister, Honey Lou, has run off from her parents' home down by New Scotia, and we're hoping against hope she has come here to stay with Axel instead of being out on the street. We all know what happens to young girls out on the street, don't we?"

"Dear, yes," Charlene said. "Did you say your grandson's name is Axel?"

Flo grabbed her hand. "Do you know him?"

"I haven't met him. The security department does its own hiring and shuttles the information to me, and I enter it into the computer. I remember the name Axel because it's so unusual." Easing her hand from Flo's grip, she applied it to her keyboard. Looking at the screen, she said, "He's off today, but he'll be here tomorrow morning at 7."

"Thank you so much, Charlene. Would you mind sharing his telephone number?"

"I really can't do that. Why don't you look in the phone book?"

Flo seemed stymied, so I stepped in. "That's a good idea, but we're in such a hurry, and there are pages and pages of listings for that last name."

"Nusbaum?" Charlene said.

"Oh, yes. You'd be surprised."

She picked up her phone. "If you don't mind waiting a minute, maybe I'd better have someone from the security department come over."

"No, thanks. Like I said, we're in an awful hurry." Flo and I bustled out the door and headed for a crowd to get lost in. "That was very good," I told her.

"Thank you," she said, grinning from ear to ear.

We found a bank of phones in one of the mall intersections, but none had directories. Using my cell, I called Oklahoma City information and was told there was no listing for anyone named Axel Nusbaum. None for Baxter Wright, either.

When I relayed that to Flo, she said, "Well, that's it, then. Now we got time to do a little shopping."

"I don't think so. We don't want to be seen hanging around here." The truth was I'd seen enough of malls to last me a great while.

"Maybe just Lane Bryant? I need some pants," she whined.

"Look, Flo, we're here for only one reason, and that's to find Honey Lou. We don't want to do anything that might mess it up."

"Well, then, what are we going to do for the rest of the day?" she asked.

"I've got a great idea. Why don't we go to your sister's?"

She folded her arms. "No."

"Why not?"

"We can't. We have to go back to the campground. I promised I'd bring the marshmallows tonight."

I thought about launching into the let's-call-your-daughter routine, but another evening spent in the warm Oklahoma out-doors singing and snacking and watching the guitar player's hands didn't sound bad at all.

I huffed for effect, and said, "OK, but only if you promise to remember your sister's address tomorrow."

"All right, I promise," she said. I checked to see if her fingers were crossed. They weren't.

"Wait outside here," I told her at the exit. "I'll pick you up."

"I have to get something in this drugstore first," she said.

I almost asked what it was but decided I didn't want to know what kind of stuff I'd be buying in drugstores when I got to be her age. When I drove back to the entrance and she opened the passenger door, I heard the *beep-beep-beep* of a store alarm. "OK, let's go," she said.

"What's going on in there?"

"Where?"

"I hear an alarm."

"I do too. Ain't it irritating?" She slammed the door. "Now let's go."

We stopped at a supermarket and bought marshmallows, hot dogs, buns, mustard, soda, and a big bag of potato chips. When we got back to the campground, Flo produced a factory-sealed deck of cards from her pocket and we played gin rummy until we got hungry. After we ate, I turned on the TV to the evening news. During a commercial, Flo, who was reclining on the bed with a cold can of root beer in her hand, said, "Dang, Jo, you sure know how to live."

From the comfy passenger seat, which I'd rotated to face Dan'l's interior, I said, "I do, don't I?"

That evening at the campfire, I got my first real guitar lesson. Our next-door neighbor said he'd seen me watching him the night before; he asked if I played. When I explained my beginner status, he told me my strumming would definitely improve as my left hand grew stronger and my fingertips became callused. As for speed, he said, that only came with practice.

He loaned me his guitar and pick and taught me what he called the bluegrass strum. And later in the evening when we sang "Tom Dooley," yours truly proudly provided the accompaniment. He even let me keep the pick.

14

The next morning, Flo and I slept late and ate breakfast out, so we didn't arrive at the Great Prophet Mall until after 11. After our second lap around, we were sitting on a bench near the upstairs Sears entrance when Flo poked me with her hot pretzel and whispered, "It's him!" She jerked her head to where a scrawny man in a guard's uniform was leaning against the rail and looking out over the walkway below.

"Are you *sure* it's Baxter?" I asked, wiping mustard off my arm.

"Sure I'm sure."

"Good going, Flo. Now he have to keep him in sight."

"You mean we have to follow him around the mall until he goes home?" she asked.

"That doesn't seem like a good idea, does it?" I said. "Would you know his car if you saw it?"

"Sure. It's a rattletrap blue Chevy. It spent three weeks at our house last year waiting for Chuck to put on a new muffler."

"Why don't we go check to see if it's parked in the employees' lot? If it is, we can just sit there and watch it until he comes out."

"Where's the employees' lot?" she asked.

I shrugged. "Maybe I could call Charlene in the office and say I'm a new employee and forgot where I was supposed to park. You don't think she'd recognize my voice, do—"

I was talking to myself. Flo had gone in a nearby jewelry boutique. Through the display window, I could see her moving around the shop and speaking with a clerk. I looked at Baxter. He was looking in my direction. I turned away, glad Flo wasn't sitting next to me. When I dared look again, Baxter's back was disappearing down the hallway.

In a few minutes, Flo came out and said, "Employees park out on the other side of the Very Big Buffet." Around her wrist was a silver chain with a tiny price tag hanging from it.

"Nice bracelet," I said.

"This old thing?" she said. "Come on. Let's go look for Baxter's car."

The Very Big Buffet was a square building on the other side of the main mall drive, and beyond it was a big group of parked vehicles. I drove up and down the rows until Flo spotted Baxter's Chevy. While she took a picture of it, I wrote the license plate number in Weezie's notebook for future reference.

"How long do you think we'll have to wait?" Flo asked.

"Didn't Charlene tell us he started at 7 this morning? He should be done at 3, 4 at the latest."

"That's a good idea, Jo," she said, pointing at the Very Big Buffet.

"What's a good idea?"

"That we go have ourselves some lunch while we wait. If we sit by the window, we can watch for Baxter at the same time."

Since it was almost two and my waffle was wearing off, I said, "Why not?"

By 3:30 we had eaten our fill a couple of times over and were on our sixth glass of iced tea. The plate-collector was probably wondering if we were going to segue right into dinner.

Flo was away on her umpteenth bathroom visit when I spotted the still-uniformed Baxter walking in the direction of his car. Handing the plate-collector a ten-dollar bill, I asked her to go tell Flo to hurry up. I paid the check, ran to Dan'l, and drove him to the restaurant's door. By the time Flo emerged, Baxter's car was headed toward an exit.

I followed him, staying several cars back so he wouldn't spot us—Dan'l wasn't exactly a stealth vehicle. After a few blocks, Baxter slowed and turned left into a motel called The Nitey-Nite Inn. I pulled into a fast-food place across the street and watched him park in front of a motel room and go in. After a few minutes, I drove over and cruised past the room. "Did you get his room number?" I asked Flo.

"Seventeen," she said.

I parked at the end of the building. We were out of sight of Baxter's window but had a full view of his car.

"I wonder which name he registered under, Wright or Nusbaum," I said.

Flo picked up her purse. "I'll go to the office and find out."

"No. He might see you. I'll go, and you keep watch. If he drives out, be sure to notice which way he turns. I'll be right back."

The office was at the front of the building, with windows on three sides. There were two couples ahead of me in line. The first couple was standing so that their bodies made contact at every possible point. In the time it took the clerk to process their credit card, they kissed six times.

The second couple was middle-aged and road-weary. They

asked for a room with two queen-size beds and Pay Per View.

While waiting, I made several trips to the window to make sure Baxter's car was still there. Then, remembering I'd left my keys in the ignition, I checked to make sure Dan'l was still there too. I was as positive Flo wouldn't take off with him as I was positive she had paid for the deck of cards and the bracelet.

Finally the two couples went off to engage in their diverse pleasures, and it was my turn at the counter. The clerk looked natty in her burgundy vest with NITEY-NITE, SLEEP TITE embroidered over her heart. "Do you know if Baxter Wright or Axel Nusbaum has registered yet?" I asked her. "I'm supposed to meet them for a family reunion."

She typed the names in her computer and said, "No, sorry, neither of them even has a reservation. Are you sure you have the right motel?"

I pulled out my receipt from lunch and stared at it. "Yes, it says right here, 'Nitey-Nite Inn.' Wait..." I smacked my forehead. "I just remembered Axel told me he'd be in Room 17."

She tapped a couple of keys and said, "Room 17 is registered to a Mr. Jed Proust."

"Uncle Jed?" I gushed. "I didn't even know he was coming. Thanks so much. By the way, do you know if he brought Aunt Honey Lou?"

"No, I don't. Would you like me to ring the room for you?"

"Not yet. I've got to fix myself up before I let them know I'm here." She looked me over and solemnly nodded.

When I got back to the motor home, Flo was leafing through a back issue of *The Advocate*. Why hadn't I thought to hide it? Living in a house with two other lesbians had spoiled me for the real world. "Did Baxter come out of his room while I was gone?" I asked.

"I didn't see him. Did you know Truman Capote was gay?"

"I think I've heard that. Does the name Jed Proust mean anything to you?"

"No. Is he gay too?"

"That's the name Baxter's room is registered under. Maybe it's another alias."

She turned a page. "Why would Baxter have two aliases?"

"I haven't even figured out why he has *one*. I sure would like to know if Honey Lou is in that room."

She dropped the magazine and reached for the door handle. "Let's go find out."

I grabbed her arm. "No!" Keeping Flo from blowing our cover was a full-time job. "We'll sit tight and watch for a while. If we see him leave, you can go knock on the door."

"OK." She sat back down. "Do we have anything to eat?"

15

It was after 11:30. Flo had finished off a couple of cold hot dogs and was lying on the bed and snoring up a storm. I was in the driver's seat fighting drowsiness by reciting things they'd made me learn in school The Gettysburg Address was easy, but I got stuck in the middle of Hamlet's Soliloquy. I'd just decided to skip it in favor of "Tiger, Tiger, Burning Bright" when two men emerged from Room 17. One was Baxter, and he was still in his guard uniform. The other guy wore tight jeans and a black tank that showed off his muscles.

Instead of getting in Baxter's Chevy, they walked toward me. I hunched down and watched through the top of the steering wheel as they climbed in a dirty white truck with an empty flatbed parked a few spaces away. I wanted to follow them in the worst way, but first I needed to find out if Honey Lou was in that room.

As soon as their taillights had disappeared down the street, I ran to the door of Room 17 and knocked. Nobody answered, but I thought I heard voices. I knocked again and called "Hello?" No answer. "Hello? Anybody in there?"

The door to Room 16 flew open, and a guy stuck his head out. "Can the noise," he hissed. "My wife's asleep." It was the male half of the queen-size couple.

"The bastard locked me out," I told him.

"Then go get another key." He pulled his head back in.

"Hey, thanks," I said, and went to the office. They'd had a change in desk clerks since my last visit. This one's nose was buried in some sort of textbook. He looked up, annoyed.

"Hi," I said. "I'm Mrs. Jed Proust in Room 17, and I'm afraid I've lost my key."

He checked the computer. "Proust, you said?" I nodded, and he handed me a key. I went back to the room, unlocked the door, and peeked in. The TV was on, but nobody was in sight, so I proceeded in, calling, "Room service. Who ordered coffee?"

The bathroom door was closed. I thought I'd better open it in case Honey Lou was bound and gagged in the tub, like a woman on a *Law and Order* episode I'd seen once. Problem was, the *Law and Order* woman had been sitting in a tubful of bloody water, dead as a doornail. I pondered that phrase, wondering how an inanimate object like a doornail could be considered dead. What was a doornail, anyway? *Open the door, Jo!* I reluctantly turned the knob.

Honey Lou wasn't in the tub, or hanging from the shower, or engaged in any of the other blood-chilling scenarios I'd seen on TV. I allowed myself a deep breath and looked around the bathroom. There were no personal items anywhere, just two rumpled towels, a wee bar of soap, and some used tissues in the wastebasket. I returned to the room.

In the interest of hearing if anyone were to approach, I used the screwed-down remote to turn off the screwed-down TV. The only articles in the room that weren't screwed down were four pillows and two closed suitcases, one fabric and one vinyl. I opened one of them. A small bag on top held an electric razor and the usual toiletry items. Underneath were three stained T-shirts, a rumpled pair of khakis, a leather belt with a bucking bronco on its oversize buckle, six white sports socks, and five pairs of jockey shorts, three of which obviously had been worn. *Eeeew.*

After washing my hands with the wee bar of soap, I poked in the other bag, wishing I'd brought rubber gloves. It was filled with a similar assortment of goodies, similarly soiled. There was nothing in either of the bags that a woman like Honey Lou Wright would have put on her body if she were freezing to death.

I peered under the two double beds, and I would have checked in the closet too, but there wasn't any closet, only a wall-mounted rack with four empty screwed-down hangers. Since there was nowhere else to check, I left.

I ran to Dan'l, jumped in, and started the engine as quietly as possible so as not to disturb Flo. Then I turned in the direction the panel truck had gone, the direction of the Great Prophet Mall. Maybe Baxter was working a night shift. Otherwise, why was he still wearing his uniform?

Pulling in the all-but-deserted parking lot, I drove slowly around the enormous structure. It was spooky at night. Yellow pools from the security lights were surrounded by vast regions of darkness. Like those eerie paintings of Jesus, mannequins in display windows seemed to turn their eyeballs as I passed. The few vehicles that remained in the lot were scattered randomly, as if their owners had literally shopped till they dropped.

About three-quarters of the way around, I pulled to a stop

and switched off my headlights. A truck just like the one I'd seen at the motel was backed up to the dimly lit loading area of an electronics store. The flatbed wasn't empty anymore—eight or nine large cardboard boxes had been placed on it, and a couple more were waiting next to a propped door. As I watched, a box emerged through the doorway carried by someone in a guard's uniform. As he set it on the truckbed with painstaking care, I saw it was Baxter. Without looking my way, he went back in.

I eased into motion and drove around the mall, trying to come up with an explanation for the scenario. Maybe Baxter was moonlighting as a deliveryman. Or maybe the store manager had hired him to cart away overstocked goods. Or maybe he was using his job as a security guard to front a heist. I voted for the last one. It certainly explained his use of an alias.

When I approached again, the flatbed was full of boxes. I looked around for Baxter or the other guy but didn't see them. Flo had left her camera on the seat, so I pulled close, thinking to take a photo of the license plate, but there wasn't one. Instead, I took a picture of the truck with the store's sign in the background. As I started to drive away, Baxter ran out of the open doorway, yelling, "Hey, you!"

I stepped on the gas and turned the wheel sharply. In my rearview mirror, I saw the truck's lights flash on then head in our direction.

I had a decent head start, but they weren't far behind. As I looked for the nearest exit, I heard a small explosion—a gunshot? Holy shit, what if they hit one of my tires? What if they hit *me*? Fighting an innate urge to flee, I drew to a stop.

The truck passed and pulled at an angle in front of me. In the light of my headlights, I could read the printing on some of the boxes. One held a computer and another a plasma TV.

Baxter and the other guy, the one with the muscles, climbed

out and approached my window. Baxter had a pistol in his hand. "Whatcha doin' here?" he demanded.

I lowered the window two inches and aimed my mouth at it. "Do you fellows work for the mall?"

"What do you care?" growled the other guy. His pecs were awesome, and he wasn't even flexing.

"I was hoping you could give me permission to park in the mall lot for the night. I can't find a campground, and I've been driving all day." I listened for Flo's snoring, but all was quiet back there. *Don't stick your head up,* I pleaded silently.

Baxter stared at me. I wondered if he was remembering my face from the mall this afternoon. I drew it back in the shadows. Finally, he said, "Well, you can't stay here. This is private property, ain't it, Jed?"

"Sure is," Jed said.

Private property like the stuff on your truck? "OK, sorry," I said. "I'll go stay someplace else."

Jed was giving Dan'l the once-over. "You ever seen one of these RV things?" he asked Baxter. "They got johns and everything. You got a john in there, lady?"

"Yes." *What if they asked to use it?* "But it's all plugged up right now." I pinched my nose to show how bad it was. "Well, I'll be on my way then. Sorry to bother you." After backing up, I made a beeline for the nearest exit. For the next several blocks, I kept checking in the rearview mirror, but the truck wasn't following. "Flo?" I said. "Did you hear all that?"

When she didn't answer, I pulled in a driveway and looked back at the bed. Flo wasn't there. "Flo? Are you in the bathroom? You can come out now."

I swung between the seats and opened the bathroom door. No Flo. *Did she wake up and leave while I was in Baxter's motel room?*

I got back in the driver's seat and headed for the motel. Sure enough, there was Flo, sitting on a concrete barrier, hugging her purse to her chest. I came to a stop and she got in, saying, "Where in tarnation did you go?"

"I've got a better question," I said. "Why did you get out?"

"I was thirsty. Those weenies were salty, and we were out of root beer, so I went to the pop machine."

"We're out of root beer? We had four cans last I looked. Did you drink them all?"

She sniffed. "What's it matter? Out is out."

"Well, buckle up, we've got to get going. Baxter could be here any minute." But it was too late—the loaded flatbed was pulling into the lot.

I thought about driving around back of the motel, but that might attract their attention, and they'd be sure to recognize Dan'l. Would they believe I just happened to pick the motel as my second choice to spend the night? Not a chance. I decided to stay where I was and pray they wouldn't look our way.

They didn't. The truck pulled into a space across from Room 17 and sat there, its motor rumbling. After a minute, the passenger door opened and Baxter hopped out and made a dash for his room. I tried to remember if I'd turned the TV back on when I left.

"Was that Baxter?" Flo asked.

"Yes."

"Who's driving the truck—Honey Lou?"

"No," I said, "it's that Jed Proust guy. I haven't seen Honey Lou. She's not in the room."

"I know."

I looked at her. "How do you know?"

"After I drank my soda, I had to tinkle, so I thought I'd kill two birds with one stone. I went to the office and told the guy behind the desk I needed a key to Room 17."

"And he gave you one?"

"Yes."

I made a mental note never to stay in this hotel—the security was lousy. "When you went in the room, was the TV on or off?" I asked her.

"Off. Why?"

"No reason." At any moment I expected to see police cars zoom in the lot, sirens blaring. The *CSI* guys would dust the TV remote for fingerprints. When they ran them through their computer, they'd be a perfect match for mine, on file from when I worked as a home health aide. The desk clerk would tell them that both I and my accomplice had obtained room keys under false pretenses. They'd arrest us, and I'd have to call Mom for bail. No, wait, I'd call Weezie. She's the one who got me into this mess.

On the other hand, the last thing on earth Baxter wanted to see right now was the police. I breathed a little easier.

Before long, Baxter came out carrying the two suitcases I'd gone through. After throwing them in the trunk of his car, he got in the driver's seat and took off. The flatbed truck followed.

"Are you going to let them get away?" Flo said.

"Yes. They have guns. What we're going to do now is go to your sister's house."

She looked at me out of the corner of her eye. "We still got some marshmallows…"

"We do not. I threw away the empty bag last night. What we're going to do *now* is go to your sister's house." I was surprised to hear Mom's Jo-this-is-the-very-last-time-I'm-telling-you voice coming out of my own mouth. It worked as well for me as it had for her. Flo looked pouty, but she gave me directions.

16

Fiona was pissed. She folded her bathrobed arms across a chest so generous, her elbows were level with her chin. "Flo," she snapped, "where have you been? You were supposed to be here *days* ago. I was sure you'd vanished into thin air like our poor Honey Lou. I've been calling Sylvie every hour on the hour to see if she's heard anything. How could you do this to me, Flo?"

I wondered why Fiona wasn't including me in her diatribe. Maybe because she knew Flo well enough to know I wasn't to blame. But I was sure blaming myself. I should have been calling Sylvie every hour on the hour until she answered and gave me Fiona's address. What was I thinking?

Flo, however, wasn't fazed. "Oh, I had the best time, sis. We went camping, and we sang, and we spied on Baxter. I even went in his room and tinkled."

"It *was* Baxter, wasn't it?" Fiona said. "I told you so. I'd know him anywhere—what did you just say? You went in his room and what?"

"I'll tell you about it tomorrow. I'd better go call Sylvie, or there'll be hell to pay when I get home."

While Flo chattered away on the phone, I asked Fiona if I could stay in her driveway overnight. "I'll set my alarm and be out early," I told her.

"Why do you have to be out early? Do you have an appointment?"

"No, I don't have an appointment. I thought you'd like to have me out early."

"Not at all. You at least have to stay for breakfast. What kind of hostess do you think I am?" she asked.

"OK, then. What time do you want me to come in?"

"From where?"

"From the driveway."

Fiona threw herself against the door. "You're not planning to sleep in your car!"

"It's a motor home," I said. "There's a bed in it."

"I've got plenty of beds. You can't sleep in your car. What would the neighbors think? I know what they'd think—they'd think I wouldn't let you sleep in the house. I could never face them again."

I considered driving back to the campground, but I was exhausted. "OK, let me get my toothbrush," I said.

"No, no," she said. "There's a toothbrush in the bathroom drawer. It's used, but I boil it between guests. I have extra night-clothes too."

After stopping in her bedroom for a nightgown, she showed me to a room fit for a princess. It really was. It had pink walls, white carpeting, and a four-poster bed with a ruffled canopy. In order not to dirty the carpet, I took off my sneakers at the door and balanced them on top of a small pink wastebasket.

"I fixed up this room for my granddaughter. Do you like it?" she asked.

"It's a little fancy for me," I told her.

"It's a little fancy for me too," she said. "My granddaughter's all grown up now, and I'd sure like to paint it. On one of those home decorating shows a while back, they painted a room aqua. It was the sweetest aqua I ever saw, not dark—it was more pastel. I wouldn't want dark aqua."

I yawned and looked longingly at the bed in spite of the fact that the comforter was decorated with little Cinderellas dressed for the ball.

Fiona crossed to it and fluffed the lace-edged pillows. "I already bought the paint," she said. "I had to have it specially mixed. Unfortunately, I'm too old to climb ladders anymore."

"You can get rollers with long handles," I said.

She clapped her hands. "I knew it! You know about painting, don't you, Jo? You've painted rooms before."

"Just for my mom."

"Was she happy with your work?"

"Well...yeah, I guess."

"Good. Hope you sleep well." She shook out the nightgown she'd brought in for me. It was a red-and-white-striped flannel muumuu. "It's way too big for you," she said, "but who's going to see? Good night, Jo."

17

When Fiona dragged a ladder in the room the next morning, the noise fit right in: I was dreaming I was on a train chasing Baxter from car to car. By the time I woke all the way and remembered where I was, she was laying drop cloths.

"Morning, Jo," she said.

I peered at the bedside clock shaped like Cinderella's carriage. "It's only 6," I said.

She moved the wastebasket with my shoes to the middle of the room and draped a newspaper page over them. "I brought you some coffee." She pointed to a cup on the dressing table. "I thought we'd better get an early start because of the appointment."

"I told you I don't have an appointment."

"Well, maybe I do," she said, grasping one side of a chest of drawers. "Here, help me move this away from the wall."

I rolled out of bed and grabbed my Levi's from the floor.

"The muumuu too fancy for you?" she asked.

"Sort of," I said.

"Me too," she said.

By 10 A.M., the room was all painted and Fiona was leafing through a mail-order catalog while I demolished a stack of pancakes. "Jo, what do you think about these flowered curtains?" she asked. "Will the green of the leaves clash with the aqua?"

I was saved from manufacturing an opinion by Flo, who came in rubbing the sleep from her eyes, saying, "What time do we start painting?"

I took the Interstate back from Oklahoma City—without Flo the trip was fast and uneventful. The Shoreville exit came up so quickly I missed it. (I was busy checking out a car with a rainbow sticker.) The next exit was for New Scotia, so I thought I'd have a look at the Wright house to see if Baxter had by any chance gone home after he'd left the motel the night before.

Parking two blocks away, I walked down the opposite side of his street with the bill of my cap pulled low, peering out with one eye. As before, there were no cars in the Wrights' carport and no sign that anyone was about. I glanced at Spitman's house, but he wasn't on his porch this time.

When I reached the end of the block, I crossed the street and walked back. At the Wrights' driveway, I made a sudden turn and sprinted to the backyard.

Everything looked exactly the same—the weeds still needed weeding, the glider was still broken, and the grill was still rusty. I looked in the kitchen window and, *wow*, things in the house were *not* the same. Factory-sealed cardboard boxes covered every surface I could see. I was reading the brands—Sanyo, Hewlett-Packard, RCA—when Baxter came in from the other room. I froze. He navigated between the boxes, picked one up, and carried it back the way he'd come.

As soon as he was out of sight, I bolted, running across backyards until I was stopped short by a chain-link fence, which was a blessing since a pit bull was snarling on the other side. I retraced my path to a driveway and escaped.

When I got back to Dan'l, my first thought was to call the police. The problem was, my cell phone wasn't in my pocket or in its charger or anyplace else. I tried to remember when I'd last seen it. Was it when Flo tried to call Sylvie for Fiona's address, which she'd known all the time? No, it was the next day in the mall when I called information.

What had I done with it after that? Maybe Flo would know. She may have even filched it. In any case, I needed to call her at Fiona's and ask. But since I didn't have Fiona's number, I'd have to call Sylvie first. Everything was so doggone *complicated*.

I drove to a drugstore and bought a phone card. When I asked the clerk if she knew where I could find a pay phone, she said I could try the nearby gas station, although the phone there was usually broken. She was right.

The gas station guy said there was probably a phone at the nearby Nichol's Market. The checker at Nichol's said they didn't have a payphone, but the library branch down the street might. The librarian at the branch said they'd had their taken out because of vandalism but said I could use her desk phone. She then busied herself at the counter so my conversation would be private. I made a mental note to start supporting our public libraries.

"Jo, thank goodness," Sylvie said when she answered. "I've phoned you a thousand times, and all I get is a *message* that I should leave a *message,* so I leave yet another *message.* But you never called me back…well, you just did, I guess."

"The reason I didn't call is because I lost my cell phone. I need to ask your mother if she knows what happened to it."

"Ma's not here. She's at Fiona's. You should know that—you're the one that delivered her there, although it took you long enough."

"I know, Sylvie, and I'm sorry. We sort of got wrapped up in following Baxter and stuff. I should have called you. I feel bad that you had to worry."

"Oh, I wasn't worried. Ma's tougher than an armadillo. It was all those calls from Fiona that drove me nutty. Ring, ring, ring—all hours of the day and night. I thought Chuck was going to pack up and move out, and it's *his* house. So it really was Baxter at that mall?"

"It was. He was staying in a motel near there. I checked in his room, but Honey Lou wasn't there."

She sighed. "I guess I didn't really think she would be. I was hoping against hope. Ma told me Baxter is using the name Axel. Why do you think that is?"

"I *know* why that is. It's so he and this other guy can steal things without anybody knowing his real name. I saw them load a bunch of boxes from a store onto a truck, and now those very same boxes are in Baxter and Honey Lou's kitchen."

"They are? Where's Baxter?"

"He's there. I just saw him. I was going to call the police and that's when I found out my phone was missing."

"But Jo, how do you know Honey Lou isn't in the house too?"

"If she is, the cops will find her, won't they? Isn't that what you want?"

"Well, yes, but would they charge her as an accessory?"

"Sylvie, I was at the mall. I saw the whole thing. I can testify that Honey Lou wasn't there." It suddenly occurred to me that Jed Proust had a fringe of reddish hair around his baseball cap, and his round face looked very much like Honey Lou's in the photo. *Could it have been her in drag? Nah.* "Look, Sylvie, I've changed my mind," I said. "I'm going to stay out of it. If you want Baxter to pay for his sins, *you* call the police."

"What would I say?"

"Say you got an anonymous tip. If you call right now, they'll be able to catch Baxter red-handed."

"OK," she said.

"Oh, yeah, I almost forgot, I used your mother's camera to take a picture of the truck. Give the film to the police; the print will have the date on it. I hope it turns out—there wasn't a lot of light."

"Jo, did you say there was another man at the mall?" she asked.

"Yes. His name's Jed Proust. Flo said she'd never heard of him."

She gave a breathy whistle. "She probably hasn't, but I sure have. Holy moly, I didn't know he was…back in the area."

"You know Jed Proust?"

"When my son Ralphie the Third was in high school, I once went to wash his jeans and found a fake driver's license in his pocket. The name on the card was Jed Proust. I figured Ralphie was probably using it to get into bars, so I threw it away, but he got another one just like it—I saw it one day in his desk drawer."

"So Jed Proust is your son? Why wouldn't your son let you know he was…back in the area?" I'd almost said "out of prison" but caught myself in time.

"I don't know, Jo. I'm sure he will, sooner or later—wait a minute, if I call the cops on Baxter, they'll arrest Ralphie too, won't they?"

"Probably. I suppose you don't want to turn your own son in."

"Well, of course I don't," she said huffily. "Anyway, how do you know those boxes you saw had stolen stuff in them? Maybe they were bone-empty, and Baxter took them to pack his stuff in because he's thinking of moving up to Oklahoma City for good. And maybe Ralphie's helping him move."

"If the boxes were empty, they'd be open, wouldn't they? The boxes I saw were sealed, like they'd come straight from the

factory. And when Baxter was carrying them, they looked heavy."
Sylvie was quiet for so long, I thought she might have hung up.
"Are you there?" I said.

"I'm here, Jo, and what I'm thinking is that it wasn't Ralphie
at all. There are probably hundreds of those fake licenses around.
Thousands."

"Who knows?" I said.

"Damn. I hate to let Baxter get away with anything,
but...I'll have to give it some thought. Don't worry, Jo, if I do
end up calling the cops, I won't tell who told me. Like you suggested, I'll say it was an anonymous tipster, and I'll stick to it
even if they try to beat it out of me."

"Would they do that?"

"Once Ralphie told me...oh, never mind."

"Do Ralphie and his sister get along?" I asked, wondering
where he was when she disappeared.

"Of course they do! They dote on each other. You know what,
Jo? You may as well go on back to New York now. Honey Lou's
probably OK, and she'll show up when she's ready. I don't think
there's anything we can do."

I felt sorry for Sylvie. She'd thought I was going to find her
daughter, and instead I was digging up dirt on her son. The thing
was, although I would have loved to go home, I couldn't face
Weezie until I'd done absolutely everything I could. "How about
if I give it a couple more days, Sylvie?" I said. "I want to talk with
Mr. Proudflesh again, and I'm hoping to contact someone at the
woman's shelter if I ever figure out how to find it."

"Well, all right, but I won't think any the less of you if you
leave right now."

"We'll see," I said.

"Goodbye, then."

"Goodbye, Sylvie... Wait! I need Fiona's number."

She recited the 10 digits and hung up.

Fiona answered after a couple of rings. After telling me how great the room looked—as if I hadn't seen it a few hours ago—she called Flo to the phone.

"Hi, Jo," Flo said. "You coming back? You can go bed-shopping with us. Fiona's thinking cherry."

"Sounds like fun, but I can't. I'm calling to ask if you know the whereabouts of my cell phone."

"Oh," she said. Followed by a long silence.

"Well, do you?"

"It might be in that cabinet under the sink in your little bathroom in your motor home behind the extra toilet paper."

"Why did you put it there?" I asked.

"Did I say I *put* it there? I *saw* it there."

Rolling my eyes, I said, "Are you sure? I just talked to your daughter, and she said she tried to call me a whole bunch of times. If the phone was in the bathroom, we'd have heard it ring, wouldn't we?"

"Maybe when I saw it there, I noticed it had got turned off."

"Well, that was convenient, wasn't it?" I said. "That way nobody could call and give me directions to your sister's house."

"I got to go, Jo. Fiona's already in the car. By the way, I had a wonderful time. If you ever want to take an old lady camping, give me a ring. Fiona wants to come too."

There were still plenty of minutes on the card, so I called home. When the machine picked up, I said, "Hi, Mom and Rose. I'm still in Oklahoma. The weather is sunny and warm. I'm planning to take a swim later. Sorry I missed you. Love you both. Goodbye."

When I got back to Rube's, her truck was gone. Maybe she was on one of her runs for parts—or over at Jenny's, cuddled up in the little houseboat.

After hooking Dan'l up, I changed to a tank top and shorts. I thought I'd better take a swim—Mom and Rose would be sure to ask about it. They probably listened to my messages with pen in hand, composing a list of questions as I spoke. That was why I hadn't mentioned Baxter, sneaking into his motel room, or even painting Fiona's bedroom. That last one would have been sure to garner a bunch of painting projects when I got home. The water was cold, but no worse than Lake Erie in July. I waded to mid thigh before my feet cramped and my mind started screaming, *No way. Way,* I told it, and dove in.

It was after 6 when Rube pulled in. "Look who's back!" she said. "How did the trip go?"

"Don't ask," I said.

"Yeah, I've had a crappy time too. Want to go get some supper?"

The chili had looked good when Jenny and Gus had it, but hoo-wee, was it spicy. By the time it was gone, I'd finished off every package of oyster crackers in the place—that's what the waitress told me anyway. After draining my fourth glass of ice water, I asked Rube if she knew Ralphie the Third.

"Honey Lou's brother? Not really. He was older than us by a couple of years and didn't want anything to do with his little sister's friends. But I do remember he was always in trouble for something or the other. Why? Did you meet him?"

"Briefly. I saw him with Honey Lou's husband in Oklahoma City. It looked like they were stealing things from the mall."

"That doesn't surprise me. I heard Ralphie was in prison once."

"Twice. Baxter Wright was in at least once too."

"Ah, what classy company you keep," she said, and dug into her dish of chocolate ice cream after winking at me.

I had my favorite, pecan pie. It was so rich, I choked on every bite. It was heaven.

18

Trailing Baxter, managing Flo, and painting Fiona's room had worn me out. I spent the next morning resting up and practicing guitar. Using the pick from the guy at the campground, I tried the bluegrass strum on every song in the instruction book from "Up on Cripple Creek" to "Jesu, Joy of Man's Desiring."

Rube came in as I was putting the guitar back in her closet.

Jo," she said, "I need a favor."

"What?"

"I can't find my 1990 Johnson shop manual, and I need one right now. I called Jenny at the marina, and she said I can borrow theirs, but she's too busy to bring it. Will you go pick it up so I can keep on working?"

"Sure. How do I get there?"

"It's easy. After you pass the breakwater, turn to starboard, and in a few minutes you'll see their flags. The repair shop is to the left of the docks." She held out a ring that held a short key and a red and white bobber.

Breakwater? Starboard? "You don't want me to take your boat," I said.

"Of course I do. It's five times as far by car."

"I've never driven a boat, Rube."

"You haven't?" By her tone, you'd think I'd said I'd never learned to use the potty. "Well, I could teach you, but it'll take less time to go myself." She grabbed her cap from a hook. "Want to ride along?" she asked. "I can give you lessons as we go."

"No thanks," I said, and mentally kicked myself. *You're turning down a boat ride on this beautiful lake? Spray in your face, wind in your hair, etc.? Next thing, Jo, like cousin Lorena's mother-in-law, you'll be refusing to cross bridges.* I ran for the dock.

Rube had boarded the *Big Fix* and was inserting the key in the ignition. "Do I have time to fetch my cap and cell phone?" I asked.

"No. If you're coming, get in."

"Want me to untie this rope first?"

"Not yet. And on a boat, rope is called line," she said.

"OK," I said and climbed in the boat. *Lesson One: line, not rope.*

"Grab yourself a PFD," she told me.

"Will do." I looked around for something with the letters PFD on it.

"PFD: personal flotation device. There, in the bin." *Lesson Two: PFD, not life vest.* I donned one, pulled it snug, and offered one to Rube. She shook her head, so I put it back.

She started the engine and told me I could free the line now. After I did, she put it in gear. The boat leaped forward, and I fell heavily into a passenger seat. *Lesson Three: Sit before accelerating.*

After a few minutes on the lake, Rube said, "It's chilly out here. I think there's a couple sweatshirts in the cuddy. Want one?"

"No, thanks. I'm fine."

"Well, I want one. Take the wheel for a minute." *Lesson Four: how to steer.*

"Geez, I don't know," I said.

"Come on, Jo. It's a straight shot to the marina. See those buildings? Just head for them."

I scanned the lake. There were only two boats in sight, and both were way over by the shore; I couldn't run into them unless I was trying. "Well, OK," I said, sliding into the driver's seat as she slid out.

"Try it out," she said. "Turn the wheel to starboard—that's to the right." I did, and the boat turned gently in that direction. "Now turn it to port." I nudged it left, and the boat responded.

"You're doing great. I'll be right back." Rube opened a little door and disappeared into what in a car would be the engine compartment.

I performed the wheel-nudge again, and the boat responded as before, so I unhooked one hand from its death grip on the wheel, leaving the other death grip intact. Hey, this was a bit of OK! I sat back, letting the warmth of the sun radiate through me. I looked out to the right—oops, starboard—to make sure the two boats were still close to shore. They were, but there was another boat in sight now, a long white one. As I watched, it suddenly made a large arc and headed toward us at a high rate of speed.

Doesn't he see us? I waved wildly with my free arm as I turned the wheel with the other, trying to steer the *Big Fix* away from him. He made another arc to adjust. He was closing in fast. "Rube!" I screamed, jerking the wheel sharply.

Rube popped through the doorway at the same time the boat hit. The blow wrenched my hand from the wheel. I fell to the deck, landing painfully on my arm. With a loud grinding noise, the white boat's nose rode up over the *Big Fix*'s side and ground to a stop, hanging a few feet above me. Cold drops peppered my face. The *Big Fix* heaved under me as the two engines battled for control.

I heard a fierce grinding of gears, and the other boat shuddered and started backing up. His nose dragged over our damaged side and hit the water with a great splash. Changing gears again, he turned and took off with a roar. With a horrible groan, the *Big Fix* righted itself and started moving forward. Where was Rube?

I scrambled to my feet, searching for a brake, but I didn't see one. Grabbing the key, I turned it, and there was blessed silence except for the sloshing of water against the hull.

"Rube?" I called. No answer. Maybe she had fallen into the—what had she called it?—cuddy? I stuck my head through the small door. In the light from two portholes, I saw an ice chest sitting on a bunk and some odd-looking hardware, but no Rube.

I stood and called her name again. This time I heard a faint "Jo?" coming from the water. I looked over the *Big Fix*'s damaged side. Rube was 50 or so yards away, submerged except for her face. The water around her was swirled with red. I jumped in and quickly swam toward her. "Where are you hurt?" I asked when I reached her.

"Leg," she said.

Furiously dog-paddling, I dragged her to the rear of the *Big Fix*, where there was a narrow platform with a metal ladder.

"Here, hold on," I told her, but I could have saved my breath—she was out of it. Looping my arm around a rung, I undid my PFD and slid it off. With difficulty, I wrapped it around her midsection and used its Velcro bands to fasten her to the ladder. Then I climbed back in the boat and searched for a radio or CB or something. Why had I agreed to come without my cell phone?

Hearing a motor, I spun toward the sound—was the white boat coming back to finish us off? Roaring in our direction was a small outboard, fishing lines streaming from mounted poles. I waved my arms at the man who was steering, and pointed at Rube. As he got closer, he decelerated and held up a CB mike. "I called the Lake Patrol," he yelled over the noise of his motor.

The water around Rube was turning red. Her skin had a blue tinge, and her chest was barely moving. I lowered myself in the water and gathered her close, whispering, "Stay with me!"

The patrol boat arrived in a few minutes and took us aboard. One of the guys tended to Rube while the other handed me a green blanket and told me to sit tight. We sped toward the marina, the *Big Fix* tied to our rear. I pulled the blanket close against the wind and asked, "What's wrong with her leg?"

"It's a bad gash," one said. "But don't worry. We're getting the bleeding under control. How are you doing?"

"My arm hurts," I told him, sticking it out of the blanket. It was seriously scraped from elbow to shoulder, but not near as bad as when I was 12 and tried to ride my bike down a set of concrete stairs at the mall. Being 12, I'd gotten right back on and rode it home. Now, however, I had no intention of ever stepping on a boat again. Once my feet hit solid ground, they weren't leaving.

"The arm can wait until you get to the hospital," he said, "but let me put a dressing on your cheek."

I touched my cheek, and sure enough, it came away bloody. While he applied the dressing, I asked, "What will you do with Rube's boat?"

"After looking it over and taking pictures, we'll leave it at the marina dock. You should have someone call in tomorrow and arrange for it to be moved," he said.

"I'll take care of that. Did you catch the person who rammed us?"

"No. We're treating it as a hit-and-run. You'll be interviewed about it on your way to the hospital."

We were near enough to the marina that I could see an ambulance waiting with flashing lights. "Which hospital?" I asked.

"Let's see, this end of the lake? Most likely Bituminous County in New Scotia."

A bunch of gawkers watched the EMTs rush the blanket-wrapped Rube to the ambulance. I tried to follow, but one of the guys from the patrol boat held me back until it took off with a blood-chilling wail.

"I wanted to go with her," I told him.

"Don't worry," he said, "you'll get there." After trading my wet blanket for a dry one, he ushered me to a car with a sheriff's department logo on the side and introduced me to Officers Laird and Manypipe. Officer Laird took the driver's seat, and Officer Manypipe sat next to me in back, a pad of forms on her lap and a pen in her hand.

"I know you've just been through a bad experience, Jo," she said as Officer Laird put the car in gear and started up the marina driveway, "but if you don't mind, I'll need to ask you some questions about your accident. It'll help us apprehend the other boater involved."

"It wasn't an accident," I said. "He aimed right for us."

"He? The driver was a man?"

"I was referring to the boat—I think of vehicles as male." When she didn't say anything, I added, "It's a feminist thing."

"I see." She wasn't as impressed as Rube had been. "So was the driver a man or woman?"

"I didn't notice. I was too busy trying to steer out of his way."

"Then you were the one in control of your boat?"

"Um…yes." Was I going to be getting a ticket for reckless boat driving? "It's not my boat, though. It's Rube's."

She paused to write on the form. Then she said, "Do you remember seeing a name, number, or identifying mark on the other boat?"

"No, it happened way too fast. All I saw of the Ram Boat up close was its bottom."

"Ram Boat?"

"That's how I've come to think of it—you know, because it rammed us."

"Ah. Can you describe it at all?"

I tried to picture the Ram Boat before it hit us, but all I got was the image of a gleaming white hull hanging over me. "It was white," I said, "and long, longer than a regular…" At that moment the Ram Boat in my mind started backing up. As it fell to the surface of the water, I saw a dark blur on its side. My mind's eye squinted, but the blur wouldn't come into focus.

"Are you all right?" Officer Manypipe asked.

"I'm trying to remember something."

"About the white boat?"

"Yes. There was something dark on its side."

"Letters, numbers?" she asked.

"I don't know."

"Could it have been damage? It must have incurred some."

"I really don't know," I said. "Maybe the man who called the Sheriff's Patrol saw it."

"We'll be interviewing him," she told me. "Do you remember if the boat was being driven erratically, as if the driver was under the influence, for instance?"

"No, it wasn't erratic at all. He saw Rube's boat and aimed directly for it… I wonder if Rube has any enemies."

"It's possible. What's her last name?"

"I don't know, but she runs a boat repair shop in Shoreville."
I was beginning to shake. First, it was just my jaw, and then it
spread to my whole body. I hadn't noticed how cold the water
was when I was in it, but the chill was sure hitting me now. My
arm ached, and my sore cheek began to throb. Officer Manypipe
pulled the blanket closer around me and told me she had enough
information for now.

As she filled in blanks on the form, I looked out the window
and watched the world go by in fast-forward. By the time we
turned into the emergency entrance of Bituminous County
Hospital, my shaking had abated, leaving me wet-noodle limp.

Officer Manypipe walked me into the waiting room, handed
a slip of paper to a woman at a desk, said goodbye to me, and left.
Still wrapped in the blanket, I fell into a chair. Heads turned and
eyes stared. I ignored them.

A few minutes later I heard a voice call timidly,
"Ja...*CUT*...zo?" It was the woman at the desk. I figured she'd
been taken to task so many times for mispronouncing people's
names, she was almost afraid to try.

Gathering the blanket tails, I crossed to her, my sneakers
going *squish, squish, squish.* As gently as possible, I said, "The
name's Jacuzzo, Ja-*coo*-zo."

"Oh. It looked like 'pizza,' so I thought..." She ended the sen-
tence with a sigh. "Your insurance company?" she asked.

"You know," I told her, "if you're thinking I need to see a doctor, I really don't. All I have is a scrape or two—it's nothing compared to my friend Rube, who was brought here in an ambulance. Can you help me find her?"

"Rube? What's the last name?"

"I don't know."

"Sorry, then. You'll have to check at the information desk."

"Fine. Where is it?" I asked

"You can do that *after* you see a doctor. You really do need to see one, you know. What if somebody sues?"

"How can they sue?" I said. "*They* hit *me. I'm* the one who should be suing."

"Exactly. Picture this." She made a frame with her hands. "You're in the witness seat, hoping to be awarded a million dollars…no, two million. The defense attorney asks, 'And *where* is your official medical report, Ms. Jacuzzo?'" Her eyebrows went up half an inch.

She had a point. "OK, I'll see a doctor."

The eyebrows descended. "Your insurance company?" she asked again.

I retrieved my sodden insurance card from my sodden wallet and handed it to her. I was glad to be using it, since I'd paid a fortune for the coverage and was hardly ever sick.

After typing in the info, she hit "enter" with a flourish and said, "Please have a seat in the waiting area. A doctor will be with you in a few minutes." My blanketed butt was hardly off the chair before she was calling another name, much more confidently this time. But then, "Robert Johnson" is hard to mess up.

Since the blanket was now damper than me, I hung it over the back of a chair and sat in the one next to it. A woman across the aisle peered over her paperback. "Fall in?" she asked.

"Yes," I said.

"It must have been cold."

"Not too bad," I told her, and turned my attention to a dog-eared copy of *Harper's*. I had time to read one scathing letter to the editor before the woman said, "What did you hit on the way?"

"Excuse me?"

She tapped her cheek.

"Oh, that. I can't talk about it," I said.

"You poor thing, of course you can't. Well, you may as well get comfortable. I've been here an hour and a half."

"Two and a half for me," said a man three chairs down. "A person could die."

"What's wrong with you?" the woman asked him.

He held up a bandaged hand. "Rat bite."

Her eyes got wide. "Really?"

"It's my son's pet—she got out of her cage. We had her cornered behind the bookcase, and like a dodo I stuck my hand in. The bite isn't bad, but my tetanus is out-of-date."

The woman tsk-tsked and told him about the time her neighbor's Siamese gave her cat-scratch fever. "I almost died," she said.

"My grill exploded once," he said, rolling up his sleeve and displaying a couple of ugly red spots.

"Oooh," she said, "so did my pressure cooker." This led to a mutual show and tell of every scar that could be shown without breaking decency laws. I couldn't help but look.

One by one, my seatmates were called to the treatment area. Finally, a guy in green scrubs called my name—correctly, on the first try—and led me into a tiny cubicle that was divided into even tinier halves by a yellow curtain. On the other side was a wailing child. His mother drew the curtain aside and apologized. "He hated the X-ray," she told me, "but he had to have one. He swallowed a quarter. It fell from my hand, and whoosh, it was gone."

As she finished speaking, a nurse arrived and told her the X-ray had shown no quarter in the kid's digestive tract. As they left to go home, the mother was asking, "Then what did you *do* with it?"

Soon, a cute doctor arrived, patted and squeezed me, then sent me to the subbasement for X-rays. After viewing them, she told me I seemed to be OK except for contusions and abrasions. "No million-dollar lawsuit?" I asked.

"Fifty bucks, tops," she said, putting a butterfly bandage on my cheek. Then she wrapped my arm and told me to take something over-the-counter if there was any pain.

Before she left, I asked how I could find out about Rube.

"You'll have to go to the information desk," she said, giving me so many directions, I wondered if it was in another country.

19

There was a noisy to-do at the information desk when I finally got there. Jenny was leaning across the counter yelling at the clerk, and the clerk was yelling right back. I thought about leaving until it was over but decided that if Jenny found out anything about Rube, I wanted to hear it. I stood back and watched them go at it.

"Ma'am, I'm telling you this for the last time," the clerk fumed. "The only thing my computer tells me about Ms. Kelly is—"

Jenny pounded her fist on the countertop. "It's Kiley, not Kelly. Her name is Rube *Kiley!* Put *that* in your computer."

The clerk narrowed her eyes and continued: "Is that Ms. *Kiley's* condition hasn't been posted. She hasn't been assigned to a room yet, and she certainly can't have visitors. Now please go home and call in tomorrow."

A man stepped up and took hold of Jenny's arm. It was her

coworker at the marina, Gus. He tried to ease her away, saying, "Come on, Jen, let's go get us a beer. We can come back later."

She jerked her arm free. "Go get *yourself* a beer. I'm sure it won't be your first today."

Gus flinched like she'd slapped him, and Jenny turned back to the clerk. "I want to see Rube right now, and don't give me any more of your bullshit."

The woman picked up her phone. "I'm calling security."

"Who cares?" Jenny turned and stomped in my direction, muttering, "I'm going to find Rube if I have to search every room in this..." She spotted me and stopped short. "Jo!" she said. "Where's Rube?"

"I don't know," I said. Gus and I exchanged nods.

"You've *got* to know!" she said. "You were on the boat with her. That's what Gus told me." She turned to Gus and said, "Isn't that what you told me?"

He shrugged. "They were both on the patrol boat when it came in."

"We were on the *Big Fix*. Another boat rammed us," I said.

"But what was Rube *doing* out there?" Jenny demanded.

"She needed a manual. I thought she called you."

A door opened, and two uniformed guards came in. They looked at the information clerk, and she pointed our way. "It's the taller woman," she said.

"Jo," Jenny said, talking fast, "if you see Rube before I do, tell her I'm going to take a bunch of vacation days from the marina and keep her shop going. Tell her she's not to worry, OK?"

I nodded. She started to say something else, but the guards grabbed her arms. She struggled but was no match for the two of them. "Hold on a minute," Gus told them. Looking directly in Jenny's eyes, he said, "You know, love, you won't be able to do Rube one bit of good from a jail cell."

She stopped struggling, and the guards let go. Gus put his arm around her and they walked through the lobby with the guards following close behind. As they went through the door, one of the guards turned and came back to where I was standing. "Ma'am," he said to me, "were those people bothering you?"

"No. Not at all."

"You know, you don't look too good. Do you need a ride? Is there someone I can call to come get you?"

It hit me that I *did* need a ride. I wondered if I could catch Jenny and Gus before they drove off.

"We have a women's shelter in town, you know," he went on. "I could get an officer to take you there."

Jenny's words from last week popped into my head: *I know how you can find the shelter: Get someone to beat you up.* Well, I guess I *looked* beaten up. "Yes, please," I told the guard. "I'd like to go to the women's shelter."

"I'll take care of it." He settled me in a nearby chair, then walked several yards away and spoke into his radio.

In a few minutes, a policeman came in the front door. After exchanging words with the guard, he approached me, asking, "You need a ride to the shelter?" I told him I did, and he led me to a police car out front. I looked around for Jenny and Gus, but they were gone, thank goodness.

Before starting the engine, he picked up a pen and asked for my name.

"Jo...Jones, Jody Jones." In the nick of time, it occurred to me I couldn't be Jo Jacuzzo. Jo Jacuzzo just got hit by a boat.

"Who did this to you?" he asked, writing on a pad attached to the dash.

"My husband."

"His name?"

"Archie Jones."

"Do you and Mr. Jones live together?"

"Yes."

"Here in New Scotia?"

"No. We live in…" *What was the last state I'd come through before hitting this one?* "Arkansas," I said.

"Which town?"

"Uh, Riverdale."

"Where's that? Near Little Rock?"

"Yes."

"Ah," said the policeman, like he'd had prior experience with wife beaters from Little Rock. "You'll want to press charges, of course."

"No."

"You really should."

"I'll have to think about it."

"I hope you will." He slammed his pen down and radioed to someone that he was taking Jody Jones of Riverdale, Arkansas, to the New Scotia Women's Shelter.

He didn't speak to me again, but the trip was anything but quiet—my conscience was screaming bloody murder. *I can't believe you're doing this, Jo. It's totally against your principles. What if some poor woman really does get beaten up, and they have to turn her away because they gave the last empty bed to you?* I thought about opening the door and bolting at the next red light, but I simply didn't have the energy.

The shelter was a big old house in a neighborhood of big old houses. It differed from the others in that the backyard had been converted to a parking lot. Sylvie's Chuck could have used a parking lot like that to store all the vehicles he hadn't got around to fixing.

The policeman didn't drive away until a thin woman with

short grayish hair opened the shelter door and ushered me in. "Hi," she said. "You must be Jody. I'm Phyllis Noyes. No kids?"

"No."

"Well, come on in." Her unspoken *anyway* hung in the air. After locking the door behind me, she turned and went down a short hall, limping slightly.

We passed through an archway and came out in a gigantic kitchen wrapped with cupboards and oversize appliances. All the lower doors were open, and hundreds of cans of all sizes and brands lay on the floor in front of them. It looked like the cupboards had eaten a bad can and barfed.

In the middle of it all sat two 30-ish women. One had a fresh track of stitches across her forehead. "Jody, this is Wren and Courtney," Phyllis told me without indicating which was which. Wren and Courtney looked up, smiled, and returned to their task.

"Green beans, French cut, 16-ounce," said the stitched one as she placed a can in one of the cupboards.

"Roger," said the other, making a mark on a clipboard. She saw me looking over her shoulder and said, "Inventory."

"Where'd all these cans come from?" I asked.

"I don't know," she said. "Phyllis might."

Phyllis shrugged. "Church collections, clubs, merchants— you name it. Are you hungry, Jody?"

I must have been in shock, because I wasn't. "No, but thanks," I said.

"Then let's go up and find you a room." She led me into a dining room, where two women and a boy of 4 or 5 were gathered around one end of a long table playing Jenga, a game in which you try to remove rectangular logs from a tower without toppling it. I used to be pretty good at it, back in the day.

Their tower was on its last legs, so I stopped to watch. The boy was in the process of easing out one of the crucial logs millimeter by painful millimeter. He was barely breathing. When he finally got it free, the tower trembled, seemed to stabilize, then collapsed with a thunderous bang. The boy buried his face in the lap of one of the women and cried. It was exactly what I would have wanted to do if it had happened to me.

"Good try," I told him.

The other woman at the table looked at me with undisguised curiosity. "Want to play?" she asked. She was young, couldn't have been much older than 20. Her skin was brown with gold highlights, and her thick hair floated around her head like a black thundercloud.

"I can't right now," I said. "Maybe later."

"I'm Nicki," she said, sticking out a long-fingered hand. "And this is Rachel and her son Todd."

I shook it. "Nice to meet you. I'm Jody."

Nicki held my hand a nanosecond too long. I looked in her eyes. They were coffee-colored and glinting with laughter. Was she a sister?

I pulled my hand away and looked around for Phyllis. She was waiting at the foot of a wide staircase. I squelched the impulse to glance back before following her up. At the top of the stairs was a tiled hall with half a dozen doors on either side. Stopping before the first door on the left, she opened it. "You can have this room," she said. "It's a single."

"Are you the manager?" I asked.

"No. Ms. Calhoun will be here Monday to interview you and arrange for counseling."

Counseling? Was I expected to talk with a counselor about my fictitious husband? Guilt ran from my brain to my belly, puddling with the guilt already there because of the woman who would be forced to go back to her nonfictional husband because I was in her rightful room. "Is this the only one available?" I asked.

"No, it's a light weekend. You've already met everyone who's here except Hannah and the rest of the children. Why do you ask? Don't you like this room?"

"Oh, yes, I love it." *It's way too good for the likes of me.*

"OK, then, I'll leave you to get settled. There are bathrooms on either side of the hall. You'll find toiletries in the top dresser drawer. If you need something to wear, try the community closet at the end of the hall. Do you want your door open or closed?"

"Open, please."

"I'll be around if you need me," she said, and left. I heard her irregular gait descending the uncarpeted stairs.

The room was about a third the size of my bedroom at home, barely large enough to hold the narrow bed and tall dresser. A wall-mounted clothes hook held two plastic hangers and a washcloth and towel.

A thick drape was drawn across a narrow window. I pulled it aside and looked into the neighboring backyard. Nothing was moving except leaves fluttering in the breeze.

"Breaking out already? I'll help tie your sheets together."

Startled, I dropped the drape and turned. The coffee-eyed woman from the Jenga game was standing in the doorway, her angular face softened by a wide grin.

Why hadn't I heard her shoes on the stairs? I looked at her feet. She wiggled bare toes and laughed.

Embarrassed, I quickly asked, "Is your game over?"

"*That* one is. I'm Nicki, in case you forgot. It's got an 'i' at the end when you go to write it. What's your name again?"

"It's Jo." *Whoops.* "...dy."

"Where you from, Jo...dy?"

"Arkansas."

"And where before that?"

"What do you mean?"

"That's no Arkansas accent. I'm guessing Ohio. I'm from Ohio, and you sound a lot like me. May I sit down?"

"Sure."

She crossed to the foot of the bed and folded her long body into a sitting position, pulling her feet under her wide skirt. I perched at the other end, leaning against the gray metal headboard.

Gazing at me so intently it was unnerving, she said, "So where *are* you from, Jody?"

"I'm a native of New York state, but when I married Archie, we moved to Arkansas. Where are you from in Ohio?"

"Sandusky. Ever hear of it?"

"Sure, I've heard of it." I said. "When I was a kid, we used to go to Cedar Point Park a couple of times a summer to ride the Corkscrew."

"I used to do that too. Sorry I missed you."

"You couldn't help but miss me. When I was a kid, you weren't even born yet."

"How old *are* you?" she asked.

"Twenty-nine. How old are you, Nicki?"

She smiled slyly. "Well past the age of consent, my dear."

I didn't know what to say to that, so I didn't say anything. In fact, the less I said to this woman, the better—if anyone might blow my cover, it would be her. I resolved to give her a wide berth, which wouldn't be easy because the next thing she did was reach over and place her hand on my cheek near the bandaged cut. I felt a buzz of pleasure—it had been a while since anyone touched me softly like that. "How'd it happen?" she asked.

"I can't talk about it," I said. The ploy had worked in the hospital waiting room.

"I can't talk about this either," she said, pulling her hand away to hitch up her peasant blouse and push down her waistband. On her midsection was a deep purple bruise fading to red at the edges, a couple of days old at least.

I forced my eyes from her navel and said, "That's terrible, Nicki. How long have you been here at the shelter?"

"Since Tuesday. Why?"

"A friend of mine was here a couple of weeks ago. I'm trying to find her. I was wondering if you might have met her."

"A couple of weeks ago? I don't think anybody's been here that long except Phyllis. I hear she's been here forever."

"Forever? Why is that?"

"I don't know. I was talking with Rachel—you know, Todd's mom? She told me Phyllis and Ms. Calhoun, the manager, are real close. I wonder what *that* means." She gave me a big-eyed innocent look.

"I have no idea," I said. "But it sounds like Phyllis is the one I should be talking to. And Ms. Calhoun, of course."

"I'd ask Hannah too, if I were you. She's been here before, a couple of times, and each time went back to her abuser."

"Really? Why would she go back?" I asked.

"It's hard to make it on your own, especially if you have kids. I'll never go back, though, will you?"

"Definitely not." Archie and me were history.

"What's your lost friend's name?" she asked.

"Honey Lou Wright. It's an odd name, isn't it?"

"You think that's odd? You haven't lived in the South long at all, have you, Jody?" When I didn't say anything, she said, "Well, if Honey Lou was in the shelter and now she's missing, it's a good bet her abuser's involved."

"That's very possible," I said, "but what I'm hoping is she's in a safe place hiding out from him. Unfortunately, I have no idea where to look. If she got close to somebody here, she might have told them where that place is."

Nicki leaned forward. "Are you a detective, Jody?"

"No," I said, "I'm just doing her mother a favor."

"What *do* you do?"

"For a living?"

"Well, yeah."

"Not much right now. I used to be a nurse's assistant," I said.

"Really? TLC and all that? I'm with the Oklahoma DMV. I sit at a computer all day. Bo-ring. But, wow, this is exciting. A womanhunt! How can I help?"

"I don't know. Keep your ears open, I guess."

"Well, if you think of anything more challenging, let me know." She stretched, and stood up. "I've got supper duty tonight, so I'd better go get started. Do you like grilled cheese?"

"Very much!" Hunger pangs attacked with a vengeance. Guess I was out of shock.

After pausing at the door to throw a kiss, Nicki left. I found myself smiling for the first time in a while.

20

After collecting a towel and toiletry items, I went down the hall to find a bathroom. I hoped there wasn't a mirror in it—I didn't want to know how bad I looked after my dunking. I wasn't vain, but...OK, I was vain.

The bathroom didn't have *a* mirror, it had *three*—one above the bank of sinks and two full-lengths, so there was no way I could avoid seeing my reflection. It was even worse than I'd feared. My hair lay in clumps with bits sticking up here and there. My Levi's were creased as if I'd slept in them, and the neck of my T-shirt was stretched way out. If I was the kind of girl Nicki liked, she had abominable taste.

I washed around my bandages and wetted down my hair, which helped a lot. Then I remembered what Phyllis had said about trying the closet at the end of the hall if I needed something to wear.

Although the door was labeled COMMUNITY CLOSET, it wasn't really a closet; it was a room full of all sizes of clothing—clothing on shelves, on tables, hanging from racks. There were piles and piles of T-shirts, both used and brand new. Some of them I wouldn't be caught dead in, like a midriff-barer from Hooters, or the one that proclaimed TROJANS RULE! I finally settled on a blue and white baseball jersey with YOU GO, GIRL on it. The imprint was faded, but the sentiment was sound.

None of the jeans came within a mile of fitting, so I decided I'd have to make do with my wrinkled ones until I got back to Dan'l or had a chance to go—*ugh!*—shopping.

As I started to leave, a suede jacket caught my eye, so I pulled it off the hanger to try on. Then I told myself, *Absolutely not— you can't afford the guilt.* While replacing it, I spotted a fuzzy red sweater a few hangers down. It looked exactly like the sweater Honey Lou had been wearing in the photo. How significant was that? If I'd had Weezie's notebook, I would have written on the CLUES page FOUND HONEY LOU'S SWEATER AT SHELTER. But unfortunately, the notebook was back in Dan'l. Unfortunately? What was I thinking? It would have been totally ruined if I'd had it on me when I hit the water.

And on second thought, finding Honey Lou's sweater, if it *was* Honey Lou's sweater, wasn't significant at all. What it told me was that Honey Lou had been in the shelter, which I already knew. She may have traded the sweater for something Baxter wouldn't recognize, which would have been a smart move, in my opinion.

In a last effort to wring something from the moment, I took a fistful of the red knit sweater and pressed it to my cheek, in case my recent injuries had made me psychic, like the guy in *Dead Zone.* When no visions appeared, I patted it back into shape and left.

The hallway was still deserted. The only sound was a faraway conversation drifting up the staircase. It was a perfect time to nose around. I didn't know what I expected to find, but I wouldn't find anything if I didn't look, would I? I tried a door. It opened easily. The room was identical to mine and appeared unoccupied—there were no clothes on the hooks, no personal items in the dresser drawers. Then it occurred to me there weren't any in mine either.

The next room was definitely inhabited. Someone had tossed a purple velvet jacket on the bed, and two pairs of sandals were scattered on the floor. A brush on the dresser was full of black curly hair. A filmy blouse and a long cotton skirt hung from the clothes hook. In a drawer, I found a pair of short shorts and a rainbow tank top. It all screamed Nicki. I found myself smiling again. *Danger, danger, Will Robinson.* I got out of there fast.

Across the hall was a larger room with four beds lined against a wall, dorm-style. The floor was strewn with clothes, puzzles, and parts from building sets. On a nightstand sat a framed photo that would have brought the religious right to simultaneous orgasm—on the landscaped lawn of a split-level, a man and woman stood behind three children who closely resembled them. Mom and daughter wore pastel print dresses, Dad was conservative in a brown suit and muted tie, and the two small sons stood military-stiff in crisp slacks and short-sleeved shirts buttoned up to their chins. They all wore smiles, but a close look at the children's eyes made me think the abuse had already started. In the years before my father left, I'd seen those same anxious eyes in the mirror.

Phyllis had told me I'd met all the women in the house but Hannah; I figured Hannah was the woman in the photo. Extending her an apology in advance, I went around the room pulling out drawers at random, finding nothing but more clothes and toys.

The door to the next room was ajar, so I slid in. It was another dorm-style room, much neater than the last one. I was about to open a drawer when a voice said, "Who are you?" A young boy was sitting cross-legged on the bed nearest the window. How could I have missed him?

I took a much-needed breath and said, "I'm Jody."

"Hi, Jody, I'm Raymond. Want to play Battleship?" He held up an electronic game.

"I can't right now. I thought you kids were all down watching TV."

"I was, but Craig hit me," he stuck out his left arm in evidence, "so I had to hit him back, and Mommy sent me up here to think about it."

"Is Craig your brother?"

"No!" The word was drenched with *thank goodness.*

"I'm sorry I bothered you," I said. "I'm new here and got the doors mixed up. I thought this was my room."

"Do you have kids my age?" he asked.

"I don't have any kids at all."

"Oh," he said sadly.

I tried to think of a subject that might cheer him up. "Do you go to school, Raymond?"

"I was supposed to go to kindergarten next fall at Dunbar-Ortiz Elementary, but now Mommy and Daddy..." His lower lip quivered.

I started backing toward the door. "I'm sorry. I've got to go now."

"Are you going downstairs?"

"Sooner or later."

"Will you tell Mommy I'm sorry?"

"Shouldn't I be telling Craig?"

"OK, but watch out, he hits—hard. And be sure to tell Mommy too."

"What's Mommy's name?"

"Courtney Walther."

The kitchen-inventory women were Wren and Courtney, but I didn't know which was which. "What does she look like?" I asked.

"Like a mommy." *Duh, lady.*

"OK. I'd better be going now. Bye." Waving, I backed out and hurried to my room, my heart still pounding from getting caught snooping. *To hell with the other rooms,* I thought. *Maybe tomorrow.* I put away the toilet articles, changed into the YOU GO, GIRL shirt, and headed for the stairs.

The dining room was uninhabited, the Jenga blocks picked up and put away. I went into the kitchen. Nicki was standing at one of the counters, buttering bread. Wren and Courtney were still sitting on the floor. It was almost empty of cans now, and all the cupboard doors were closed but one.

"Courtney?" I said.

The one with the clipboard said, "Yes?" *One mystery solved, anyway.*

"I just spoke with Raymond."

"That scamp! I told him to stay in our room."

"That's where he is, up in your room on his bed. I opened your door by accident." Nicki turned her head and winked. Ignoring her, I told Courtney, "Your son seems like a very nice boy."

"He has his moments," she said.

"He's sorry he hit Craig. He asked me to tell you that."

"Yeah, I'll bet he's sorry."

"No, really. He's thought it over, and he's very, very sorry."

"Thanks for telling me, but he's still got half an hour left." She turned back to her clipboard.

I didn't want Raymond sitting up there thinking I'd blown him off, so I said, "He's really, really sorry. He promises he won't ever do it again."

"All right," she said. "I'll go get him in a minute."

"Great. Did Craig really hit him first?"

"I don't know—I wasn't there. But Craig does seem to do a lot of unprovoked hitting. Somebody should put the fear of God in him."

"Maybe they should," I said. "Do any of you know where I can find a pay phone?" I needed to call the hospital. Maybe they'd know something about Rube by now.

The one who, by default, was Wren looked up from her can-counting. "There's a phone in the front hallway. Local's free, but you have to have a card to call long distance."

"Thanks. My call's local. By the way, have either of you ever met a woman named Honey Lou Wright?"

"I haven't," said Wren. Courtney shook her head.

Telling them thanks anyway, I left and went through the dining room into a large room with four sofas and twice as many chairs. Homer Simpson's voice blared from an open doorway to my right. I peeked around the jamb. Two women and several children were sitting on mismatched furniture and the floor, watching a big-screen TV. The only ones I recognized were Jenga-players Rachel and her son Todd, who were sharing a recliner.

The other woman was curled in a beanbag. It was hard to tell in the semi-dark, but she could have been the one in the photo I'd seen upstairs.

"You opened Courtney's door by accident? I don't think so, Ms. Gumshoe." It was said directly in my ear, and I jumped. "Did I scare you?" Nicki said. "I'm sorry."

"My nerves are shot," I told her. "Is that your hobby, Nicki, going around startling people?"

"Only people who ignore me."

"I don't mean to. I've got a lot on my mind. Do you happen to know which one of those kids is Craig?"

She peered in the room. "Floor. Brown stripes."

I waited for a commercial and went in. Kneeling before the brown stripes, I said, "Craig, Raymond is very sorry for hitting you." Then I closed in on him, dropping my voice to a raspy whisper like Marlon Brando's in *The Godfather*. "I also promised him you'd never hit him again, and I *never* break a promise. Understand?"

He stared at me openmouthed and finally nodded.

"Good," I said, and left.

Nicki was waiting for me. "Maybe it's not so bad that you ignore me," she said. "You scared the stuffing out of that kid."

"Do you think his mother will come after me?"

"To give you a medal, maybe. Hannah's at her wit's end about what to do with him. Kids from abused families can have major problems."

"Believe me, I know," I said. "Was that Hannah in the beanbag?"

"Yes. She's really nice."

"Glad to hear it," I said. "Now where's that phone again?"

She pointed in the direction of a foyer. "See you at supper," she said. "And no more startles. I promise."

I asked the person who answered at Bituminous Hospital for information about Rube Kiley, offering a silent thanks to Jenny for supplying her last name. He said her condition was stable and she could receive visits from family members starting tomorrow.

"Does she have a telephone?"

"Not yet. They'll probably move her to a room with a phone in the morning."

"Thank you," I said, wishing I knew who Rube's family members were. Maybe Jenny knew and had already notified them. In any case, there was nothing I could do from here.

I returned to the kitchen, where Nicki was busy frying sandwiches and Wren was filling glasses with milk and iced tea. I asked if I could help and was set to folding paper napkins. When Hannah came in, I ducked into the back hall. At some point I was going to have to ask her if she'd ever met Honey Lou, but it could wait. In spite of the nice things Nicki had said about her, a lot of parents didn't take kindly to somebody else reprimanding their children. Unfortunately, my mother hadn't been one of them.

After Hannah filled a tray and left, I grabbed a plate and took it to the stove. As Nicki slid a sandwich on it, I asked her if she had seen Phyllis Noyes recently.

"She went out for a fish fry. We could go out too, if you don't feel like grilled cheese. I have a car, you know."

"Thanks, but the sandwich is fine."

"Care for an iced tea?" she asked.

"Sure. Is there any rule against eating in my room?"

"Not that I know of," she said. "Want company?"

"I don't think so, Nicki. I'm really tired."

When I turned at the kitchen door to say good night, she had her arms folded and was regarding me through narrowed eyes. "Is it because of my skin color?" she demanded.

"No, I like that part," I said, and took off.

The bedroom was way too warm. I pushed at the window but it wouldn't open—they'd probably glued it shut against human predators. After eating my sandwich, I lay on the bed sweating and thinking about boat crashes, hospitals, and missed opportunities with sexy young women until I fell asleep to dreams of the same.

The next morning, by 6 A.M. I was showered and wearing the YOU GO, GIRL T-shirt and my wrinkled Levi's. I'd hung my socks on the headboard overnight to dry, but they got damp again when I stuck them in my sneakers.

There was a rap on the door. It was Phyllis Noyes. "Good

morning, Jody, I saw your light was on," she whispered. "Did you sleep well?"

"Yes, thanks. Come in, Phyllis. I need to talk with you about—"

"Not right now. I'm in a rush. I just wanted to see if you'd mind helping Rachel make breakfast this morning. Wren was going to do it, but she can't."

"Sure, I'd be glad to."

"Thanks. And I need to talk with *you* too. On weekends and whenever Ms. Calhoun's not here, I'm authorized to conduct the preliminary interviews—you know, get your emergency numbers, et cetera."

Hmm. I could make up emergency numbers, but the "et cetera" worried me a little. "When do you want to do that?"

"I'll be in Ms. Calhoun's office anytime after 10:30. It's off the back hall," she said, then hurried off.

I gathered my dishes from last night and headed for the kitchen. Rachel was already there, measuring coffee into a large electric urn. Her son Todd was perched on a stool at the counter, eating a bowl of Trix while having a lively conversation with the rabbit on the box.

"Hi, Jody," Rachel said. "Have you come to help me, I hope, I hope?"

"I have," I told her. "Where would you like me to start?"

"How about making the orange juice?"

Making the orange juice was harder than it sounded due to the fact that the concentrate was frozen solid. The can-shaped iceberg remained a can-shaped iceberg no matter how hard I stirred. Finally, I put the plastic pitcher in the oversized microwave. That melted the iceberg all right, but I left it in too long, resulting in a misshapen pitcher and lukewarm juice. While I was adding ice cubes, I saw Todd watching me and giggling. Guess I was even more entertaining than the Trix rabbit.

While Rachel and I arranged an assembly line of eggs to be fried and bread to be toasted, she thanked me again for helping and said that Wren couldn't do it because she was busy packing—she had decided to go stay with her sister for a while. "It's just an apartment, so they'll be pretty crowded, but she thought it would be better for her kids than here."

"I'm glad to know she isn't going back to her abuser," I said.

"Yeah, but he'll still probably harass her. He's done it before."

"Can't the police keep him away from her?"

"A guy can do a lot of damage in the time it takes the police to come." Her tone was bitter, like she'd been there..

We worked in silence for a while, then I said, "Have I asked you if you've ever met Honey Lou Wright?"

"The name isn't familiar. Who is she?"

"Just a woman I'm looking for. Hannah might know her. I'll ask her when she comes down."

"Hannah's not here, Jody. She left last night to deliver her kids to some out-of-state relatives—she wanted to drive while they were sleeping. But she'll be back sometime tomorrow, because she's got an appointment with an attorney first thing Monday morning."

"Thanks. I'll try to catch her then."

While washing dishes, I realized Nicki hadn't shown up for breakfast. Maybe she liked to sleep in on weekends. Or maybe she had to work Saturdays. What did I care, anyway?

21

At 10:30 sharp I was knocking on a door in the back hall with a plaque on it engraved ESTHER CALHOUN, HOUSE MANAGER. After a minute, Phyllis opened it, saying, "It's a total fabrication!"

"What is?" I asked, getting ready to run. Then I saw she was holding a cordless phone to her ear.

She motioned me to a chair, saying, "But there's *never* a time when nobody's here. Maybe he went to the wrong address. In any case, we need that order delivered by noon or we're going to be looking for a new supplier... All right, then. Goodbye." She slammed the phone in its charger. "Excuse me, Jody," she said. "Prevarication brings out the worst in me." She took a seat behind the sturdy oak desk that nearly filled the small room.

"Nice desk," I said. It was the kind of desk I'd have wanted to work at if I had to work at a desk. Actually, the thought of working at any desk made me slightly nauseous. The only part I hadn't liked about being a nurse's assistant was the mountain of paperwork.

"Yes, isn't it beautiful?" Phyllis said, running her hand reverently across the grain. "Ms. Calhoun brought it here from her own home. I'm so sorry you came to us on a Friday and won't get to meet her until Monday. She's a wonderful person."

"I'm sure," I said.

"What we're going to be doing this morning, Jody, is filling out a form." She indicated a piece of paper in front of her. "We really should have done this last evening, but by the time I got back, you had gone to bed."

"I was tired," I said.

"Understandably," she said, picking up a pen.

In case the interview didn't go well, I thought I'd better get my own business out of the way, so I said, "There was a woman here a few weeks ago named Honey Lou Wright. Do you remember her?"

"Of course. Why are you asking about Ms. Wright?"

"I'm a friend of her mother. She told me Honey Lou was staying here when she disappeared."

She frowned. "I really can't talk to you about that; it's confidential. I'm sure you understand."

"I was just wondering if she made any friends when she was here."

"I can't tell you that." Her voice was growing steadily colder.

"Did she happen to leave any belongings behind?" I asked.

"No, she didn't."

"I saw a red sweater in the closet room that looked just like hers."

"Really? Well, I wouldn't know. Now, let's get this form filled out. I have other things to do today. You say your name is Jody Jones?"

"Yes."

"And why have you come to us?"

"I was physically abused."

"By whom?"

"By Archie, my husband."

"Do you and Archie live together?" she asked.

"Yes, in Arkansas. That's where he abused me, at our home in Arkansas."

"What town?"

"Riverdale."

"I never heard of it." She was staring at a filing cabinet in the corner. I wondered if there was a map of Arkansas in it.

"It's a *very* small town," I said quickly, "not even incorporated.

"And Archie's last name is Jones too?"

"Yes," I said, suddenly realizing that Archie, Jones, and Riverdale were all names from *Archie Comics*. They must have bubbled up from the days when I used to sneak up to the attic and practically memorize my mom's tissue-wrapped collection. I hoped Phyllis wouldn't catch on.

I guess she didn't, because she went on to the next question. "Do you have children, or have you ever had children?"

"No." Jughead and Betty were still gleams in their daddy's eye.

"What is your occupation?"

"We have a farm." That should be safe—I'd seen lots of farms in Arkansas. I went on to give her the farm's address and a bunch of other faux statistics.

Then she said, "I'll need a description of your husband."

"Why?"

"In spite of our best efforts to keep the location of the shelter a secret, abusers occasionally show up."

"Archie won't show up." I told her. "He's too cheap to come all this way."

"I'll *need* a description," she said, tapping her finger on the form.

"Well, he's about six feet tall and has an unusually large Adam's apple," I said, picturing the policeman who'd brought me here.

"Caucasian?"

"Yes."

"Eye color?"

I tried to picture the policeman's eyes, but all I got was brown hair sticking out from under a blue hat. "Blue," I said, "and his hair is brown."

"Brown," she echoed as she wrote. The next paper on the stack had an outline of a woman's body. She handed it to me. "Now I want you to draw your injuries on this diagram."

The diagram had more curves than I did, but I shaded in my abrasions and made a slash for the contusion. Handing it back, I said, "Is that it, then?"

"Not quite. If you come from Arkansas, how do you happen to be a friend of Ms. Wright's family?"

"That's an interesting story," I said, trying to think of one. "Guess I should start at the beginning." While Phyllis wrote furiously, I told her how Archie and I had been married for three years before he started beating me. At first it was because I wasn't getting pregnant and he wanted kids to help with the chores. But lately he'd been hammering on me for any stupid reason he could think of, like if the hens hadn't laid enough eggs for his breakfast. So yesterday morning, I decided I'd had enough. When he went out to the field to plow, I flagged down a passing car. The driver happened to be Mrs. Sylvie Lemming, who told me about this wonderful shelter in New Scotia where her daughter had stayed. She said if I happened to end up there, would I please find out if they had any information about Honey Lou's disappearance.

I thought it sounded pretty good, but as soon as I finished, Phyllis picked up the phone and punched in a number. Then she swiveled until her back was to me and started talking in low tones. The only words I caught were *Arkansas, Honey Lou,* and *preposterous.* Suddenly she swiveled back, offered me the phone, and said, "Ms. Calhoun wishes to speak with you." I felt like a kid being sent to the principal.

"Hello?" I said.

"Ms. Jones, this is Esther Calhoun. I understand you've been asking Ms. Noyes for information about one of our former residents." It was the voice of a woman-in-charge. I should know, I lived with two of them.

"Yes, ma'am. I was trying to help Honey Lou's mother, who…"

"We *cannot* give out information of *any* kind about anybody. Do you understand?"

"Yes, ma'am."

"We'll talk about this further on Monday, when I'll be interviewing you and arranging for counseling." Her tone implied I sorely needed it. "Now put Ms. Noyes back on the line, please."

"Yes, ma'am." I handed the phone to Phyllis and walked out of the office. I wanted to keep going out the back door, but I also wanted to talk to Hannah when she returned tomorrow. She was my last hope for information that might lead me to Honey Lou. Then it occurred to me that if Hannah could leave the shelter and return again, why couldn't I? After making sure the door was securely locked behind me, I walked up the driveway and up the street. A few blocks later, I found a Citgo station with a pay phone and called a taxi. When it came, I told the driver to take me to Bituminous County Hospital. As he dropped me off, he told me I must be on a lucky streak because he couldn't remember ever hitting so many green lights in a row.

I told him I was due for a lucky streak.

The clerk at the information desk was the same one who had been in the grudge match with Jenny yesterday, but she turned out to be quite nice if you didn't scream at her. Without any kind of hassle, she told me Rube was in room 42B on the third floor, her condition was stable, and if I was family I could go right up.

"Thank—42B, you said?"

"That's right. You *are* family, aren't you?"

"Yes, I am," I said, hightailing it for the elevator while singing under my breath, "*We* are fam-i-*lee*."

All the staff members on the third floor had their noses in charts, so I tiptoed past and went looking for Rube. She wasn't hard to find—her name was handwritten on a card next the door of room 42: RUBE KILEY, BED B, it said, right under PENELOPE WOOSTER, BED A. Ms. Wooster looked up with a happy smile when I came in, but her smile turned upside-down as I passed her bed and crossed to the other side of the curtain. Rube was lying in a cranked-up bed, looking out the window. Her right leg was bandaged from her ankle to somewhere under the hem of her short hospital gown.

"Hey, buddy," I said.

"Jo!" she said. "I was hoping you'd come. How *are* you? I didn't have your cell phone number, and all they would tell me was that you had been treated and released."

I hugged her gingerly and pulled up a chair. "That's more than they'd tell me about you. I'm feeling OK, just a little sore." I showed her my wounds.

"Shit, I'm sorry. I should have never left you alone on deck," she said.

I wanted to scream, *No, you shouldn't have!* Instead, I said, "So what happened to your leg? I was worried—there was so much blood."

"They tell me it was sliced, most likely by a propeller. It's a bad cut way into the muscle. I've got stitches over stitches."

"Geez," I said.

"I can't remember anything after I went down in the cuddy.

Tell me what happened. All I know is what I read in the paper."

"We're in the paper?" I asked.

She handed me the New Scotia newspaper folded open to a short article under the headline: "Women Injured in Boating Accident." The first line gave our names, which made me doubly glad I'd used an alias at the shelter. The story went on to say it was a hit-and-run, and the Lake Patrol was looking for the other watercraft involved in the accident.

"Why do they keep calling it an accident?" I said.

"It wasn't an accident?"

"No, and I told the officers that too!"

"Jo, what *did* happen?" Rube asked.

I told her the whole gory story, finishing with, "I was so scared for you, Rube—you lost a lot of blood."

"Yeah, guess I was down a few pints," she said. "So what did that boat look like, the one that hit us?"

"It was long and white. Like I told them, I couldn't see who was driving or any writing on its side." As I spoke, the dark blur on the Ram Boat's side flashed in my mind again and disappeared. I tried to call it back, but it wouldn't come.

Rube sighed. "Long and white? That describes a good percentage of the boats on the lake. Are you sure we were hit on purpose?"

"I'm sure. It was like he knew your boat and was aiming for it. Does someone have it in for you?"

"I can't think of anyone."

"Do you have any unsatisfied customers?"

She shrugged. "Well, every business does. But if something goes wrong, I always try to make it right. Nobody's ever threatened me or anything."

"How about a business rival? Who would gain by putting you out of action?"

"Nobody specific. If I were to close up shop, I suppose my

customers would go to one of the other small engine repairs or to the marina."

"Who owns the marina?" I asked.

"It's a corporation. I don't see how the value of their stock would be pushed up by my death or dismemberment." She winced. "Did I say 'dismemberment'? That's a little too close to home."

I patted her ankle. "Your members are all present and account- ed for, thank goodness. How long before they let you out?"

"They won't say. I'm still on IV pain meds, and they want me to be able to get around on crutches. But even when they send me home, I don't know when I'll be able to get back to work."

"Geez." I hit my forehead with the palm of my hand. "I'm sorry. I forgot to tell you: Jenny says not to worry. She's going to keep the shop open for you."

"I know. She was here this morning—she brought the paper. I feel bad that she has to use up her vacation days, but I'd be los- ing a lot of business otherwise."

"It's great that she's going to do that," I said."

"It is," Rube said, "especially since she already works way too hard. This morning she had bags under her eyes like she isn't sleeping nearly enough. She told me she has plans to work on the *Big Fix* too, but I told her to leave it till I'm well enough to help."

"Geez, that's another thing I forgot," I said. "I was supposed to call the marina and arrange for the *Big Fix* to be moved from where they towed it."

"That's OK. Jenny took care of it. She's storing it at the mari- na until she can get it in their fiberglass shop."

"Jenny really cares about you, doesn't she, Rube?" I was hop- ing she'd take the cue and enlarge on their relationship, but an aide brought in her lunch tray, setting it on the over-the-bed table. Rube peeked under the plate cover and made a face. "Plain old chicken breast. What I wouldn't give for a cheeseburger from the Happy Crappie."

"What's the Happy Crappie?" I asked.

"You know, that place in Shoreville where we ate the other night."

"Funny, I don't remember seeing that name anywhere."

"Actually, it's not called that anymore. It changed hands, and now it's called the Feather and Fin or something dumb like that, but everybody still calls it the Happy Crappie."

"Well, why don't I drive down to the Happy Crappie or whatever and get you a burger?" After saying that, I remembered I didn't have a vehicle to drive to the Happy Crappie. I thought about telling Rube about being at the shelter, but I wasn't sure she'd understand. *I* didn't understand.

"Thanks, but no," she said. "They're downright anal here about the patients' diets. They inspected my breakfast tray this morning, checking off little boxes on a form—I felt guilty for leaving my crusts. But now I'm sorry I didn't eat 'em. I'm so hungry I could eat…well, a chicken breast."

Figuring she wasn't going to start eating until I left, I rose, saying, "I'll try to visit again soon. Is there anything I can bring you?"

"No, but you could do me a really big favor."

"Anything, as long as it doesn't involve boats," I said.

"No boats." It was good to see her smile. "What I need is for someone to go to my sister Fran's and ask if she'll come stay with me for a while after I get home. She lives with her husband outside Washburn, and they don't have a telephone. It's south of Tulsa, about an hour from my place." She handed me a set of keys from the top drawer of her bedstand. "Take my truck. No sense driving your gas guzzler all the way up there."

"I'll go tomorrow, no problem." *Problem, Jo. You still have to get to Shoreville.* Oh, well. I'd worry about that tomorrow.

Rube wrote directions to her sister's house on half a paper

napkin and tore it off. On the other half, she asked me to write my cell phone number. I did, making a mental note to fetch the phone from Dan'l when I picked up her truck. Taking my half of the napkin, I said, "You eat those crusts now, hear?" and headed for the elevators. As I waited, an attendant wheeled up a man who was hacking up a storm. Each hack sounded like it might be his last. I looked at the attendant with concern, but all he said was, "Don' worry, it ain't catchin'."

Since I wasn't ready to go back to the shelter, I took a taxi to the cinema. Their marquee had changed, and they were playing another film I'd been waiting for, *Holes*. I bought a ticket and watched the movie with a couple hundred rowdy kids. I might have enjoyed the film if I hadn't missed so many of the lines.

When it was over, I walked to a nearby Wal-Mart and called a moratorium on my boycott long enough to buy a couple of new T-shirts and a package of underwear. I also bought a copy of *Time* because it had a story on Internet piracy, a story I was seriously interested in. I would have bought jeans and sneakers too, but they didn't have anything I liked. After eating a tepid hotdog in their depressing little café, I took another taxi to the Citgo and walked back to the shelter.

Before I could ring the bell, Nicki opened the door, saying, "Jody, thank goodness you're back! I thought you were gone for good. Don't you know you're supposed to sign out when you leave?" Seeing my blue plastic bag, she added, "Did you walk all the way to Wal-Mart? I guess that explains why you were gone all day."

It was sort of nice knowing that someone in this part of the world cared where I'd gone and whether I was coming back. "I took a taxi," I told her. "I went to visit a friend in the hospital."

"You have a friend in the hospital? Is he or she going to recover?"

"She'll be OK."

Knowing the gender of my friend triggered a slight frown. "Well, good. Did you eat? There's some vegetable soup left. I could nuke it for you."

"Thanks, but I did eat, and I'm really tired. I think I'll go to go up to my room and read."

Nicki's frown deepened. "Do you think it's good for you to be spending so much time alone, Jody? I mean, after all you've been through?"

I almost wished I really was Jody Jones. I'd have loved to begin my emotional healing in the company of this engaging young woman. But there were only so many lies Jo Jacuzzo could tell. I hoped that was true, anyway. "I'll be fine," I said, and headed for the stairs.

Nicki caught up with me and gently held my arm so that I'd look her in the eye. "You know, it's silly for you to take a taxicab to visit your friend in the hospital when I've got a perfectly good car sitting out back," she said. "If you want to go again tomorrow, I'll be glad to take you—I'm not doing a thing. Or if you'd rather visit her alone, you can borrow my car. And on Monday when I have to work, you could drop me off and keep it all day if you like."

"Really?" I said. "You'd trust me to borrow your car? How do you know I won't drive it back to Arkansas, or New York, even?"

She leaned toward me and said in my ear, "Hell, if you're going to New York, take me with you."

I caught a whiff of warm vegetable soup. Comfort food. I found myself wishing she'd touch my cheek again…and a couple of other spots. *Wide berth, Jo, wide berth!* "I'll think about it," I said. "Borrowing your car, I mean." I edged around her and ran up the stairs.

After showering and donning a new T-shirt and undies and

the old, wrinkled Levi's, I lay on the bed and opened my new magazine. A few pages in, I noticed I was itching all over my upper torso. I threw the magazine to the floor and pulled the T-shirt off, cursing the manufacturer, Wal-Mart, and life in general. While examining my skin for a rash, I noticed my nipples were rock-hard. I touched one and got a clear image of a mouth that tasted of vegetable soup. The reason I knew how it tasted was because, in the image, it was open and pressed against mine.

I pulled on the YOU GO, GIRL shirt and ran downstairs. Nicki was in the TV room, but she came over when she saw me in the doorway. "I'd like to take you up on your offer," I told her. "I need to go to my hospitalized friend's place tomorrow. It's in Shoreville."

She shrugged. "OK. I'll get my car keys for you."

"No, I want you to come too…if you don't mind."

Her eyes widened. "Of course I don't. What time should we leave?"

"Early. I'd like to leave early—8?"

"We can leave earlier if you want," she said, finally daring to grin.

"Eight will be fine." I touched her cheek and said, "Good night, Nicki." Then I went upstairs and took care of myself, which made me sleep so well, I didn't want to wake up the next morning. When we finally got going, it was 10 minutes after 9.

22

While I filled Nicki's gas tank, she paced the island and looked up and down the street. "What's the matter?" I asked her.

"It's Sunday, Dove's day off. She might be driving around looking for me."

"Dove?"

She sighed. "My abuser."

"Damn. I've been hoping it wasn't a woman," I said.

"And I've been hoping yours wasn't a man."

"Yeah, well, I need to talk to you about that."

"Great. Something to do on the way," she said. "Do you mind driving?"

"Not at all."

We were several miles out of town before she stopped swiveling in her seat to check out all the vehicles around us. Then she relaxed somewhat and said, "OK, Jody, spill. Were you beat up by Archie or Arlene? Because, baby, you are one dykely dyke, and don't try to tell me anything different."

"Before I tell you anything at all," I said sternly, "you have to promise you won't tell anyone at the shelter."

"Why should anyone care?" she asked. "You were battered—it doesn't matter who did it. They know all about me, and they didn't kick me out. Anyway, Phyllis and Ms. Calhoun are way more than friends. You should see them together, all shoulder pats and torrid glances. I sure would like to know what goes on behind that office door. Do they lie on the desk, do you think, or does Ms. Calhoun sit in the chair, and…"

"Stop!" I said, trying to maintain my sternness. "Do you promise or not?"

"No, I won't promise. I refuse to help you stay in the closet."

"Fine. Forget it."

"Fine, I will… Dyke!"

"Brat!" I said.

She turned white. "Please don't call me that," she said quietly. "It's what Dove always said just before she hit me."

"Geez, I'm sorry, Nicki. I didn't know."

"Of course you didn't. How could you? It was a shock, that's all."

"But I shouldn't have said it," I told her. "I'm too old to be calling people names."

"That's right, you are," she said. "Grandma!"

"Whippersnapper!" I said, winning a laugh. After that, we stuck to less controversial topics, like politics and Anna Nicole Smith.

When we got to Rube's, Nicki said, "Wow, your friend's place is right on the lake! She repairs boats?"

"Yes, she's good at it too. Do you have a boat?"

"No. I don't care much for boating."

"Me neither," I said pulling beside Rube's pickup. I looked

around for Jenny's truck, but it wasn't there. Opening the car door, I said, "Thanks, Nicki, I appreciate the ride. See you tonight."

"Will you? Are you really coming back?"

"Yes, I am, really." We both got out of the car, but instead of getting in the driver's side, Nicki took off around the building. "Where are you going?" I called, running after her. No way did I want her to see Dan'l. How would I explain my being in the shelter when I had such a sweet little hideaway?

"I want to have a look at the lake," she said, slowing down.

"I thought you didn't like the lake."

"It's boats I don't like. I love the water." She rounded the back corner and stopped. "What's this?"

"It's Rube's motor home," I said.

"Cool. Do you think she would ever let you use it?"

"I don't know."

"Can I see the inside?"

Pride overrode my common sense. "Sure. I happen to have her keys." I needed to get my cell phone and Weezie's notebook anyway.

"Wow," Nicki said as she climbed in. "This is rad."

"Isn't it?" I said, pointing out the microwave and refrigerator. While she was oohing and aahing over the bathroom, I pocketed the phone and notebook and buckled on my sports watch. "I have to be on my way now," I told her.

"Where are you going?"

"I'm driving Rube's pickup to her sister's house in Washburn."

"Washburn? That's up by Tulsa, isn't it?" she said. "It's a bit of a drive."

"That's why I have to be on my way."

"Oh, Jody, can I go with you? Please? It's such a nice morning, and I have nothing to do today but go back to the shelter and worry about Dove finding me."

"In the shelter? How could she do that?" I asked.

"She's a woman, isn't she? She could injure herself and tell the police some guy did it. She'd have to use a false name, of course, but I wouldn't put it past her."

"How low!" I said, feeling like the world's biggest hypocrite. "So even though you're in the shelter you might still be in danger?"

"Yeah," she said. "So can I go with you?"

"I guess I wouldn't mind some company," I told her.

It was a lovely warm morning, Rube's truck was fun to drive, and traffic was light—all the cars were in church parking lots. After a while, I started noticing that every church we passed was Protestant. "I haven't seen a Catholic church since I hit Oklahoma," I told Nicki.

"Are you Catholic?" she asked.

"I was raised that way."

"Does this mean you'll need a papal dispensation to divorce Archie and marry me?"

I laughed so hard, the truck's right tire dropped on to the shoulder. I eased it back, and said, "You are the brassiest thing! What makes you think I'd want to marry you?"

"Never mind then," she said. "We'll live in sin." When I didn't comment, she groaned. "Jody, I'm dying here. OK, I won't tell anyone at the shelter. I don't see why I can't, but I won't."

"Promise?"

"I swear on my latest issue of *Girlfriends*. By the way, remind me to change the address on my subscription."

"To where?" I asked.

"Wherever we're going to live. Will you get the house, do you think? Or will Archie get it?"

I sighed. "You were right, Nicki, Archie doesn't exist. But there's no Arlene, either."

"Oh, my God," she said, "you're a nun? Well, that explains a lot."

"What? What does it explain?" I asked.

"Well, you seem to be so…unreachable. I mean, I assume you have emotions…"

"Of course I have emotions!" This was starting to sound like a conversation that ended one of my relationships. "Look, Nicki, if I'm unreachable, it's because I'm under a lot of stress. You see, I didn't get these wounds from being battered. I lied about that to get into the shelter so I could ask around about Honey Lou. I'm sorry I had to do it that way, but that's the way it was."

My ears were hot with embarrassment. I couldn't look at her. All I could do is wait for her recriminations, the accusations that I was no better than Dove.

After a minute, a hand snaked around the back of my neck. "So you're not celibate?" she said.

I told Nicki everything, starting with Weezie's request and ending with the horror of the boat collision.

"Somebody ran into you on purpose?" she asked.

"That's sure what it looked like."

"Well, *I* call that abuse, don't you?"

"What do you mean?"

"You said you lied to get into the shelter. But you were abused as surely as I was. That boater was trying to kill you, and he might try again. If that's not a good reason to be in a shelter, I don't know what a good reason would be!"

"Thanks, Nicki. That helps, it really does. But it was Rube's boat, so I think she's the one who's in danger." I wondered if there shouldn't be a guard posted outside her hospital room. Why hadn't somebody thought of that?

Houses and small businesses were beginning to appear on

both sides of the road. "Where did you say we were headed—Washburn?" Nicki asked.

"That's right."

"I think you missed your turn. We're in the outskirts of Tulsa."

"Hell and damnation!" I said, pulling to the side of the road.

"Why, Jody, you *do* have emotions," Nicki said, unbuckling her seatbelt. She leaned over the gearshift and pressed her lips on mine. The kiss was gently sensuous, full of promise, better than any vegetable-soup fantasy.

Suddenly, she pulled away and said, "Let's get going."

I turned on the engine and made a U-turn. "What happened?"

"A guy in a black pickup going the other way slowed down and took a hard look at us."

"You had your eyes open?"

"This isn't New York, you know." She turned in her seat and watched through the back window. After a few blocks, she said, "I don't see him, but turn at the light. We'll find another route to Washburn. Do you have a state map?"

"I don't know. Try the glove box."

There was no map in the glove box, but Nicki pulled a dirty, dog-eared map of Oklahoma from under the seat. It was torn at the seams, but she held it together long enough to get us to Washburn. Then she folded the map and started reading aloud from Rube's directions on the half-napkin. "After you pass the Sunoco station, take Fairview Street south. In a few miles, it turns into a county road. Around a sharp curve is a white farmhouse with a big red barn. Turn left on the first gravel road."

It all went like clockwork until we got to the farmhouse. It was around a curve all right and there was a big red barn behind it, but the house wasn't white. It was dark green. I took the first gravel road past it anyway.

"What are you doing?" Nicki said. "That house wasn't white."

"Maybe it's been painted since Rube was here."

"Maybe it's the wrong house."

"I guess we'll find out," I said. "What's the next instruction?"

"Turn left at the tree in the road."

"The what?"

"That's what it says. Turn left at the tree in the road."

"Are you sure? Maybe it says the *fork* in the road. Let me have a look." I grabbed for the half-napkin, but she wadded it in her fist.

"I guess I know the word *tree* from the word *fork*," she said.

"O-*kay*." I rolled my eyes—one little kiss and we were having a lover's spat. *Oh, to be single again.*

After a mile of stony silence, Nicki shrugged and said, "Of course, they could both mean the same thing. Trees have forked branches, don't they?"

"You're right, they do. Good thinking, Nicki," I said, happy to be making up. Taking my right hand from the wheel, I laid it on her knee, and she covered it with her palm. We rode that way, bumping along on the rutted gravel, until we came to a big oak tree growing smack in the middle of the road. In order to turn left, I had to drive around it.

Nicki unwadded Rube's directions and announced that Fran lived in the second house on the right.

The first house was fairly new. It had shiny aluminum siding and baby trees planted here and there. The second house, a quarter-mile down, was old, small, and weather-beaten. I pulled in the dirt driveway and parked behind a blue Chevy sedan that had something wrong with its underpinnings. The passenger side hung so low, I wondered how the driver would keep from sliding over.

"Should I come in with you?" Nicki asked.

ANNE SEALE

"You may as well. I'll have to tell Fran what happened, and then if she wants to call Rube, I'll have to loan her my cell phone, so it might take a while."

There was no doorbell, so I knocked. The woman who answered was holding a fretful infant, while a slightly older child gazed up from his seat on the floor.

"Hi," I said. "I'm a friend of Rube's." She stared at me blankly, so I added, "Your sister."

"Unless she died and left me money, I ain't got no sister," she said.

Nicki whispered, "I told you we shouldn't have turned at the green farmhouse."

"You're not Fran?" I asked the woman.

"I wouldn't be Fran if you paid me. You want the next place down."

"But that would be the third house, and Rube said Fran lived in the second house."

"Then Rube ain't been here to visit in the two years since they built that fancy-schmancy place at the corner, has she? Some sister!" She humphed loudly and slammed the door.

The third house was indeed where Fran lived, but Fran wasn't home. "She's to work right now. I'm her husband, Cyrus," said a gangly fellow with George W. Bush ears. When I told him I was there on behalf of Rube, he whisked us in and poured us glasses of orange Kool-Aid. "Wish it could be something better," he said, "but we're not buying sody these days. I bin laid off my job." His tone was so pitiful that if my mom had been there, she would have needed a Kleenex.

"I'm sorry," Nicki and I said in unison.

"That's why Fran had to go get herself a job. She waits tables in one of them restaurants up in Tulsa. That's where she is today. She'll be fit to be tied when she finds out she missed you. So what's going on with Rube?"

185

I told him what happened and how Rube had hoped Fran would come stay with her when she got home. "I don't think she knows Fran has a job," I said.

"She don't know, but it don't make no matter," he said. "Family ties is what's important. You tell Rube to whistle, and Fran'll come running. I'll probably come too. Maybe I can find some work down in New Scotia."

"But how can Rube get hold of you if you don't have a phone?"

"Give her this." He wrote a number on a scrap of paper. "It's the place where Fran works. Tell her to call anytime but meal-time and, if a woman answers, leave a message. If it's a man, she should pretend it's a wrong number and try back later."

I pocketed the paper, and we left. "Rube's apartment is really tiny," I told Nicki as I drove around the tree. "I don't know where she'll sleep two extra people."

"Can't they sleep in her motor home?" she asked.

I took a deep breath and said, "The motor home's not Rube's, Nicki. It belongs to me. I'm sorry I lied to you about it. I'm all through lying now. To you, anyway."

"So is this truck yours too?"

"Nope. This truck belongs to Rube. Check the registration." To my surprise, she did. "See?" I told her. "No more lies."

"Well, we all lie when we have to, Jody. I can't tell you how many times I lied to my parents about where I was going and who I was going with. And after I hitched up with Dove, I had to lie to my boss and coworkers about all my bruises. I told them I fell a lot because there was something wrong with my inner ear. And then, of course, I had to lie to Dove about anything that might set her off."

"I'm so glad you left her," I said.

She laced her fingers in mine and leaned as close as her seat-belt allowed. "Are you wondering why I stayed as long as I did?" she asked.

"It's probably the same reason my mom stayed so long with my dad. She told me that when he wasn't beating up on her, he was a pretty good husband and father. And when he *was* beating up on her, he convinced her she deserved it."

"That's it, pretty much," she said with a catch in her voice. I let go of her hand and touched her cheek. It was wet.

"You don't deserve anything but the best, Nicki," I told her.

"Thanks, Jody," she said.

I decide to wait until another day to tell her my name wasn't Jody.

We stopped for a meal in a town that was far enough from New Scotia to make Nicki comfortable. She still insisted on taking a booth with a clear view of the door.

"Would Dove attack you in public?" I asked.

"I don't know, but she might attack *you.*"

"Geez, I never thought about that. What does she look like?"

"She's 5-foot-11, 200 and some pounds, with a blond buzz."

I ordered the roast chicken Sunday special, but I don't remember eating it—I was too busy keeping an eye on the door.

When we got back to Rube's, I led Nicki to Dan'l and we made slow, sweet love. She was good at it—patient and eager to please. "Is this what you like?" she murmured. "More of this?"

She, in turn, was as delicious as I'd fantasized. I couldn't get enough of her smooth brown skin or her wet, sweet warmth.

We took a swim break and then made love again. After that, we ate microwave popcorn and watched a couple of DVDs before spending the night wrapped close in each other's arms—the only way two people *could* sleep in Dan'l's narrow bed.

23

We got up early, because Nicki wanted to stop at the shelter to shower and change clothes. "Do you want to use my car while I'm at work?" she asked through the steam of her coffee.

"I do need to do some running around," I told her, "but I can use Rube's truck."

"No, no. Use my car. Then you can pick me up after work. It'll give me something to look forward to."

I grinned. "Are you still afraid I'm going to ride off into the sunset?"

"Baby," she said, "it's obvious that I like you more than you like me, so I'll do anything I can think of to keep you around." She took my hand, turned it palm up, and kissed it.

"What are you talking about?" I said. "Didn't I prove I liked you last night?"

"You proved you liked sex, but I'm not sure about the liking me part."

"Look, Nicki, we've only known each other a couple of days," I said. "I may end up liking you lots more than you like me."

"Super. That gives me something else to look forward to. But meanwhile, take me to work this morning. Please?"

"All right. I'll try to catch Hannah at the shelter while you're getting dressed. I can grab a shower too." I threw a change of clothes into my backpack.

As soon as we got to the shelter, Nicki ran off to her room after telling me we'd need to leave in an hour. I went directly to one of the bathrooms and stood in line behind a woman I hadn't seen before. Since she wasn't 5-foot-11 with a blond buzz, I struck up a conversation. She told me her name was Mia, she'd come to the shelter last night, and no, she'd never met anyone named Honey Lou Wright.

While Mia was in the shower, the bathroom door opened and Phyllis came in. "I heard you were back, Jody," she said. "You signed out for the day yesterday, but you were gone all night."

"I'm sorry, Phyllis. I couldn't get back."

"Then you should have called," she said.

"You're right, I should have. I'm sorry."

She narrowed her eyes. "Nicki didn't come back either. Was she with you?"

"You'll have to ask Nicki where she was."

"Very well," she said in a clipped tone. "Don't forget your appointment with Ms. Calhoun this morning. Be in her office at 9 sharp." She strode out before I could tell her that nobody had told me about the appointment and I'd be gone by then.

By the time I had dressed and thrown the rest of the stuff from my room into my backpack, there wasn't much time left in which to find Hannah. Luckily, it wasn't hard. She was in the kitchen frying eggs.

"Hannah?" I said. "Do you have a minute? I need to talk to you."

"Sure. Hope you don't mind if I keep cooking. Want some eggs?"

"No, thanks. My name is Jody."

"I know. You scared the bejesus out of my son the other night."

"I'm sorry."

"Don't apologize. He's been toeing the line ever since... I'm thinking of hiring you as his personal trainer. So what do you want to talk about?" She used her wrist to push her bangs out of her eyes.

"I've heard this isn't your first time at the shelter."

"I been here so many times, they're thinking of naming it after me," she said. "I won't be back, though. I've got a line on a job in another state, and I'm taking it."

"That's great," I said. "So when you were here before, did you by any chance meet a woman named Honey Lou Wright?"

"Honey Lou? Sure. How's she doing?"

"Well, that's the thing, Hannah, she's disappeared. She was staying here, and one day she went to work and nobody's seen her since."

"That's right. I remember now. She was here and then she wasn't."

The woman named Mia came in, ordered two eggs over-easy, and went off to get coffee. While Hannah cracked eggs in the sizzling pan, I said, "When Honey Lou didn't come back to the shelter, weren't you worried about her?"

"Not really. People take off all the time. I've done it myself. Ms. Calhoun doesn't like it much—but what's she going to do?"

"How well did you know Honey Lou?" I asked.

"We talked sometimes, you know, about our husbands and

all the things we'd like to do to the sons-of-bitches." She shoved the spatula under the eggs with such force the yolks exploded.

"When you were talking with her, did Honey Lou by any chance mention places she might go to get away from her husband? Besides here, I mean."

"Sorry," she said. "I didn't know her that well. But she was real chummy with a woman named Kayla. She might know."

"Do you know Kayla's last name?" I asked. The smell of food had made its way from my nose to my brain to my stomach, which gave a hungry growl.

"No, but she was an Avon lady, if that helps. I remember because she gave us a bunch of samples. Actually, she knew Honey Lou from outside—I think she used to date her brother."

"Ralphie the Third?" I said.

"Is that her brother's name? Well, it makes sense, doesn't it—coming from the same mother who named her daughter Honey Lou?"

Mia came back for her eggs. Wrinkling her nose, she said, "You broke the yolks!"

"Sorry, I'll make you new ones," Hannah said. She slid the eggs on a plate and yelled, "Anybody want these?"

"I do," I said, grabbing the plate and heading for the toast and jelly station.

"What are you going to do today, Jody?" Nicki asked as I drove her to work.

"I want to go to the hospital to see how Rube's coming along, and after that I'm not sure."

"I get off at 4. Call me if you're going to be late or anything. I'll write down the number for you. Do you have something I can write on?" I pulled Weezie's notebook from my pocket and handed it to her. "Cool," she said, removing the little pen and turning to a blank page. "Where'd you get this, from one of your girl-friends?"

"If you mean that in a platonic sense, yes. Weezie, the one who sent me to find Honey Lou, gave it to me. She said it was for keeping track of clues." Saying Weezie's name reminded me I should call her today with a progress report. Monday was her day off, so hopefully she'd be able to talk this time.

Nicki flipped through the pages. "Look at the notes you've made! I'm impressed, Jo. You're so organized."

"Thanks," I said, wondering when all the organization was going to start paying off.

I stopped as close as I could get to the DMV's door. Nicki kissed her finger and laid it on my lips. "See you later, baby," she said.

"You too," I said, checking my sports watch. It was only 7:30, too early to go to the hospital. I drove to a McDonald's drive-through, ordered an orange juice, and pulled into a parking spot. Opening the notebook to a blank page, I made a to-do list:

1) VISIT RUBE AND GIVE HER FRAN'S NUMBER.

2) CALL WEEZIE WITH A PROGRESS REPORT.

3) TALK WITH HONEY LOU'S BOSS AGAIN. WHY HADN'T HE MENTIONED GIVING HER A RIDE?

4) FIND KAYLA THE AVON LADY. IS THERE A LOCAL AVON CONTACT NUMBER?

5) ISN'T KEN KANE'S BOAT WHITE? CHECK ITS HULL FOR DAMAGE.

I thought I'd better do the last one first since I didn't know how I 'd get a look at the boat if Rita wasn't home. As I turned onto their street, a car backed out of the Kanes' garage and came in my direction. The car wasn't yellow, so it had to be Ken's. I veered into the nearest driveway, pulling way up to the closed garage. Scrunched down, I watched in the side mirror as Ken passed without a glance in my direction.

Hearing the mechanical grinding of a rising door, I shot up in the seat and exchanged startled glances with a gray-suited man who was about to get into a BMW. I whipped Nicki's car into reverse and peeled out, leaving black stripes on the driveway. As I sped past the Kane house, I noticed the garage was still open and the yellow Honda was inside. I kept going, parked around the corner, and walked back.

Ken's boat was indeed white. It didn't seem to be quite as long as the Ram Boat, but who knows how the stress of the moment may have skewed my perceptions. I circled the boat a couple of times but didn't see any damage.

I heard a door open. It was Rita in a reverse playback of the first time I'd seen her—she was wearing the same navy suit and carrying the same diaper bag, and, of course, the same baby. Without noticing me, she opened the door of the Honda and placed the baby in the car seat.

As she messed with the buckles I darted to the driveway and acted as if I were just arriving. "Hey, Rita," I called. "Is that you?"

She pulled her head out of the car. "Jo? What are you doing here?"

"I was in the neighborhood and thought I'd stop by to see how you are."

She eyed me warily. "Why? How was I when you left me that night?"

"The night we went to the bars? You were fine."

"Was I acting...rational?"

"I'd say so. Don't you remember?"

"No, I don't. I don't remember coming home at all, and

when I woke up the next morning…well, it wasn't exactly morning anymore…there was a note from the sitter saying that since she thought I wasn't in any shape to care for Sophie, she took her home. I had to pay her for *18* hours." She stuck a pacifier in Sophie's mouth and closed the door.

"She didn't tell Ken, did she?" I asked.

"No, but even if she had, he couldn't be any madder at me. And it's so unfair! I mean, I didn't even know it was missing."

"You didn't know what was missing?"

"Remember that bar above the fried chicken place where I took out my MasterCard?"

"Oh, no," I said, "you lost your MasterCard?"

"Yes, and didn't they wait until Ken was home from his fishing trip to call and say they'd found it? And didn't they tell him *where* they'd found it?"

"Geez," I said.

"Yes, and he hasn't let me out of his sight ever since, except to go to work." She opened the driver's door and got in. "Look, Jo, I've got to get going. I'm going to be late for work."

"Wait, Rita—so Ken hasn't been fishing since that night?"

"Did I say that?" she asked.

"You said he hasn't let you out of his sight."

"You bet he went fishing, and he made me go *with* him." Glaring at me like it was all my fault, she started the engine and put it in gear.

I jumped out of the way. "Where did you go?" I asked. "Lake Eudora?"

Without answering, Rita slammed the door and took off. I had to scramble to keep from getting flattened by the descending garage door.

24

The meatpacking-plant office wasn't open yet, but a silver Porsche was parked under a big shade tree; it had to be Mr. Proudflesh's. I pounded on the office door and jumped to the side. If he spotted me through the glass, he probably wouldn't unlock it.

But it wasn't Mr. Proudflesh who answered; it was a woman holding a feather duster to her breast like a wedding bouquet. Unlocking the door a crack, she said, "They ain't open yet."

"I'm from FedEx," I told her. "I'm supposed to pick up a package."

"I don't know anything about that. Come back at 9."

"Is Mr. Proudflesh here?" I said. "He's the one who called us to come get it."

"He's here, but he's out in the plant right now."

"It's an extremely important package," I said. "Time-sensitive."

"What's that mean?"

"If it doesn't get to Chicago by tomorrow morning, the payroll will be late."

That hit her where it hurt. She flung the door open, ushered me in, and told me she'd go look for him. As soon as she'd rounded the corner, I tried Mr. Proudflesh's office door. It pushed right open, so I went in and scanned the labels on his file drawers. I pulled open the one called PERSONNEL W-Z and flipped through until I found WRIGHT, HONEY LOU. The HONEY LOU part was handwritten on the tab, but WRIGHT had been typed on a sticky label and pasted over whatever last name had been there originally. Evidently, Honey Lou had worked at the plant longer than she'd been married to Baxter.

I returned to the reception area and picked up the New Scotia newspaper from Shoulder-Pad Woman's desk. I'd barely got it around the file when Mr. Proudflesh walked in. His gaze swung around the office and reluctantly settled on me. "Where's the person from Fed Ex?" he asked.

"She realized she had the wrong address and left," I said.

"I see. Well, what are *you* doing here?"

"I'm still looking for Honey Lou. I've been informed that you gave her a ride the day she disappeared. Why didn't you tell me that when I was here before?"

"I don't believe I have to tell you anything, Miss…"

"*Ms.* Jacuzzo. And you're right, you don't have to tell me a blessed thing. I'll be noting that fact in my full report to her mother, which she in turn intends to hand over to the police."

"Since I had nothing to do with Mrs. Wright's disappearance, that doesn't scare me in the least," he said. "However, in the sole interest of getting rid of you, I'll tell you what happened. I was getting in my car that afternoon when Mrs. Wright ran up. She said her abusive husband was in the parking lot, and she needed a ride to a friend's house on the west side of town."

"What was the friend's name?"

"I don't believe Mrs. Wright mentioned her name. I did see her, though. She arrived home at the same time we got there, but I didn't stay around to be introduced."

"What kind of car was she driving?" I asked.

"I don't know, but it was bright yellow."

"Did Honey Lou mention where she might go to hide out from her husband?"

"No, she didn't," he said. "If she had, I would have told her mother."

"Just like you told her mother you gave Honey Lou a ride that day?"

He flicked a piece of lint from his tie. "You're correct. I should have told her that. At the time, however, I was sure Mrs. Wright would show up soon." Lowering his voice, he added, "To be frank, Miss…*Ms.* Jacuzzo, I didn't want it getting back to my wife that I gave a female employee a ride, no matter how innocent. She's the suspicious sort."

"Without reason, I'm sure."

He narrowed his eyes and said, "Of *course.*"

There was a *tap-tap-tap* on the door. Shoulder-Pad Woman was outside, holding a gigantic box of doughnuts.

Mr. Proudflesh crossed and let her in. She nodded to me and hurried to her desk to set the box down. She immediately lifted it again and peered under it. "Where's today's newspaper?" she asked.

I slid out the still-closing door and made a clean getaway.

As I passed Penelope Wooster on my way to Rube's half of the hospital room, she waved like we were old friends. I was surprised to find Rube sitting in a recliner, dressed in a T-shirt and shorts. She was watching one of those house-makeover shows. A homeowner was trying to mask her horror at her new checkerboard carpet by saying, *How…unique!*

"Jo!" Rube said, switching off the TV. "I've been wondering if you ever got to Fran's, but I wasn't able to call you."

"Why not?" I asked. "I gave you my cell number."

"Yes, but I forgot it's a New York number. For long distance, I'd need a phone card."

"Your wish is my command." I whipped out my phone card and handed it to her.

"Really? Thanks," she said. "So did you see my sister? The powers-that-be tell me I can go home Wednesday if someone will be there to help me out."

"Fran wasn't home when I got there, but Cyrus told me they'd be glad to come." I gave her the piece of paper with Fran's work number on it and explained the caveats.

"Thanks," Rube said. "I owe you."

"Nah," I said, perching on the bed. "Here, I brought you today's newspaper, or has Jenny already been here with one?"

"No. She came last night with my clothes—I can't tell you how much better it feels to be up and dressed. She won't be coming today because she wants to spend a long day working in my shop. Didn't you see her there?"

"I left early. I have a bunch of stuff to do."

"Like what?"

I held up the file. "Like borrowing this. It's Honey Lou's personnel file from the plant."

"They let you take it?"

"Sure, her boss has taken a real shine to me. We can go through it together. I thought I'd bring it here. You know her a lot better than I do. Actually, I don't know her at all."

"If you did, Jo, you'd like her. She's a genuinely nice person.

The evening she showed up at my door, we picked up our friendship right where we'd left off years before. So what's in the file?"

I opened it. The paper on top was Honey Lou's original application, dated six years ago. Her age was 23, and her last name was Bosco. "Was Bosco her first husband's name?" I asked Rube.

"It wasn't her maiden name, so it had to be. She told me about that marriage. She said it ended after she had a miscarriage and tried to dull the emotional pain with drugs and alcohol. Her husband couldn't handle it and divorced her. Not long after that, she met Baxter, and it was all downhill from there."

"When did she tell you all this?"

"The night she spent at my place. We did some talking after..." She put her hand over her mouth.

"After what?" I asked.

"You won't tell Weezie, will you, Jo? It's been ages since they were together, but it would really hurt her, I know it would."

"Tell her what? Did you and Honey Lou have sex?"

Rube picked up her glass of water and twiddled with the straw. "Well, you know, my sofa's not very comfortable. It's too short to stretch out on, and it's hard as a rock. Honey Lou started out there, but pretty soon she said she heard noises outside and came over and crawled in bed with me."

"What kind of noises?"

"I didn't hear them, but it was probably the neighbor's dog. She comes over all the time looking for Elvis—they had a litter together. Anyway, maybe it was just a pretext, because as soon as Honey Lou hit my pillow, she started kissing on me."

I didn't know what to say. Finally I stammered, "So, uh, after...uh...that, she told you about the miscarriage?"

"Yeah. We lay there a long time and talked. Between you and me, Jo, I was sweet on Honey Lou since grade school but was afraid to do anything about it because I was afraid of my folks catching on—I told you how religious they were. They're both dead now, up in their heaven walking the streets paved with gold."

"Where everybody's straight," I said.

She laughed. "That *would* be one of their main requirements. Anyway, in our freshman year I couldn't stand it anymore and was about to make a move on Honey Lou, when all of sudden she and Weezie got together. It broke my heart, but I never told anybody."

"And then you met Rita?"

"Oh, I'd known Rita forever, but I never *dreamed*. She was such a *girl,* you know. When she came on to me at a drive-in movie, I about fell over."

"But, Rube, there's one thing I don't understand," I said.

"What?"

"How could you have let yourself have sex with Honey Lou when you and Jenny are lovers?"

"Jenny and I aren't lovers," she said quietly.

"You're not? Forgive me, but you sure act like you are."

She sighed. "I adore Jenny. I'd be lovers with her in a minute, but whenever I try to take it past the...playful stage, she always draws away. So last Wednesday when you were gone to Oklahoma City, I had a serious talk with her. I asked her please not to be flirting and touching on me anymore, that it was too hard. I told her I needed to move on with my life."

"What did she say?"

"She said she understood. And she's been good ever since."

"Good?" I said.

"You know, keeping her distance. Thing is, Jo, when she was teasing me all the time and wrasslin' with me, it kept me in a constant *state*. So when Honey Lou came on to me that night, I was *ready*—you know what I mean? I hadn't been laid since Beth."

"Beth?"

"Remember when you first got here, Jo? Jenny was telling you

I had *two* friends that disappeared? Beth was the other one, the one from El Reno."

"You and Beth were lovers?" I asked.

"Sort of. I met her in a lesbian chat room, and we were trying it out. I don't think it would have worked, though. She liked her job up there, and I sure didn't want to move."

"But if you and Jenny aren't lovers, why would she have a photo of you that says 'Us Forever' or something like that?" I asked.

"I'm sure she has lots of photos of me. She's always taking them. But what do you mean, it says 'Us Forever'?"

"It was written right on the photo. I can't remember exactly what it said. It looked like it was taken several years ago."

"Where did you see this photo, Jo?"

"Remember that evening I borrowed Jenny's truck to drive to the dam? While I was adjusting the seat it fell out."

"I can't think what you could be talking about," she said. "It must have been a photo of somebody else."

"Sure looked like you."

"I tell you, it wasn't me. I never write on photos."

"Well, OK," I said, "but another reason I thought you were lovers is I saw a pair of strappy sandals in your closet. Don't tell me *you'd* ever wear anything like that."

She furrowed her brow. "Strappy sandals?"

"Black patent with silver buckles."

"Oh, I know the ones you're talking about. They're Fran's. She bought them in New Scotia last time she was here and forgot to take them home." She frowned. "Aren't they in a shoe box shoved in the way back?"

"It was the day I was looking for a guitar tuner. I thought maybe it might be in there. People put all sorts of things in shoe boxes." I opened the newspaper to hide my red ears. "Holy cow," I said. "Where's Missouri from here?"

"Northeast. Why?"

"It says 94 tornadoes touched down last night, killing 19 people."

"Well, it *is* the season," she said, clicking on the TV.

I took the hint and said goodbye, thinking I should be getting myself out of Tornado Alley, and the sooner the better.

This time as I passed Penelope Wooster, I got no smiles or waves, just a wide-eyed stare. Whatever was wrong with her, it wasn't her hearing.

25

My next project was to find Honey Lou's Avon Lady friend, Kayla. The pay phones in the hospital lobby didn't have directories, so I went to the information desk. The clerk heaved two enormous phone books onto the counter. "Use them right here and don't tear out the pages," she said.

I didn't see any "Avons" in the white pages at all, not even anybody with the last name of Avon, so I opened the Yellow Pages and tried "Beauty Supplies." No Avon Ladies there either. I stared at the book, wondering which category to check next. It might have looked like I was about to tear out a page, because the clerk came over. "Are you finding what you need?" she asked.

"Where do you suppose I would find an Avon Lady?" I asked her.

She brightened. "Actually, I'm one. Can I give you a catalog?"

"Is your name Kayla?" I asked hopefully.

"It's Gretchen."

"Do you happen to know a Kayla?"

"Sorry," she said. "Try the back of the white pages, there's a section of business numbers."

She was right. Sandwiched between Avis Rent-A-Car and Awesome Vacations, I found six numbers for Avon, five local and one 800. None of them had names attached, so I took out my cell and started at the top. All the five local numbers turned out to be answering machines, none of them mentioning the name Kayla.

The woman who answered the 800 number said she'd *love* to help me find Kayla, but without a last name it might take some time. "Are you completely out of your favorite product?" she asked.

"No," I said, hoping she wouldn't ask what my favorite product was.

"Then give me some time to track her down. It shouldn't take more than a day or two. What's your phone number, dear?"

"I don't have a day or two. Can't you do it now?"

"No, I'm sorry. I could give you the number of another representative, whom I'm sure you will like just as well as Kayla."

"That won't work," I told her.

"All right, dear," she said in a customer-is-always-right voice. "What I'm going to do is give you the number of our area manager. Perhaps she can help you find Kayla. And if not, the manager will find someone in your neighborhood who will be glad to fulfill your Avon needs."

My only Avon need was to find Kayla. I dialed the number she gave me and got a woman's taped voice saying that if I was calling about Avon or wanted to speak with any of the Malones, I should leave a message, but I shouldn't talk too long or the blasted thing would cut me off. While waiting for the beep I rehearsed my spiel so I could get it out fast. As it turned out, I didn't have time to say more than "This is," before the phone was picked up and the same voice said, "Is that you, sweet stuff?"

"Excuse me?" I said.

"Oh, lordy, lordy, I'm sorry, you sounded just like my daughter. Oh, dear."

"That's OK," I said. Are you the Avon area manager?"

"Why, yes, I am. Are you thinking of taking a route? We have some choice ones available. Where do you live?"

"No, thanks. I'm trying to find one of your representatives whose first name is Kayla."

"Have you bought from her before?" she asked.

"No, but my friend Hannah did. She says Kayla is absolutely the best salesperson—Hannah says her face never looked so good. Unfortunately, she forgot Kayla's last name, so I don't know how to reach her." I thought about adding, *So I can place my several-hundred-dollar order,* but then there's probably only so much even an Avon area manager will swallow.

"I know who Kayla is, of course," she said, "but I can't remember which neighborhood she works in. I really need her last name. Where does Hannah live? I could search that way."

"She wasn't at home when she bought from Kayla."

"Was she at a place of business?"

"Yes, but I don't know which one."

"Hmm. Well, hang on, dear. I'll scan my list. Kayla isn't a real common name. I mean if it were Diane, for instance, it would be like a needle in a…oh, wait, how lucky. Here it is right at the top. 'Kayla Aaron.'" She gave me Kayla's phone number and told me to have a *lovely* day.

Kayla Aaron was right at the top of the white pages too, and without even consulting a map, the information clerk told me how to get to her address. This was a woman who had clearly found her calling.

Kayla's house was in an eastern suburb and had an Avon sign in the window and another pounded in the front yard. A car that was backing out of the driveway had AVON CALLING stenciled on the door. I quickly parked and ran over. The driver lowered her window halfway and asked if she could help me. When I told her Hannah had said she was friends with Honey Lou Wright, she lowered it the rest of the way.

"How do you know Hannah?" she asked, squinting green-mascaraed eyes against the sun.

"I met her at the women's shelter. We're both staying there at the moment."

"Hannah's there again? Damn. She promised she wouldn't... oh, well. Yes, I know Honey Lou. I haven't seen her since I left, though. We said we'd keep in touch, but we haven't."

"So she was still at the shelter when you left?"

"Yes. Why?"

I started to tell her the Honey Lou saga, but she interrupted. "Look, I've got to make a delivery. A customer has a job interview this afternoon, and she's completely out of gel. You can either wait here or come along."

I went along, telling her the story on the way. "So can you think of anywhere I should be looking for Honey Lou that I haven't already?" I asked her.

"I'll be right back," she said, stopping in front of a two-story colonial. Grabbing a little bag, she got out and ran to the front door. I was too far away to hear the doorbell, so I supplied the *ding-dong* myself. The woman who answered took the bag and gave Kayla a check and a big hug.

"As far as I can remember," Kayla said when we were back on the road, "Honey Lou mostly hung out at bars or at her mother's house when she wasn't working."

"Did she tell you of any place she might go to get away from her husband? Like a friend's house, or a boyfriend's maybe?"

She pursed her lips thoughtfully and finally said, "No. If she had a boyfriend, she didn't tell me."

"How about a favorite spot somewhere?"

"Like what?"

"I don't know, I'm trying to jog your memory."

"My memory is pretty good. I remember that she grew up over on Cable Street and was raised by her mother and grandmother. I remember she always carried a big purse with a zipper pocket in which she kept a pint of whiskey—we took hits on it after supper in her room. Every day she had a new one. And I remember exactly which tooth that ex-con husband of hers knocked out."

The word "ex-con" reminded me of something Hannah had mentioned. "Did you used to date Honey Lou's brother?" I asked.

She sighed. "I didn't just date him, I *lived* with him. But that was years ago. Do you know Ralphie?"

"Not well."

"Take my advice and keep it that way. He's bad news. It took me a long time to get away from him. You'd have thought I would have learned, but along came Mr. Goodbar…"

"Who?"

"It's a book. You should read it."

"Do you think Ralphie would ever hurt his sister?" I asked as she pulled back into her driveway.

"Not unless she crossed him."

"One last thing, Kayla," I said before getting out. "Do you know Honey Lou's first husband?"

"I knew him way back. Royale Bosco was a nice guy."

"Was?"

"He moved to Montana or somewhere like that, not long after Honey Lou had the abortion and they split."

"Abortion? She told my friend it was a miscarriage."

"That's what she told Royale too. I don't know if he ever found out the truth."

After giving me a goodbye hug, Kayla said, "Just look at those dry lips! I've got some balm in stock. Want to buy one?"

"No, thanks," I told her, feeling discouraged. My last great hope for finding Honey Lou had just gone up in smoke. I'd lied my head off, gone places I had no business going, and had absolutely nothing to show for it. *Wait a minute, you've got Nicki to show for it,* I told myself. *That's not nothing.*

As I drove back to New Scotia, I thought about Nicki and her fear that I was going to disappear from her life. Was it valid? *How do you really feel about her, Jo?* But my emotions, as usual, screamed at me to go away and leave them alone. So I did.

It was barely afternoon, and I had only one item left on my list of things to do today: CALL WEEZIE WITH A PROGRESS REPORT. *And just what progress would that be, Jo?*

I was happy when she didn't pick up right away—her answering machine wouldn't ask questions. But both Weezie and the machine picked up at the same time. "Don't hang up," she said, sounding like she was down in a well. There were a bunch of clicks, two "shits," and a "damn," then finally she said in her normal voice, "Are you still there?"

"Hey, Weezie, it's Jo."

"Jo, hi. Want to buy an answering machine? Cheap?"

"That one too tricky for you?" I said.

"Ha ha. Glad you called. I was beginning to think you got sucked into the Lake Eudora triangle."

"No, but I did get eaten by the Loch Eudora monster."

"Yeah, I used to date her too. But seriously..."

"Seriously, I'm at an impasse. I've followed every lead I can think of and talked to everyone I can find. Mrs. Lemming told me

I should go on home, so I guess I will, unless Rube needs me to take care of her until her sister gets here."

"Take care of her?"

"Yeah, well, she's in the hospital right now. She's going to be all right, though."

"The hospital? Jo, what's going on down there?"

"Rube and I were out on her boat, and somebody rammed into us."

"Who?"

"I don't know. It was a hit-and-run. I figure it must be somebody who has a grudge against her."

"Holy shit! Jo Jacuzzo, don't you dare leave Rube right now. I can't afford to lose any more friends."

"But Weezie, I don't know what else I can do."

"Find out who's trying to kill her."

"But…"

"You're already there. It isn't going to hurt to stay a while longer, is it? Give it another week. Please?"

"Five days?"

"OK. And Jo, be careful. Maybe it's you they're after."

"Why would anybody be after me?"

"You've been nosing around, haven't you? Maybe it's whoever…whoever…" She couldn't bring herself to say it, but I was glad to know she was considering the possibility that Honey Lou might not be among the living anymore.

I quickly said goodbye and broke the connection—I didn't want to witness any more tears from Weezie, even over the phone. There was something about a big butch crying that really unnerved me.

But could she be right? Was I in danger down here from something other than a tornado? Nicki had raised that possibility too. My stomach started roiling, but it could have been because I hadn't had lunch.

I took Honey Lou's personnel file into a sandwich shop and flipped through the rest of the pages as I downed a BLT. The only items of interest were half a dozen warnings for tardiness and unexplained absences. On two occasions she had been sent home because of "erratic behavior due to suspected substance abuse." She must have been a wonderful butcher to have kept her job through all that drama.

Taking a cue from *Without a Trace,* I arranged the pages from the file on the table in chronological order, hoping to discover some kind of gestalt. Nothing appeared, however, except spots of grease from a smear of mayonnaise. I wiped them off as best I could. After leaving the restaurant, I stopped at a post office, bought an envelope, and mailed the file back to the meatpacking plant. Then I drove to the cinema and saw *Holes* again.

Nicki stayed in the DMV foyer until I came to a complete stop, then she made a beeline for the car. "How was work?" I asked while she belted up.

"It was OK," she said. "How was your day?"

"It was OK." We sounded like an old married couple. As I eased into rush-hour traffic, I asked, "Do you need to stop anywhere before we head for the lake?"

"I don't want to go to the lake tonight," she said. "Why don't we sleep at the shelter?"

"Come on, Nicki. I wasn't planning to go back to the shelter. If you'd told me this morning that's what you wanted to do, I would have driven Rube's truck."

"I know, and I'm sorry," she said. "But I had a serious talk with myself this afternoon and decided I can't go through life like this. I need to get a restraining order against Dove, and I need to do it now. At the shelter they can help me with that."

"Then how about taking me out to Rube's first?"

"I don't think so."

"Look, Nicki, I can't go back there and face Ms. Calhoun. I blew off an appointment with her. She's going to be pissed."

"She won't be there. She's never there when I come in from work. Anyway, do you think you're the first person who ever blew her off?"

"I suppose not," I said.

"Just one more night, OK? I'll file the restraining order in the morning and drive you back to the lake before I go to work. Then you'll be rid of me, if that's what you want."

"I don't want to be rid of you," I said.

She regarded me with a sad expression. "I wish I could believe that."

"OK, OK," I said. "One more night."

I drove to the shelter and was about to turn into the driveway when Nicki hissed, "Keep going, keep going."

"Why?"

"I just saw Dove's truck."

"Where?"

"Back there, the green one."

I glanced over my shoulder. A dark green pickup was parked about three houses down. "Is she in it?"

"No. Maybe she's in the shelter," Nicki said. "Let's get out of here."

I accelerated and turned left at the end of the block. "Are you sure it was Dove's truck?"

"I *guess* I know Dove's truck," she huffed.

"Shall we go to the lake, then?"

"All right. But first I want to go out to her house and get my things."

"Dove's house? Is that a good idea?"

"Sure, it is," she said. "With Dove at the shelter waiting for me to show, it's the perfect time."

"I don't think so," I said. "Why don't you wait and do it some other time?" *Sometime when I'm not with you.*

"OK, stop," she said.

"What?"

"Stop the car. I'll drive."

"Nicki…"

"It's my car. I want to drive."

"Look, Nicki…"

"Now!"

I pulled to the curb and got out. She slid across the gearshift into the driver's seat. "OK, get in," she told me.

"I don't think we should do this right now," I said.

"I'll need your help. Get in!" she said.

Back when I was studying to become a certified nurse's assistant, one of the courses I took for easy credit was Assertiveness Training. As it turned out, it wasn't easy—and it sure didn't take.

I plodded around to the passenger side and got in.

26

Dove's house was out in the country a few miles west of New Scotia, all alone on a quiet road. The driveway was empty, but Nicki didn't pull in; she parked in front on the shoulder.

All the windows I could see were small and shaded by metal awnings, making it impossible to tell if someone was looking out. This made me nervous—I wasn't convinced that just because Dove's truck was at the shelter, *she* was. If I were Dove, I'd have left my truck at the shelter for Nicki to see and have a friend take me back home. Then I'd sit inside waiting for her to show up. When I shared this with Nicki, she said Dove wasn't that smart and, anyway, she didn't have any friends.

"C'mon in," she told me. "I'm going to need help carrying stuff." She took a key from under a mat and used it to open the front door.

I followed her into a living room, my eyes darting around for a 5-foot-11 woman with a blond buzz. The room was elegant, with thick green carpet and burgundy leather furniture. "Nice place," I told Nicki.

"Dove decorated this room. I hate it." She pointed to a giant glass ashtray on the coffee table. "That's mine. Put it in the car. I'll be in the bedroom packing."

"The ashtray?" I asked. "Do you smoke?"

"Not anymore, but it's *mine*. That floor lamp's mine too."

Glad there were no neighbors around to watch, I carried the ashtray and floor lamp out to her car. The lamp wouldn't fit in the trunk, so I pulled the passenger seat forward and tried to cram it in the tiny backseat. Even with the shade removed, there was no way. I left them sitting on the grass next to the door. Nicki could do the logistics.

It was easy to find her when I went back in—all I had to do was follow the sound of cussing. She was in a bedroom staring at a bed on which was heaped a mountain of rags. "What's that?" I asked.

"My clothes. She cut them up. Damn, damn, damn!"

"You have that many clothes?

"I *did*. Oh, no—look, my Renaissance Faire costume!" She held up some flowered strips and a fragment of velvet. "That was expensive!" She rummaged through the mess. "Oh, no, my favorite jeans."

"Um, Nicki," I said.

"Oh, no—my Melissa Etheridge Breakdown Tour shirt!"

"Nicki?"

"What?"

"Is this the bed Dove sleeps in?"

"Yeah, why?"

"Then she must have done this since she got up this morning."

"So?" she said.

"So she knew you'd be coming today. You've been set up. I think we'd better go."

She sighed. "OK, just let me get my clock radio."

As she reached to pull the plug, we heard someone call, "Nicki, where are you? Baby Doll, I'm so sorry."

"Stay here," Nicki hissed. "I'll take care of it." She took a deep breath and walked out of the room.

I looked around for something to use as a weapon. The only thing remotely weapon-like was a pair of sturdy hiking boots half shoved under the bed. I grabbed one of them, tiptoed down the hall, and peeked around the corner. In the middle of the living room stood a Goliath of a woman in green overalls over a green-striped T-shirt. There was an enormous white bandage on her forehead. In one hand she held the glass ashtray and in the other, the floor lamp. "Nicki, sweetie, lover," she was saying, "I didn't mean to hurt you. I'm so sorry."

Nicki shook the clock radio at her. "Why did you ruin my clothes, Dove?"

"I was mad at you. But now that you're here, I'm not mad anymore. I'll buy you new clothes—lots of new clothes, anything you want. And I'll never hurt you again. That's a promise. I love you, baby, you know I do... Hey, is that my knife?"

Knife? I craned my neck. In Nicki's other hand, the one that wasn't holding the clock radio, was an open switchblade.

"Of course, it's your knife," Nicki said. "It was in the bathroom, where you left it after you cut your forehead. That was a really dumb thing to do."

"You're right, it was." Dove said. "It bled down into my eyes. I should have cut my arm."

"It was a dumb thing to cut yourself at all. And it was *very bad* to go to the shelter," Nicki told her.

"I know, Baby Doll, but I missed you so much. I wanted you

home with me, that's all. And it worked, didn't it? So come on, give me my knife." Setting the ashtray down, she grabbed for it.

Nicki leaped backward. "Stay away from me, Dove, or I really will give it to you."

"You little brat!" Dove said, lunging at her.

I ran into the room, yelling, "Stop!"

Dove froze in mid lunge and stared at me. Finally, she said, "Is that my boot?"

Nicki said, "Dove, this is Jody, a woman from work. I brought her here to see your hiking boots, and then I was going to take her home."

"You brought her to see my boots?"

"That's right, Dove," I said. "I told Nicki I've been looking for some boots just like this. Would you mind sharing where you bought them?"

Dove looked at Nicki and back at me, processing the situation.

"I've got an idea, sweetheart," Nicki said quickly. "Why don't I tell Jody to take my car on home, and you can take me to work tomorrow? That'll give me time to fix you a nice dinner tonight before we...you know."

I saw what she was trying to do, and there was no way—I wasn't leaving here without her. I grabbed her arm and ran for the door.

Dove bellowed and hit me with the lamp. I rebounded, turned the knob, and pulled...and pulled. It was locked! I braced for another blow.

Dove bellowed again. *Now, now, now.* Nicki pushed me aside, turned the deadbolt—*duh, Jo*—and threw the door open. We ran for the car. The passenger seat was still tilted forward. In one motion, I righted it, jumped in, and locked the door. I was still carrying Dove's boot.

The green pickup was backed tight against Nicki's front bumper. "Damn," Nicki said from the driver's seat.

"You can back up, can't you?" I asked.

"I could if I had the keys."

"Where'd you leave them?"

"If I knew...!" She gave me a look so scornful it made her cross-eyed.

"You used a key from under the mat to get in the house."

"That's right... I remember now, I left my keys in the ignition, but...oh, no!" She stared at a point on the other side of me.

I turned. There was a field of bloodstained green denim outside my window. It served as a backdrop for a key-ring swinging from a plump index finger. I stared at the shiny keys. *Back and forth. Back and forth.* If someone had said right then, "You are getting very sleepy," I would have been down for the count.

"Those bloodstains are fresh," I said. "Did you stab her?"

Nicki grunted. "Not nearly as deep as she deserved."

"Where's the knife?"

"Sticking out of her shoulder, last I looked. I have to go get those keys." She opened her door.

"*No!*" I said.

She closed the door and folded her arms. "What, then?" she said.

"I'm going to call 911." As I took my cell phone from my pocket, it rang, making us both jump. I hit the button and put it to my ear.

"Jo, is that you?" Mom said. "How are you doing, dear? Did you get to go swimming the other day?"

"Geez, Mom, I can't talk right now."

"We leave messages, but you never call back."

"I'm sorry. I can't figure out how to retrieve them." It was true: The process of retrieval was extremely complicated, involving a secret code I could never remember.

"Rose knows how to do that... Ro-ose, get on the extension!" she yelled.

Nicki hit me on the arm. I looked out the window. One of the keys was on its way toward the lock. "Mom, are you there?" I said in the phone.

"Of course I am."

"I'm here too," said Rose's voice.

"Hi, Rose. Now, I want you both to pay absolutely no attention to what I'm going to say, OK? I'm playing a game."

The key entered the lock, turned, and the car door opened. I tightened my grip on Dove's boot and said loudly into the phone, "What's that, Sheriff? You say there's a squad car just around the corner?"

Dove hesitated long enough for me to shove the boot, heel first, in her face. She yelped and took a couple of steps backward. I jumped out, took the keys from the door, and tossed them to Nicki, who fired up the engine and threw it in reverse.

Scrambling onto the seat, I reached for the door, but Dove was already back, snarling mad. She grabbed my arm and pulled. I flailed with my other hand until I caught hold of something. Unfortunately, it was the steering wheel. The rear of the car veered sharply onto the lawn and hit a tree. Dove was smacked by the open door and thrown to her knees. As I wrenched my arm from her grasp, Nicki put it in drive and peeled out, hitting the rear corner of Dove's truck with the door. It slammed shut, but was too bent to latch. I hung onto it as Nicki floored it, heading toward New Scotia.

The first light we came to was red, but she didn't even slow down. An SUV squealed to a stop and laid on his horn. Nicki held up her middle finger.

I looked at her. "Why'd you do that? You're the one in the wrong."

"Adrenaline," she said. "What's that funny sound?"

I listened. Tiny voices were calling, "Jo? Jo? Hello? Jo?"

With the hand that wasn't holding the door, I picked the

phone from the floor and said, "Hi, Mom and Rose. Everything's OK. Like I told you, we're playing a game."

Rose said, "A game? What kind of a game was that?" Years of teaching had trained her to spot a falsehood a mile away—or in this case, half a continent away.

"Yes, Jo," Mom said, "what kind of a game? You said something about a squad car, and then I heard tires squealing. Are you driving recklessly, Jo?"

"I'm not driving at all. I'm in my friend Nicki's car and we're orienteering. Say hi to Mom and Rose, Nicki." I held my phone to Nicki's mouth.

"Hi, Mom and Rose," she said. "Like Jo said, we're orienteering."

I took the phone back. "See?" I said.

Rose said, "What's orienteering?"

"We saw a show on cable about orienteering a while back, remember?" I said. "It's like a scavenger hunt where you use maps and compasses."

"Why are you playing games, anyway?" asked Rose. "I thought you were there to find Weezie's friend."

Mom said, "Maybe she already found her. Did you find her, Jo?"

"No, I'm still looking," I said.

"I suppose Jo's entitled to a little fun, Rose," Mom said.

"I'll tell you all about it when I get home, and I'll send you a postcard of Lake Eudora. I love you both. Bye." I broke the connection and asked Nicki if she knew where I could buy a postcard with a picture of the lake.

"No," she said. It was her turn to look at *me* like I was crazy. Maybe we both *were* a little crazy by that point.

Still hanging on to the bent door, I turned in my seat and watched the road behind us, but the green truck didn't materialize. "Do you think Dove's OK?" I asked.

"OK? Do you mean, is she back there bleeding to death?"

"Well, yeah."

Nicki snorted. "Not likely. The knife didn't go that deep, an inch tops."

Still," I said.

"Fine." She pulled into the next gas station and opened her door.

"What are you doing," I said.

"Calling Dove an ambulance."

"Use this," I held out my cell.

"911 has caller I.D., Jo," she said, then ran to a pay phone at the corner.

Back when I took psychology, we were taught that fear can serve as an aphrodisiac. If I remember correctly, the theory was based on an experiment where interviews were held in the middle of a wobbly bridge over a deep canyon. Many of the interviewees became majorly attracted to the interviewer— and the researchers concluded that some people interpret fear as sexual arousal.

This may explain why Nicki and I barely got Dan'l's door closed before we tangled on the bed and went at it from all angles. If our previous night's sex had been a home run, this time we hit it clear out of the ballpark.

27

In the morning, Nicki asked if she could use my phone to call the shelter. "Dove may have gone there again looking for me," she said.

"Sure," I told her. "And you'd better make an appointment to have your car fixed." I dug in a bin under the bed. "Here's some rope. Use it to tie the passenger door to the seatbelt, so it'll stay closed."

"Thanks, Jo," she said with a kiss. "I don't know what I'd do without you."

"I think you'd do all right," I said. "While you're on the phone, I'm going to take a cup of coffee to Jenny, Rube's employee. I see her truck parked at the side of the building."

"OK," she said, punching in numbers.

Jenny was oiling parts at one of the workbenches. "Hey, Jo," she said. "Whose car's in the driveway, and what on earth happened to it?"

"It belongs to a friend of mine; she had a fender bender. I'll bring her in to meet you when she's off the phone."

"I'd like that. I looked for you yesterday when I was here working. Thought we might go for a bite."

"I went to up to the hospital."

"Yeah, Rube told me when I called her. Doesn't she look a whole lot better?"

"Sure does," I said, wishing I had the courage to ask Jenny about the "Us Forever" photo. In spite of what Rube had said about never writing on photos, I had a hard time believing it wasn't her in the photo. A chilling thought came to me. What if it *was* a photo of Rube, and Jenny had stolen it and written the "Us Forever" herself? How creepy would that be? I'd simply have to find it again and show it to Rube. "Are you going to be around at lunchtime?" I asked.

"I will," Jenny said, "but I won't be able to leave. Two guys are coming for their motors this afternoon, so I'll have to work right through."

"I'll be glad to fetch you a burger or something," I said, figuring I could ask to use her truck, which would give me a chance to filch the photo.

"Thanks, but I bought a sub on the way in. How about dinner? Is your friend going to be around?"

My friend. Bingo! "Maybe. I'll go ask her."

When I entered the motor home, Nicki was searching through my drawers. "Don't you have anything but T-shirts?" she asked.

"There's a couple of tanks."

"That won't help—I need something to wear to work. All my blouses are dirty, even the ones at the shelter. Well, this one might do," she said, holding up one of my new Wal-Mart shirts. "Can I borrow it?"

"If you do me a favor, you can have it for keeps," I told her.

"What kind of favor?"

"Go into the workshop and introduce yourself to Jenny. Then keep her talking."

"Why?"

"I want to look for something in her truck."

"Without her knowing? What is it?"

"I'll tell you later," I said. "Just do it."

"I haven't got time to mess around, Jo. The coast is clear at the shelter, and Phyllis said she'll help me with the restraining order if I come in right now."

"I only need 10 minutes. And not only will I give you the shirt, but I'll take you out tonight for the best fish sandwich in these parts."

"You've only been in these parts a week. How would you know what's the best?"

"Week and a half. Will you do it?"

"OK. But 10 minutes and I'm out of here."

"Deal." I waited until the shop door closed behind her, then ran to the truck. If Jenny stayed by the workbench, she wouldn't be able to see me through the window on this side of the building, but just in case, I kept my body low.

The driver's door eased open with only a few small clicks and creaks. *So far, so good.* Then I pulled the seat-adjustment lever, and the seat flew forward with a loud thunk. Silently cussing, I dropped to the ground and rolled under the truck. When Jenny didn't run outside, I rolled back out and wasted precious seconds picking gravel out of my skin.

The photo wasn't under the jack, where I'd wedged it. I peered under the seat and spent a couple more minutes coaxing out a piece of paper that looked to be the right size. It turned out to be a receipt dated June 7, 2002 for a $200 anchor. I'd had no idea anchors were so expensive.

I shoved the seat to its original position and, stretching across, opened the glove compartment. Jenny's camera was in there, along with a roll of duct tape and two screwdrivers, but no photo. I was easing it shut when I felt a tap on the back of my leg. "Shit, Nicki," I hissed when my heart slowed down.

"I'm sorry, Jo, but I'm leaving now," she whispered. "I thought you'd like to know."

"OK. I'm done anyway." I didn't want the truck door to slam, so I left it slightly cracked, hoping Jenny wouldn't notice.

"Did you find it?" Nicki asked, as I walked her to her car.

"No."

"So what were you looking for?"

"I think Jenny may have taken a photo that doesn't belong to her."

"A photo? Big whoop," she said. "I like her, she's nice. She's going to treat us to dinner tonight, so I'll take a raincheck on the fish sandwich. I'll be back here about 5." After I helped her tie up the mangled door, she gave me a quick kiss and took off.

I went back to Dan'l, opened him up to the fresh air, and surveyed the damage from our lovemaking. The sheets were pulled out and twisted, and a couple wet spots hadn't completely dried. I remembered waking up cold in the wee hours and feeling around for the blanket. Now I saw why I couldn't find it; it was bunched up under the pillows. I replaced the sheets with clean ones, put Nicki's mug in the sink, and folded a dirty shirt she'd dropped on the floor. I decided if she was going to be staying with me, she'd need a lesson in tight-space living.

When the place was shipshape, I sat down and opened Weezie's notepad to the Honey Lou Tree. It had been a while since I'd updated it. First I added A.K.A. JED PROUST, APPLIANCE THIEF to Ralphie the Third's branch and crossed off his PRETTY GOOD ALIBI.

I also added a twiglet to the Rube twig and named it BETH FROM EL RENO, ALSO MISSING. I was finding it hard to believe that when two women each had sex with a third and subsequently disappeared, it wasn't somehow related.

I added one more branch to the tree, writing in tiny letters to make it fit: ROYALE BOSCO, STILL IN MONTANA. Sylvie might know, but if I called her, she'd probably just say, "Why, Jo, are you still here?"

I turned to the CLUES page. There were still only three clues there:

1) H.L.'S HUSBAND BAXTER IS ABUSIVE.

2) RITA KANE PICKED UP H.L. FROM RUBE'S PLACE WEDNESDAY MORNING, ALTHOUGH RITA DENIES IT.

3) BAXTER RAN A CLASSIFIED AD IN THE NEW SCOTIA NEWSPAPER. THIS COULD MEAN HE'S INNOCENT. OR NOT.

I tried to think of another clue to keep them company but couldn't.

I decided to try another tack. Flipping to a clean page, I wrote at the top UNSOLVED MYSTERIES. I figured that naming it after the TV show would serve as a reminder that even real detectives didn't crack all their cases on the first try.

The first unsolved mystery was WHERE IS HONEY LOU? The likelihood of solving that one was getting dimmer by the minute.

Number two was WHO WAS DRIVING THE RAM BOAT? I had a personal interest in this one.

Number three was WHAT HAPPENED TO THE PHOTO IN JENNY'S TRUCK? I had to admit that this mystery—and number four: IS IT REALLY A PICTURE OF RUBE?—seemed rather minor compared to the other two. Like Nicki had said, "Big whoop."

I optimistically drew lines after all four unsolved mysteries on which to write the answers when they presented themselves. Then, closing my eyes, I made a circle in the air with my index finger and stabbed the page. I opened my eyes. Ta-da! The lucky unsolved mystery for today was number two: WHO WAS DRIVING THE RAM BOAT?

In order to find the driver, I needed to find the boat, but I didn't have the foggiest idea where to look. The only place I'd seen a lot of boats was at the marina—it was a place to start, anyway. Since I'd never been there by land, I thought about asking Jenny for directions. But then I figured, the marina was on the lakeshore, and Rube's shop was on the lakeshore, so if I hugged the shoreline I'd find it, right?

Wrong. I drove Rube's truck down so many circle roads and hit so many dead ends, I thought I was in some kind of diabolical maze. *Just like my search for Honey Lou,* I mused as I turned around in somebody's driveway. A guy ran out of the house, shook his fist at me, and yelled, "Didn't you see the dead-end sign, asshole?"

"Obviously I didn't, shithead," I hollered from the safety of the air-conditioned cab. When I got back to the main road, I saw that some clever person had turned the sign so it now said the county highway was a dead end.

I finally stopped at a bait shop and asked for directions.

The other time I'd been to the marina, I'd been too stressed to notice what a pretty place it was. There were two peak-roofed buildings built on a rise and several low ones down by the water, all surrounded with stately oaks and delicate willows. One of the peaked buildings had LAKE EUDORA MARINA painted on it, and the other, MARINA SEAFOOD HOUSE, ALL FISH LOCAL. (If all the fish were local, shouldn't it have been called Marina Lakefood House?)

Farther up the hill was an inviting campground with a dozen or so RVs occupying its shady sites. If Rube got sick of me, I could move Dan'l over here and bug Jenny for a while—that is, if she turned out not to be a photo-stealing psycho.

I parked and walked around the buildings to the docks. Ten long piers reached out on the water, with boat slips on either side. About half the slips were occupied. To my left was a line of wider slips for party boats and houseboats. I scanned the houseboats for Jenny's homemade one and found it right away. The house part had been fashioned from metal sheets instead of the gleaming curved fiberglass of the others. Dozens of strings of flags in primary colors had been stretched from deck to roof and back, giving it a festive flair. *Someday I'll have a closer look at it,* I promised myself, *but today I'm here to look for the Ram Boat.*

Choosing a pier at random, I encountered a sign that said BOATERS ONLY AND THAT MEANS YOU. I changed my walk to a purposeful swagger, like at any moment I was going to jump on a boat and roar off.

What I was looking for, of course, was a long boat with a stark white exterior—this narrowed the odds to nine boats out of 10. Zero out of 10, however, were *smashed* white boats. At the end of the pier, I turned and sauntered back, like I'd had my boat ride and there was nothing to do for the rest of the day but sit at the Seafood House bar and ogle women.

As I swaggered up the next pier, I amused myself by chanting the fanciful names of the boats. *"Desmond's Dream, Lips Ahoy, Floatin' a Loan, Bikini Barge, Mom's Mink, Sunny Delight, Ramboat."* I skidded to a stop. *Ramboat?* It was too weird to be a coincidence—like Rube's two missing lovers, only more so.

The *Ramboat* was white and long. After glancing around to make sure no one was watching, I stepped over a knee-high chain and walked slowly around it on a narrow walkway. There was no visible hull damage. Could the boat have been repaired already? How many days had it been? Four? Was it possible to get fiberglass repaired in four days? I'd had some minor body work done on a motor home I briefly owned, and they kept it in the shop for three weeks.

I knelt and then lay flat on the walkway, staring at the gleaming hull, hoping to force one of those flashes of memory I'd been experiencing. None came.

Flipping through Weezie's notebook, I found the page where Nicki had written her work number. She answered on the second ring, "Oklahoma DMV, Nicki speaking.

"Nicki, it's Jo," I said.

"Who?"

"Jo. You know."

"Yes. I'm at the Lake Eudora Marina, and I've spotted a boat that could be the one that hit Rube and me. If I give you the name and numbers on its side, would you be able to trace the owner?"

"Probably," she said, "but if I was found out, I'd be in a whole lot of trouble."

"Forget it, then. I don't want to get you in trouble."

"That's OK, Jody. I'll do it for you. I'll be real careful."

"Thanks, Nicki, and would you mind calling me Jo instead of Jody? Everyone does."

"I noticed that you introduced yourself that way to...what was his name? Cyrus? But you know what? I like Jody better."

"I don't," said. "Jody's not my name. My name's JoDell, so I suppose I could have been a Jody, but I'm not. I'm Jo. I'm sorry, Nicki. I should have told you before."

She was quiet for a moment. Then she said coyly, "So what if I just call you sugarpot?"

"Sugarpot? I don't know." There weren't many pet names I tolerated, and I was pretty sure sugarpot wasn't one of them.

"You are a sugarpot, you know," she said. "You're one big pot of sweet, sweet sugar, and I just can't wait until tonight, can you?"

"Um…no. Are you sure they don't listen in on your calls?

"Who?"

"Your employers. They do that sometimes."

"Well, you should have thought about that before you asked me to do something that's completely against the rules. Maybe I shouldn't do it after all." She sounded truly annoyed.

"You know, Nicki, on second thought, I kind of like the name sugarpot," I said, wincing.

"Too late," she said. "You're going to have to beg."

"OK, I'm begging."

"Are you on your knees?"

"Yes. I'm prone, in fact."

"What's that mean?"

"Flat on my belly."

"Oooh. OK, give me the info."

Fifteen minutes later, she called back to give me the New Scotia address of Stephen Richter, *Ramboat*'s owner. I thought about phoning him but decided it would be better to go to his house in person—that way I'd know what he looked like in case I had to identify him in court. But it was a middle-aged woman in tennis whites who opened one of the mammoth carved double doors of the Richter domicile. When I asked for Mr. Richter she told me her husband was out of town.

"How long has he been out of town?" I asked.

She gave me that none-of-your-business look I was beginning to know so well. "Who did you say you were again?"

"The name's Jody Jones. My husband Archie and I were over at the Lake Eudora Marina yesterday where we saw your boat, *Ramboat*. That's your boat, right?"

"Yes. Is something the matter with it?"

"Not at all." I said. "It's a beautiful boat. What kind is it?"

"It's a 36-foot Baja."

"Thirty-six foot—that's about what we figured. How long have you had it?"

"Steve bought it sometime in the late '90s. Why do you want to know?"

"Well, let me tell you, Ms. Richter, Archie fell totally in love with it. He sent me over to ask how much you want for it."

"'Want for it?' It's not for sale. Wherever did you get the idea that it was?"

"Some guy at the marina told us."

"An employee?" she asked.

"He said he was. Could your husband have given him the impression it was for sale when he was up there Friday?"

"Steve couldn't have been up there Friday. He's been in Arlington for over a week. It was only Thursday, in fact, when I called the marina and told them to take the boat out of storage so it'll be ready whenever Steve wants it." She made a sour face, like she knew all about being ready whenever Steve wants it.

"I see," I told her. "By the way, I love the name *Ramboat*. How'd you happen to call it that?"

She gave a delicate snort. "My husband's in the military. He thinks he's Sylvester Stallone."

"He's in the military? Is there a base here?"

"There's a great big army ammunition plant south of town. Where are you from, anyway? Obviously not around here."

"Archie and I are from Little Rock, but we recently bought a house right on Lake Eudora—that's why we need a boat. So neither you nor your husband has taken *Ramboat* out on the lake this year?"

"Like I said, Steve's in Virginia, and I *never* take the wretched thing out. As far as I'm concerned, boating is nothing more than an invitation to nausea or sunburn or both. Goodbye, Mrs. Jones." She closed the enormous door in my face.

28

My innards were letting me know it was way after lunchtime, so I stopped at a diner and ordered a tuna sandwich. Since there wasn't anybody else in the place, the waitress had plenty of time to hang around my table and tell me about her little boy. Seems he was almost 2 but hadn't started to walk yet. "I've taken him to three doctors," she said. "Every one of them told me there's nothing wrong with him and he'll walk when he's ready, but when will he be *ready*?"

"Dunno," I said around a mouthful of sandwich.

"Meanwhile, my back is about to break in two from carrying him everywhere. He's like an *elephant*." She picked up my half-full glass and asked, "More root beer?"

"Sure," I told her.

When she returned, she said, "I'll bet he's getting back at me for having to spend so much time at day care. But I *have* to work, don't I? Boy, let me tell you, single parenthood is the pits."

"Does he talk?" I asked.

"Sure. I mean, it's 2-year-old talk. Nothing very deep."

"Have you asked him what the problem is?"

She stared at me. "Have I *asked* him?"

"Sure. It's worth a try."

"It never occurred to me. I mean, what does a kid know? But you're right, it's worth a try. I'll do it tonight. What are you, a psychologist or something?" A man wearing a suit emerged from the kitchen, opened the cash register, and started counting money. The waitress quickly busied herself wiping the table with a cloth that smelled of strong disinfectant and did nothing for my appetite.

"No. I'm not anything like a psychologist," I said.

"What do you do, then?"

"I'm a home health aide, but I'm between jobs right now."

She wiped closer to my plate and lowered her voice. "Well, don't bother applying at the bomb factory. They've been sitting on my application for five months."

"The bomb factory?"

"You know, the ammo plant."

"The army ammunition plant?" It seemed significant that this was the second time I'd heard about it in less than an hour. "Where is that located? I'm new in town."

"South of here off the main highway. Look for the sign. If you apply and they hire you, stop by and let me know, OK? I'll go and put in another application. They have their own day care, even. It would be so convenient."

"It's a big place?" I asked

"Huge. Acres and acres, with all kinds of buildings and a big woods where they let you come in and hunt deer, although I'm not sure they still do that—after 9/11, you know. Their security is real tight because they make everything—bombs, missiles, rockets. Last year a guy got killed out there by a bomb."

"Really? It went off?"

"No, it fell on him. They said it didn't have a fuse. But if there was a fire or something…" She shivered. I wondered if she was having second thoughts about working there.

The guy at the cash register cleared his throat. It may have been merely an innocent throat-clearing, but it acted on the waitress like a work whistle. She loaded a tray with condiment bottles and hurried around the place, trading full for empty. I paid and left, thinking maybe I'd come back tomorrow so I could find out what her kid said.

I decided to go out and have a look at the ammo plant, just in case hearing about it twice had been more than a coincidence. What if Honey Lou was trying to communicate with me from—I shivered—beyond the grave?

The plant entrance was about six miles south of New Scotia. I drove past slowly. It looked like I'd need to go down a long drive and through a well-guarded checkpoint to get in.

I made a U-turn and went past again, slower this time. I probably could have bluffed my way in, but I didn't like to mess around with the feds. My cousin Kimmy's mother took part in the women's Ban the Bomb march in the early '80s at the Seneca Army Depot, and she was sure the CIA was still keeping an eye on her. Who knows, maybe they were. Anyway, if Honey Lou really wanted me to investigate something at the ammunition plant, she'd have to be a lot less vague.

I couldn't think of anything else to do in New Scotia, so I drove back to the Lake Eudora Marina, sat on the pier, and stared at *Ramboat* for a while. If this, indeed, was the boat that hit the

Big Fix, who had been at the wheel? According to Stephen Richter's wife, it couldn't have been him. Had the boat been stolen, then? I wondered how hard it was to hot-wire one of these things.

The afternoon sun was beating on my head and arms, and the humidity was stifling. Circles of sweat dotted my T-shirt. My throat was parched. I pulled myself up and walked to the Marina Seafood House, taking a barstool as far away as I could get from four scruffy men who were standing around one end of the bar, laughing loudly. Paranoia told me it was me they were laughing at. Reason told me to get a grip.

The bartender was hunched on a stool by the cash register, his arms tightly folded, looking out a large window at the sparkling lake. He was a young man with a thick neck bulging over the collar of his red-and-white striped dress shirt. The garter on his sleeve suggested the outfit was a uniform and not his personal bad taste. The scene brought to mind something I once heard about Alcatraz, that every cell in the place had been given a great view of San Francisco so the inmates couldn't help but see what they were missing. On a nice day like this, the bartender must have felt just as deprived. He probably cheered up when it rained.

"Do you have root beer?" I asked when he finally noticed me and came over.

"Sorry, not much call for that. How about a Shirley Temple?"

"Sure," I said. When he brought it and asked for $5.50, I wished I'd asked for ice water. That might have only been $3.50.

He laid down the change for my ten and turned to leave, so I quickly said, "This is a nice marina. How many boat slips are here? Do you know?"

"How many in all?" he said, eyeing my $4.50 change.

I pushed it toward him. He palmed it and walked away but

came right back carrying his stool. Parking it across the bar from me, he said, "There are more than 300 slips, and by July they'll all be full. Every day now more boats are showing up."

"It must take a lot of employees to look after them."

"Yes, it does," he said. "Why, you looking for a job?"

"As a matter of fact, yes," I said. "I put in my application in at the ammunition plant, but they haven't called." I sipped my syrupy drink through the miniature straw so I wouldn't get a pink mustache. *Got Shirley Temple?*

"I hear they've slowed their hiring way down," he said. "Maybe you'll get lucky and our government will invade another country."

I couldn't tell if he was kidding or not so I snickered and said, "Yeah, maybe."

"So what kind of work do you do?" he asked.

"I'm good with motors. Do you know if they have any openings in the repair shop?"

"I don't think so. There's four of them there already, and they've all been here for years. Never hurts to put in your application, though."

"Thanks. I'll do that."

The men down the bar exploded in hilarity. One of them laughed so hard he knocked over a stool. The bartender shook his head. "Those guys come in here all the time, swapping stories. They're catfish noodlers."

"They're what?"

"They noodle for catfish. That means they jump in the water and stick their hands in holes where catfish hide. When the catfish bite, they pull them out."

"The fish bite their hands?" I looked at him in horror.

"Yeah. It's a real art. Not too many can do it anymore, but the ones that do get enormous fish, 50 pounds and up."

I stared at the men. Their clothes were creased and mis-shapen, like mine had been after my dunk in the lake. Two of them had duct tape wound tightly around their right hands. "Seems like a tough way to catch a fish," I said.

"Tough and dangerous. There can be snapping turtles and snakes in those holes. Ready for a refill?"

"No, thanks," I said sincerely.

Back at Rube's truck, I leaned against its warm side, took out my cell phone, and called information for the marina's number. After punching it in, I could hear a phone ringing through the building's open windows. The ringing stopped abruptly and a man's voice barked, "Marina."

"This is Mrs. Stephen Richter," I said. "Can you tell me if our 36-foot Baja is ready for use? I called in the order last Thursday."

"Hold on a minute." This was followed by the sound of flipping papers. If I had walked over to the window and looked in, I could have watched him flip. "OK, Mrs. Richter," he said, "your boat's been tuned, gassed up, and lake-tested. When you come out, just stop by the office for the key."

"That's great," I said. "Would you mind telling me which mechanic worked on it? We'd like to thank him in some *small* way." No need to get anyone's hopes up.

"Let me check who signed the order... Looks like 'G.P.'— Gus Peavey."

"Thanks so much. Is Mr. Peavey working today?"

"I believe he is. Would you like me to transfer you to the repair shop?"

"No. I'll catch him later. Thanks so much. Goodbye."

Gus? I thought. *Gus Peavey had access to the Ramboat and a reason for having it out on the lake? What possible motive could he have for hurting Rube? I should call Rube and ask.* The phone in hospital room rang nine or 10 times before it was picked up and immediately hung up again.

I hit redial. This time it was picked up right away. "Rube?" I quickly yelled. "Is that you? Are you all right?"

"She's out of the room, for goodness sake," said an unfamiliar voice. "How long were you planning to let it ring *this* time?"

"Are you the nurse?" I asked.

"No."

"A nurse's assistant?

"No."

How many guesses do I get? "Is this her roommate, Penelope?"

"Yes, it is, but not for much longer."

"Oh, that's right," I said, "she told me she's coming home tomorrow."

"Are you one of those...friends?"

"Yeah, this is Jo."

"Oh, *that* one. Well, Jo, she has some kind of infection. That's where she is now, down for tests."

"Oh, no."

"They told her she'll have to stay until it's under control."

"Then why won't you be her roommate much longer?" I asked.

"I've put in for a transfer," she snapped and hung up before I could ask her to have Rube call me. I thought about calling back but really didn't want to.

I walked down to the dock, where I'd noticed a long, low building with the sign MARINA REPAIR above its door. The door was open, so I stepped in. It was too dark to see anything, but I could hear pounding from a couple of directions. As my eyes adjusted, I saw the place was an overgrown version of Rube's shop, full of boats and dismantled motors. The sound of at least one running motor bounced off the walls. Neon shop lights spotlighted two men busy at workbenches on opposite sides of the room. One was a burly guy whose black hair hung four inches past his collar. The other was a slight fellow with round shoulders. I wended my way through the nautical maze toward the round shoulders. "Gus?" I said.

He stepped out from under the light. "Jo?" he said, surprised. "Is something wrong with Rube? Or Jenny?"

"No," I said, "I just happened to be over here today and thought I'd look you up."

He smiled and wiped his hands on his coveralls. "Well, great. How about I take a break, and we go have a drink?"

"I'm not thirsty," I said, although the Shirley Temple had left me thirstier than ever.

"Then how about I show you around the marina? Or has Jenny already done that?"

"No, this is my first time here. I'd be very interested in seeing it."

"Give me a few minutes to wash up, and I'll give you the grand tour. Back in a few, Harve!" he yelled to the other side of the room.

"Gotcher fuckin' ass," Harve yelled back. Then he noticed me and said, "Oh, sorry."

While Gus hit the men's room, I hurried over to the docks, mulling over the fact that he hadn't acted like a person who had anything to hide. But of course, I was good at that too. What I really wanted was to watch his face when he got to the *Ramboat*. Would he look sly? Guilty? Would he rush on by?

"Shall we start with the boater's lounge?" he asked when he joined me. "It's real nice." He had removed his coveralls and looked clean except for the grease under his fingernails.

"I'm a little strapped for time, Gus. Why don't you show me some of the boats?"

"I'd have thought you would have had your fill of boats from staying over at Rube's."

"I'll never get my fill of boats," I gushed.

"Then why don't we go over to the houseboat area? Rube hasn't got anything so big over to her place. I can show you Jenny's."

"Is it the one with all the flags?" I pointed.

"That's it. Want to see it? She wouldn't mind, and I have a key."

"I'd like to do that if we have time. But first, why don't you show me these boats right here?" I started down *Ramboat's* pier. "What's the story with this one?" I pointed to a boat with a deck so long, it would fit a bowling alley.

"That belongs to a judge," he said, "and the *Carver* next to it belongs to some old rock star, can't remember which one."

I kept asking questions as we moved down the pier, Gus answering me amiably, until finally we reached *Ramboat*. "What about this one?" I asked him. "It's a perfect size for *hitting* the waves, don't you think?" I watched intently, but he didn't even blink.

"That's a Baja," he said, "and you're right, she's a real nice craft."

I waited for him to hurry me to the next one, but he didn't. We just stood there staring at the Baja like it might be about to produce baby Bajas. Finally, I said, "*Ramboat* is an odd name, isn't it? Do you happen to know who owns it?"

"No, I don't. Their name was probably on the work order, but I didn't pay any attention."

"You worked on this boat?"

"Uh, no, I didn't."

"I thought you said you had the work order."

He looked at me out of the corner of his eye. "I didn't say I *had* the work order, I just *saw* it," he said. It was the same ploy Flo had used when I'd asked her about my missing cell phone, and I didn't believe him any more than I believed her. I suddenly felt nervous. "I'd better go," I told him.

"Already?" he asked. "Let me at least show you the marina building. That's where the lounge is. It's right on your way to the parking lot."

I couldn't think of a reason to refuse, so I said, "OK, if it won't take too long."

The inside of the marina building looked like a ski lodge, with upholstered furniture arranged around a massive fireplace. I told Gus it was very nice.

"The store's up front here if you need any supplies," he said, leading me through an archway. He dragged me up to the counter and introduced me to the clerk, an old guy wearing a shirt printed with the slogan A BAD DAY BOATING IS BETTER, ETC. ETC. Since the guy had a pile of work orders next to his cash register, I shook his hand without saying anything. I was afraid he might notice that Jo Jacuzzo had Mrs. Stephen Richter's voice.

As we were about to leave, the clerk said, "Oh, by the way, Gus, the owner of that Baja you worked on Friday just called. She's going to be thanking you in person." He jingled some change in his pocket.

Gus turned red, mumbled goodbye, and was gone.

29

When I got back to Rube's, a note had been stuck under Dan'l's windshield wiper:

Jo: Rube called from the hospital. She's got a bad infection, so I've gone to see her. Sorry won't be able to eat with you and friend. Rain check? —Jenny

Damn, I'd planned to call Rube about Gus! Even if she felt well enough to talk about him, I sure didn't want her doing it when Jenny was sitting right next to her. Another thing I wanted to ask was if I could use her shower and washing machine again. Deciding she'd say, *Sure, Jo, go ahead,* I tried keys from her ring in the back door until one fit and turned.

When I was clean and dressed, I threw my sweaty clothes and the love-stained sheets in the machine with a good dose of detergent.

Then I practiced guitar while waiting for Nicki to come home. It sounded so good in my mind, I said it out loud, "Waiting for Nicki to come home." Then I set it to music. "Turn on the stove, throw the dog a bone, just a'waitin' for my Nicki to come home."

I was trying to figure out the chords when my cell phone rang. It was Nicki, and she wasn't coming home. All four tires on her car had been slashed in the DMV parking lot.

"It's got to be Dove getting back at me for stabbing her," she said. "The cops are filling out a report as I speak. Then when they're done, I've got to get a tow."

"Can't you leave your car in the lot overnight?" I asked.

"I guess I could. Why?"

"I'd feel better if you let me pick you up. Who knows what else she's planning to do with that knife."

"But sooner or later I've got to get some tires," she said.

"Don't get them now. She might come back tomorrow and slash the new ones. I'll come get you and take you to work in the morning. You can worry about the tires then."

"OK," she said. "Pull up to the door like yesterday. I won't come out till you get here."

As I stopped as close as I could get to the DMV's door, I glanced around for Dove's pickup. The image of her spearing those tires with the bloodstained switchblade was creeping me out. Nicki appeared and looked around in all directions before making a dash for Rube's truck. Her hands were shaking so hard, she had a tough time getting her seatbelt fastened.

"How are you doing?" I asked.

"OK, I guess. The cops called to tell me they went to Dove's house, but she wasn't home. They said I should be careful."

"We will be careful," I told her. "By the way, Jenny's rescinded her supper offer. Shall we pick up a pizza or something?"

"I'm way too upset to eat," she said. "I wish we could get in that motor home of yours and just take off."

I shrugged. "Why can't we?"

"I thought you were still looking for Honey Lou," she said.

"I've about given up. I did promise Weezie I'd give it a few more days, but she'll understand. What about your car, though? And your job?"

"I don't care about that wreck of a car, and I can always get another job, but I sure would like to get my paycheck. How about if we plan on leaving Friday night?"

"Fine with me," I said.

She undid her seatbelt long enough to plant a big one on my cheek. "Thanks, Jo," she said. "Now I'm hungry. Why don't we go get that best fish sandwich in the area?"

"I don't think I want to go to that place tonight," I told her. "You never know who you might run into."

"Are you talking about Dove?" she asked.

"No."

"Who, then?"

"This guy you haven't met—it's a complicated story. Say, how would you feel about getting the best chicken-fried steak in the area instead? My friend Weezie says it is, anyway. Only problem is, it's in Tulsa."

"As far as I'm concerned, the farther we get away from here the better."

"My sentiments exactly," I said.

After we ate, I called Weezie from a booth at the Oil City Grill. "You're right," I told her. "The chicken-fried steak here is delicious. I even liked the okra. It's *sweet*."

"I knew you'd like it," she said.

Nicki grabbed the phone. "I liked it too, Weezie. Thanks

for making Jo bring me here... I'm Nicki, Jo's lover."

I tried to get the phone back, but Nicki jumped out of the booth, saying, "You mean she didn't tell you?" She stood on the other side of the restaurant and chatted with Weezie for five minutes before coming back. Finally, after saying "See you in about a week, then," she handed me the phone.

"What's all this?" Weezie asked me. "I send you to Oklahoma to find my woman and instead you find your own?"

"Yeah, I don't know how that happened," I told her. "You can have this one, if you want."

Nicki whacked me with a spoon.

When we woke the next morning, Jenny's truck was parked in its usual spot alongside the shop. Before taking Nicki to work, I ran in to ask how Rube was doing.

"She's more frustrated than anything," Jenny said, "but the doctor thinks a few days of big-bullet antibiotics will take care of the infection."

"Good to hear. I thought I might go see her this morning."

"She'll like that. Tell her I'm thinking about her," she said.

"You're not going over there today?"

"No, I got too much work here. My unexpected jaunt yesterday put me way behind—I'll be lucky if I finish up by 10 tonight," Jenny said, looking around the shop. Then she looked me in the eye and said, "Sorry about missing our meal together. I was looking forward to getting to know Nicki. How about if we try again Sunday?"

Nicki and I would be halfway to New York by Sunday, but I didn't tell her. I was afraid she might pass the information on to her buddy Gus, and I didn't want him knowing that much about my itinerary. "Sunday sounds good," I told her.

On the way to the DMV, Nicki grimaced and said, "I hope

nobody notices I'm wearing what I wore yesterday. When you pick me up this afternoon, you'll have to take me to the shelter for my clothes, and then maybe we can stop at a laundromat so I can wash them."

"Rube's got a washing machine," I told her, "if you don't mind hanging them out on a...oh, shoot."

"What's the matter?"

"I put a load in yesterday afternoon just before you called. I forgot all about it."

"Well, you'd better have them out before I get back or I'll make you take me shopping for new clothes," she said.

I shook my head. "Sorry. I've used up my mall time for the rest of my life. I've used up my shelter time too. Why don't you just let me loan you another T-shirt?"

"No, thanks. The last one itched." She did the usual scan for Dove's truck and got out.

Penelope Wooster must have got her transfer—her bed was empty and stripped. The dividing curtain was pushed back, and Rube was lying flat on her back, staring at her IV bottle. "Good morning," I said in the cheery tone I reserve for the sick and injured.

She barely turned her head. "Oh, hi, Jo," she said. "You're an early bird this morning."

"I forgot it was so early. Do you want me to come back later?"

"No, it's all right. Have a seat."

"I'm sorry about your infection."

"Yeah, me too. I am *so* sick of this place."

"I'll bet you are." I tried to think of something optimistic to say, but all I could come up with was, "Your truck's running really good."

"Is it? Maybe someday I'll get to drive it again." She didn't sound like she had much hope.

I decided to get to the meat of the matter. "Rube, I need to ask you something."

"What?" She pushed a button on a remote control and the head of her bed started rising.

"How do you get along with Gus Peavey?"

"All right, I guess. I don't see that much of him."

"Would he have any reason to hurt you?"

For the first time since I walked in the room, she looked directly at me. "Hurt me? Why would he want to do that?"

"That's what I'm asking you. Maybe he's got a crush on Jenny, for instance, and he's jealous of her friendship with you, something like that."

"That's ridiculous, Jo. Gus is happily married. Whatever gave you that silly idea?" She smacked the sheet with her hand. If my silly idea had been sitting there, it would be dead.

"The thing is," I said, "I've been nosing around at the marina, and I found a boat that might be the one that hit us. The owner's been out of town, and Gus is the repairman who worked on it, so I thought…"

"Forget it, Jo," Rube said. "Gus would have no reason in the world to hurt me."

"What if the marina paid him to put you out of business?"

She gave a bitter laugh. "Yeah, the marina considers me a real threat. I'll bet they paid Jenny to wreck my shop while I'm in the hospital too."

"No," I said.

"It doesn't add up, Jo. Anyway, how do you know the boat you found is the one that hit us?"

"It's called *Ramboat.*"

She laughed hysterically. *Wonderful, I cheered her up after all.* After wishing her a speedy recovery, I left. I hadn't driven more than two blocks from the hospital when my cell phone rang. It was Rube.

"I'm sorry, Jo," she said. "I know you're just trying to help. This infection thing has me really bummed out, and I'm afraid I took it out on you."

"That's probably it," I said.

"You left in such a hurry, I didn't get a chance to tell you I've been thinking about that photo, the one you think is of me. Do you remember what I—the person in the photo was wearing?"

"It was a head shot, so all I could see was the top of a V-neck sweater."

"What color?"

"I think it was light brown or beige. And your hair was longer than it is now. It was pushed behind your ears."

"Was the inscription on the photo 'Us numeral-4 Ever'?" she asked.

"Yes, that's it. 'Us 4 Ever'—that's exactly it. So it *was* you, wasn't it, Rube? I knew it. Now I can cross it off my unsolved mystery list."

"Don't cross it off quite yet," she said.

"Why not?"

"That picture was taken for our high school yearbook when I was a senior. All four of us Little Dutch Girls exchanged prints, and we wrote the same thing on all of them: 'Us 4 Ever.' It was so long ago, I'd forgotten about it."

"So the only people who got those signed photos of you were Rita and Weezie and Honey Lou?"

"Yes. I can't imagine how Jenny would come to have one."

"Is there any chance she could have gotten hold of Rita's?" I asked.

"She doesn't know Rita. I'm sure of it."

"And she sure doesn't know Weezie." I said. "So I guess that leaves Honey Lou."

Rube was quiet for a while. Finally she said, "Where did you say you saw the photo, Jo? In Jenny's truck? We've got to alert...somebody." She wasn't ready to say "the police."

"It was in her truck when I saw it, but it's not there now—I looked. She must have put it somewhere else."

I heard her take a deep breath. Then she said, "You've got to find that photo, Jo. You've *got* to."

30

There were a lot more people milling about the marina today. I parked Rube's truck in one of the RV spaces on the hill and walked down to the dock, hitting it on the other side from the repair shop—I didn't want to take a chance on running into Gus.

A party of four was heading for the houseboat pier, so I joined them, staying far enough behind that they wouldn't feel threatened.

As I approached the flag-decked box Jenny called home, I saw that its front had been fitted with a sliding glass door. Next to it was a ladder leading to the roof, where she had mounted the steering column and a bench seat. Behind the seat was a row of storage bins, probably for PFDs and such.

The short ramp that led to the boat wasn't chained, so I

strolled across like I was an invited guest. Now came the hard part: making my foot actually step on the boat. *What? Are you crazy?* my foot cried. *I thought you said we were never leaving solid ground!*

This boat's not going anywhere. It's as good as solid ground, I told it.

Yeah, sure, the foot said, reluctantly stepping on the deck.

The sliding glass door was firmly locked. Peering through it, I could see a window on the opposite wall, and it looked to be partly open. Bending to avoid being decapitated by the string of flags, I maneuvered to the back.

The window wasn't large, as windows go, but I'd always been good at getting through small spaces. Problem was, *this* small space was covered by a screen on a sturdy aluminum frame. After looking around to make sure nobody was watching, I took a dime from my pocket and used it to remove the screws. Then I traded the dime for a quarter and pried at the corners of the frame. Unfortunately, by the time I got it completely free, it was bent into a shape that might fit a window in a geodesic dome. In a panic, I threw the whole thing in the water and watched it sink.

Shoving the window all the way open, I started pushing myself through. The shoulders were a tight fit, but once they'd made it, the rest of me followed like I'd been greased. I landed heavily on my sore arm. After rubbing it for a while, I got up and looked around.

The inside of the box had been paneled in white cedar edged with powder-blue molding. The blue was picked up in a round braided rug in the middle of the wood parquet floor. Mom and Rose would have called it *cozy*.

Jenny had furnished the place with a cedar chest, a small table with two pine spindle-back chairs, and a built-in bunk with drawers below. Her kitchen consisted of a microwave and a small refrigerator on a long counter. Underneath were some drawers and two cabinets. In place of a sink, a blue vinyl dishpan hung on the wall next to a cat clock that ticked the seconds away with its pendulum tail. Also on the wall was a pine-framed mirror with a row of hooks that were empty, save for a short-billed hat with gold trim, like Captain Stubing's on *The Love Boat*.

A Porta Potti with a blue padded lid was snugged into one of the corners, and a clothes rod had been mounted in the opposite corner, turning it into an open closet. Jenny had done a lot with a little, I had to give her that.

I knelt in front of the bunk and pulled out a drawer. I was sorry to see that everything in it was neatly folded—it would have been a lot easier to restore a mess. One by one, I shook out each shirt and pair of shorts, checked the pockets, and carefully refolded it. I did the same with the contents of the underwear and sock drawers and a long drawer that held sweaters and sweatshirts.

In the cedar chest were linens and four hard-back books lying spine-up between the tidy piles. Two of the books were about boats, one was a history of the Civil War, and the last was a Bible. I turned the boating and war books upside-down and riffled the pages, but nothing fell out. When I shook the Bible, however, three newspaper clippings floated to the floor, each of them about a different woman who was missing. I had never heard of two of the women, but both of them had worked at the army ammunition plant in New Scotia. The third missing woman was Beth Witherspoon of El Reno. According to the article, she'd never returned home from a weekend trip—but her car had been parked in her driveway.

I thought about sticking the clippings in my pocket, but decided not to. I was here for Rube's photo, nothing else. I'd tell Rube about the clippings, of course, but without further evidence, they would prove nothing except I had been trespassing in Jenny's houseboat.

After taking the linens from the chest and shaking them out, I did my best to return them to the mathematical perfection with which they had been folded, but they'd somehow grown thicker—in order to get the chest latched, I had to sit on it.

I searched through the bedclothes, under the mattress, and in the pillowcase. I checked the pockets of the hanging clothes. I took the utensils out of the kitchen drawers and looked under the linings. I emptied the cabinets of cans, dishes, and pans. Before putting the cans back, I carefully inspected them, in case Jenny had one of those soup-can safes I'd seen in the Harriet Carter catalog. They were all bona-fide cans.

I checked the refrigerator—it was empty except for 10 cans of Mountain Dew. The wastebasket was empty too, but I checked under the plastic liner. I even looked behind the mirror, clock, and captain's hat, and lifted the lid on the Porta Potti.

The weird thing was, I didn't find one photograph in the whole place. According to Rube, Jenny was always taking them. She'd even taken one of me.

Standing in the middle of the braided rug, I made a full turn, surveying the room for other places to search, but there weren't any, except... I leaned over and picked up the edge of the rug. My own face smiled up at me. I was sitting in a restaurant booth behind a plate that was empty except for a fish tail. The camera had been aimed so that I was over near the border, like a necessary evil. A grinning Rube was front and center.

Pulling the rug up more, I found a multitude of Rubes— Rube in her boat, Rube working in her shop, Rube swimming, Rube playing with an Irish setter.

I moved the photos on top in order to see the ones beneath, and suddenly there she was: the young Rube in a beige V-neck sweater, with the inscription "Us 4 Ever." I pulled it out and stuck it in my pocket.

As I was replacing the rug, the sliding door opened and Jenny stepped in, a pistol in her hand. I froze. I considered diving for the window, but by the time I got my shoulders through, my butt would be Swiss cheese. I had no choice but to try to talk to her.

With her unarmed hand, Jenny latched the door behind her. A length of line was coiled around her shoulder. "Hello, Jo," she said. "I *will* shoot if I have to."

I had no idea what to say. "Hello, Jenny" seemed understated, but "You'll never get away with it" was way too optimistic. I settled on "Nice place you got here."

"It *was*," she said. "What did you do with my window screen?"

"It fell in the lake. I'll be glad to pay for a new one." I reached for my billfold.

"Keep your hands where I can see them," she yelled.

"OK, OK!" I held them up, palms toward her.

"Better," she said, and pulled one of the chairs from under the table. "Sit down."

"No, thanks," I said.

She pointed the pistol at my thumping heart. "*Sit!*"

I sat.

"Now put your arms around the back of the chair," she said.

"Sorry, I can't. My arm is injured."

She stepped behind me and stuck the pistol barrel in my ribcage. It must have hit some kind of reflex point, because my arms flew back like they had minds of their own. Immediately, she wrapped line around my wrists and pulled it snug. I turned my head to try to see where she'd put the gun. "Eyes front!" she hissed, and gave the line an extra tug. Pain shot up my bad arm.

I tried to pull free, but it was hopeless: Not only had she tied my arms together, she'd tied them to the chair.

She crossed over to the silverware drawer and grabbed a butcher knife. *A butcher knife?* The optimist in me still thought I'd get out of here in one piece, but the pessimist in me started wondering if my affairs were in order.

"Don't get all upset now, Jenny," I said. "I came here because I wanted to ask you some questions, that's all. And I'm really sorry about the screen, but the place was so cute I simply had to see the inside."

"If you wanted to ask me questions, you knew perfectly well where I was. Can you imagine my surprise when Gus called me at Rube's and said he saw you crawling through my rear window?"

"Where was he? I didn't see him."

"Obviously." She tested the edge of the knife with a finger and disappeared behind me again.

"What are you doing?" I braced myself for more pain.

"Relax, I'm cutting the rope," she said with a laugh.

"Rope?" I said. "I thought on a boat it was called line."

"On *you* it's called rope." She laughed again and came around to kneel at my feet. At the same time I got the idea to kick her, she moved to the side. Laying the knife and gun on the floor, she tied my ankles together.

"Too tight," I said.

'Too bad," she said, cutting off the excess line, rope—whatever. Then she stood and picked up the gun. I wriggled and flexed my wrists, trying to create some slack. How had Houdini done it? I wished I would have watched him closer in the film— but then, that was only Tony Curtis, wasn't it?

"Where *was* Gus when he saw me?" I asked.

"Working on a boat across the way."

"So are you and he in it together?"

"In *what* together?" She seemed genuinely puzzled.

"Jenny, I know Gus was driving *Ramboat* when it hit Rube and me."

"How do you know that?"

"He had access to it. His initials are on the work order."

"Of course they're on the work order. I put them there."

"You did? Why?"

"My friend Gus has a little drinking problem. He'd gone on a bender the night before and was sicker than a dog. I sent him here to sleep it off while I worked on his orders, signing his initials to them so he wouldn't get in trouble."

"Who ran into Rube and me, then? You?"

"I didn't know Rube was on board. I'd just finished working on *Ramboat* when she called to say she was sending you over in the *Big Fix* to borrow a Johnson manual. *Sending* you, she said, not *bringing* you. I didn't know she was down in the cuddy."

"So it was *me* you were trying to kill?"

"Of course."

"Why?"

"You know why," she said.

"No, I don't."

"Well, you *should.*"

I turned my head so she wouldn't see the tears gathering in my eyes. I was terrified—and confused. This woman clearly wasn't playing with a full deck. I tested my bonds, but they were as tight as ever and my wrists were getting really sore. I blinked back the tears and said, "I should have suspected something when you weren't waiting on the dock with the manual, like Rube said you'd be," I said. "Where were you? Off hiding *Ramboat*?"

"Bingo! I took it up to my folks' house and threw a tarp over it. Then I borrowed a car and drove back to the marina. That's when Gus told me Rube had been hurt. I couldn't believe it. I'd never hurt Rube on purpose. Never."

"But how did *Ramboat* get fixed so fast? Did you do it?"

"Of course I did. After dark, I brought it here to the shop. It took me all night." She checked my knots and put the knife back in the drawer.

"What are you going to do with me?" I asked.

"Take you for a ride. Won't that be fun?" She took the captain's hat from the hook and put it on, looking in the mirror as she tucked stray hairs under the brim.

"Shouldn't I be wearing a PFD?" I asked.

Now she really laughed.

I wondered if anyone was close enough to hear if I screamed. But even if they were, it would have to be a horror-movie kind of scream, and I wasn't sure I could carry it off. I was rehearsing one in the back of my throat when Jenny stuck the gun in her waistband, cracked the door, and went out, locking it behind her.

Through the door's glass, I watched her throw off mooring lines and climb the ladder to the roof. Soon I heard a starter grind and catch. Dishes clattered in the cupboard, and the floor vibrated under my bound feet as the houseboat backed up and changed gears. *Hey,* my feet said, *you said this boat wasn't going anywhere. You said it's just like solid ground.*

So sue me, I told them.

Docked boats streamed past and disappeared, and a cool breeze from the open window bathed the back of my neck. It was time for that scream. I took a deep breath. *Eeeek!* As screams go, it was pitiful, a "Bee in my hair, get it out!" kind of scream. I took another breath, arched my back, and pretended I was Julie Harris in the original *The Haunting,* when she and Claire Bloom are alone in a locked bedroom with the lights out. Something bangs on their door. Then it bangs even louder. Julie shudders and hangs on to Claire's hand for dear life. Suddenly, Claire speaks to her from way over on the other side of the room. Whose hand is Julie holding? She screams, "AIEEEEEEEE!"

The volume was a lot better this time. Jenny stomped on the ceiling, so I did it again. And again.

In the course of arching my back, I discovered that the fingers on my right hand were able to reach into my rear pocket to the top buttons of my cell phone. With a great deal of difficulty, not to mention pain, I shoved them in far enough to push what I hoped was 911 and SEND. I couldn't hear if anyone answered, but in case they did, I yelled out my name and every particular I could think of that might help them find me.

Seventeen minutes later by the cat clock, the noise and vibrations stopped. Judging from my view of sky, water, and an extremely distant shoreline, we were somewhere in the middle of the lake.

Jenny climbed down the ladder and came back in, taking a can of Mountain Dew from the refrigerator. Sitting across from me, she laid the pistol on the table and popped the can's tab. "Shoot," she said.

I eyed the pistol, so close and yet so far. "Shoot?"

"You said you came here to ask me questions. So shoot." She took a long pull at the can.

The question on top of my mind was why she wanted to kill me, but I didn't want to enter that labyrinth again. Instead I said, "What did you do with Honey Lou Wright?"

"What I did with the horny Ms. Wright is the same thing I'm going to do with the horny Ms. Jacuzzo—I gave her a burial at sea."

"You killed her? Damn… Wait, what do you mean, 'horny Ms. Jacuzzo?'"

"You know what I mean," she said.

I wanted to scream, but I was all screamed out. "May I use

your toilet?" I asked. I didn't really have to go, but it was the only way I could think of to get untied. This time I'd kick her first and think later.

"No, sorry," she said. "Next question?"

"OK, *why* did you kill Honey Lou?"

Jenny leaned back in the chair and put her hands behind her head. "It all started when she and that blond bimbo showed up at Rube's that Tuesday evening…"

"The blond bimbo's name is Rita. I wonder if you know that Rita is Rube's ex-lover," I said.

She stared. "Rita too?"

"*Just* Rita. Honey Lou was only a friend."

"Then what was she doing in Rube's bed?"

"So it was *you* Honey Lou heard snooping around Rube's place that night."

"Sure, it was me," she said. "I left the shop after work like usual, but I went back later and peeked in the window. Honey Lou was going at Rube like an animal. It was shameful."

"Why was it shameful?"

"It's a sin," she said. "Haven't you ever been to church?"

"Yes. But they never said sex was a sin. If they thought that, where would they get the next generation of churchgoers?"

"You know what I mean," she said. "Same-gender sex is a sin and an abomination—it says so in the Bible. Leviticus 18:22—man shall not lie with man."

"So who's a man?"

"Leviticus meant man*kind*."

"You know Leviticus personally?" I asked, wishing I'd paid more attention to the Gay Pride speaker last year. She'd talked about exactly this thing, how religious homophobes zeroed in on that one verse while they totally ignored others with prohibitions against things like mixing fabrics and—oh, yeah, eating pork.

"Jenny," I said, "doesn't Leviticus tell us we shouldn't eat pork? You were putting those ribs away the other night like they were going out of style."

"Nobody's going to hell for eating pork," she said.

"How do you know? Anyway, you've committed a lot worse sins than eating pork. For instance, you bore false witness—isn't there something about *that* in the Bible?"

"What are you talking about?"

"Didn't you tell Rube a yellow car picked up Honey Lou that Wednesday morning, so she'd assume it was Rita's?" I asked.

"Well, yeah." She finally looked rueful. "I didn't like lying to Rube, but I couldn't have her suspecting me, could I?"

"OK, your friend Leviticus forgives you for that one," I said. "But you just told me you committed murder! I'm sure he wouldn't be happy about *that*."

"It was justified. Honey Lou was pure evil."

Tired of the holy histrionics, I got back to basics. "How did you manage to get her to come with you, anyway?"

"After Rube left that morning, Honey Lou came in the shop, and we got to talking. She told me she wanted to hide out from her husband for a while, so I said she could stay with me."

I looked around the tiny room. "Here?" I asked.

She laughed. "That's exactly what she said when she saw it. She didn't know she wasn't staying very long."

"How can you laugh?" I asked. "You *killed* her!"

She heaved a big sigh. Obviously Jenny didn't run into too many people as dense as me. "Like I told you, it was justified. She defiled Rube's body with her wantonness."

"You don't think Rube was a willing partner?" I asked.

"She's weak. She needs protecting from sexual predators like Honey Lou and you."

"Me?" It came out as a squeal.

She snorted. "Don't pretend you didn't sleep with her, Jo."

"I didn't!"

"I saw her leaving your recreational vehicle that morning."

"Which morning? You mean the morning after I arrived, when you waved to us from a boat? She brought me a cup of coffee, that's all." The light dawned. "Is that why you rammed the *Big Fix*? You were trying to kill me because you thought I was having sex with Rube?"

"Of course you were having sex with her. How could you *not* have sex with her?"

If my hands were free, I would have buried my face in them. "How terribly sad," I said.

"What?"

"You're in love with Rube, aren't you, Jenny?"

"Don't be ridiculous," she said

"I've seen you with her. You can't keep your hands off her."

"I don't know what you're talking about. I'm not a...*lesbian*." She spat out the word.

"No, you're not," I said. "Maybe you could have been, but something went horribly wrong. What you are is a killer. You killed Honey Lou, and you killed Beth, Rube's friend from El Reno."

"Oh, her," Jenny said.

"And what about those other two women? Did they have sex with Rube too?"

"What are you talking about?" Her pupils jerked in the direction of the chest.

"Yeah, I saw the clippings in your Bible. Two more burials at sea?"

"Those women were from way before I even knew Rube. But yes, they were sexual predators. I buried them on land. Government land, even," she said proudly.

"Government land? Like the grounds of the army ammunition plant?" *So that's what Honey Lou's ghost had been trying to tell me.*

"Sure. I used to work there. I probably couldn't get away with it today, with all the tight-ass security they have there now."

"Where on the grounds are they?" I asked in case 911 was listening.

She drained the soda can and said, "None of your beeswax."

"So altogether you've killed four women? Or are there more?"

"No, just four. Well, five with you."

"I'm not *dead*!" I cried. If I hadn't been tied to the chair, I would have dropped to my knees. "Please don't kill me, Jenny. I won't tell anyone. Let me go, and I'll get in my motor home and drive right out of Oklahoma. I'll never see Rube again in my whole life, honest."

"Sorry, Jo," she said, "I can't take that chance. By the way, where's the picture you stole?"

"What picture?"

"I saw you take a picture from under my rug. Where is it?"

Shit. "In my left pocket."

She stuck her hand in and drew out the photo. "Ah, *this* one. I should never have taken it from Honey Lou's purse, but Rube looked so young and innocent, I couldn't resist. What else have you got in there?" She took everything out of my pockets and stuffed it all back except the photo and my cell phone. Those she took outside and threw in the lake. Then she came back and said, "Come on, let's get this show on the road."

I was all argued out. My shoulders were on fire, my hands and feet were numb, and sweat was pouring out of every pore in my body.

And now I really did have to use her toilet.

31

Jenny hummed "Rock of Ages" while she opened a low kitchen cupboard and took out a bunch of cookware. After staring at it for a while, she said "Crap" and threw it all back in. Folding her arms, she looked at me. "How much do you weigh?"

"110, give or take," I said.

"I wonder how much weight I'll need to attach to your body to keep it from floating up."

"This chair should be enough," I said.

"What are you talking about? The chair's wood—it'll float. Anyway, it matches my other one. What about cans of food? I could probably tie them in a pillowcase." She opened another cupboard and surveyed her assortment of canned goods. "Nah, not enough. Unfortunately, I used my anchor on Honey Lou and haven't replaced it."

"You used a $200 anchor to weigh down a body?" I said. For Jenny, murder wasn't cheap.

She ignored me. "I got a bunch of heavy tools up on the fly-deck." Taking the pistol, she went outside and climbed the ladder. This time she left the door open. Cool air rushed in, and I inhaled it gratefully. Something else wafted in, a humming sound like the motor of a distant boat. *A distant boat!*

Ignoring shrieks from my shoulders, I scooted my rear toward the front of the chair. By pulling my upper body into alignment, I was able to stand on my bound feet in a hunched sort of way, the chair hanging from me like an awkward backpack. I took a little hop, but it made the boat bounce. Not a good idea.

The braided rug was about a foot behind where I'd been sitting. Executing a backward shuffle that would have won points in a ballroom competition—"Have you ever seen anything like that, Ginger?" "No, I haven't, Fred. How *nouveau!*"— I backed up and set the chair on it. Using my legs as levers, I pulled the rug, the chair, and me across the floor. Glancing back, I saw I was leaving a trail of photographs in my wake.

When I reached the raised doorsill, I stuck my head out and checked the ladder. Jenny wasn't in sight, and the distant hum didn't sound so distant anymore.

The coast was clear. It was now or never, do or die. I couldn't think of any more clichés, so gritting my teeth, I hoisted the chair and hopped over the doorsill. At that very moment, a leg was flung over the top of the ladder and Jenny started climbing down. She stopped in mid climb and stared at me. I took advantage of her stupefaction to take another hop, which brought me to the edge of the deck. Taking a deep breath, I leaned over the rail and rolled into the water.

I sank a few feet but bobbed right up. Jenny was right; the chair wanted to float. I heard an explosion and a splash. She was shooting at me! Forcing air from my lungs, I tried to make myself sink but couldn't.

She shot again and my ear exploded in pain. I gasped, taking in water. Without permission, my bladder started emptying. Choking and coughing, I tried to position the seat of the chair between me and the gun, but it was futile. Closing my eyes, I waited for the next shot, wondering if I'd hear it before it took me out.

The next sound wasn't a shot; it was the roaring of the houseboat's motor. I opened my eyes and watched it back up. There was a loud grinding of gears, and then it headed right for me. I flailed my bound feet, trying to kick out of its path. I could see the swirl of white bubbles generated by the churning blades between the two pontoons. Blades that could chop me into hamburger.

The houseboat moved over me, its broad bottom blotting out the sun. With a mighty effort, I pushed my arms backward, thrusting the chair at the approaching blades. There was an ugly crack as the wood shattered and my arms broke free. I dove under, and when I came up again, the houseboat was speeding away.

I gulped air and grabbed hold of the chair seat that was floating next to me, but now that I wanted it to hold me up, it wouldn't. "Damn you," I told it.

The boat that had scared Jenny off turned out to be the .Lake Patrol. After fishing me out, they applied first aid to my ear and wrapped me in a blanket. *Where did these people get all the blankets?*

One of the patrol guys told me my 911 call had got through. "Good going," he said.

"But Jenny's getting away," I told him.

"We radioed for another boat to take up the chase. They'll get her. That klunker is no match speed-wise for our boats."

"Did 911 hear the part where she admitted to killing four women?" I asked.

"I'm not sure what they heard, but it's all on tape."

"That's great," I said. My cell phone had finally paid for itself.

"Do I have to stay here for the trial?" I asked. "I was planning to go back to New York real soon."

"You can go after we record your statement, but you might have to come back," he said.

"OK, unless it's tornado season."

He laughed. "It's always tornado season."

While I was at the hospital getting my ear dressed, I stopped to see Rube.

"Jo, guess what?" she said. "They're letting me go home tomorrow! Fran and Cyrus are coming to pick me up." Then she *really* looked at me. "What happened to you?"

As I explained the day's events, the color drained from Rube's face. She sat for a moment, stunned into silence, then said, "I can't believe it. Jenny admitted to killing Honey Lou and Beth and those other women? And she rammed the *Big Fix*? And she shot at you? My God! Why?"

"She said it was to protect you, but I'm sure jealousy had a lot to do with it."

"There was no reason to be jealous. If she would have crooked her little finger…"

"She couldn't have. In her eyes, that would have been a quick ticket to hell."

She took a deep breath. "It's too horrible to think about," she said. "Why did I ever tell you to go looking for that photo?"

"But, Rube, the thing is, I found it! Just when I thought I was a complete bust as a detective, I found the photo, and because of it, I solved the whole mystery!"

"But you almost lost your life."

"Well, yeah, there is that," I said.

32

I used Rube's phone to call Nicki. "I'm leaving for New York today," I told her. "If you want to come, get a taxi and pick me up at the hospital."

She didn't ask how or why. She just did it. By bedtime, we were parked in a truck stop on the other side of Memphis. Nicki snuggled up to me and ran her hand across my breast, but I said, "Give it a few days," and moved to the cushions on the floor. "I'm so sore," I told her, "I'm like an exposed nerve."

"You *are* an exposed nerve," she said.

When I couldn't sleep, I took out Weezie's notebook, turned to the UNSOLVED MYSTERIES page, and took great satisfaction in filling in the blanks.

1) WHERE IS HONEY LOU? <u>AT THE BOTTOM OF LAKE EUDORA</u>

2) WHO WAS DRIVING THE BOAT THAT RAMMED US?
<u>JENNY</u>

3) WHAT HAPPENED TO THE PHOTO IN JENNY'S TRUCK?
<u>SHE HID IT IN HER HOUSEBOAT, AND NOW IT'S AT THE
BOTTOM OF THE LAKE WITH MY CELL PHONE AND HONEY
LOU.</u>

4) IS IT REALLY A PICTURE OF RUBE? <u>YES</u>

I still had room on the page, so I added:

5) WHO STOLE APPLIANCES FROM THE GREAT PROPHET
MALL AND MAY NEVER HAVE TO PAY FOR THE CRIME?
<u>BAXTER AND JED, A.K.A. RALPHIE THE THIRD</u>

On the morning of our second day on the road, Oklahoma
was in the news. A tornado had swept through the middle of
the state, destroying vehicles and structures and injuring people. I'd got out of their just in time.

I bought a phone card at a truck stop and called Rube at her
shop. She answered on the second ring. "Good, you made it
home!" I said. "Did you get any of those tornadoes?"

"No, that was all west of here. You *do* have a thing about
tornadoes, don't you, Jo?"

"Well, I can't deny I'll be glad to be back in tornado-free
Buffalo."

"Why don't you ever answer your phone?" she asked. "I
tried to call you quite a few times."

I had a vision of fish gathered curiously around my ringing
cell phone. "I forgot to tell you—"

She interrupted. "Jo, where's my truck?"

"Oh, geez! I'm sorry. It's in the RV area at the marina, if it
hasn't already been towed."

"Where are the keys?"

"Oh, geez! They were in my pocket when I hit the water and I haven't seen them since. They're probably down there with my cell phone. I'm sorry."

"Don't worry about it," she said. "I got another set."

"Good. How are you doing healthwise?"

"Not too bad. Fran waits on me hand and foot, and Cyrus is helping in the shop."

"Tell him I said hi."

"I will. One more thing, Jo. Where shall I send your laundry?"

"Oh, geez," I said again.

Nicki and I didn't talk much that day, just the basics. ("Next rest area, please." "Are we ever having lunch today?") We made it almost to Cleveland by midnight. In my younger, healthier days, I would have pushed it to Buffalo, but not this time, even with Nicki doing most of the driving. She pumped gas at a Flying J and found us a fairly level parking spot far away from the noisy semis. Then without saying good night, she turned her back on me and went to sleep, or pretended to. After a few minutes feeling guilty for not being what she needed, I downed a couple of pain pills and hit my cushions on the floor.

Mom and Rose were at work when we got home the next day. I didn't want to take up their spaces in the driveway, so I pulled as close as I could behind a neighbor's car parked in front of our house. Nicki and I unloaded our stuff—well, my stuff, really; she didn't have any stuff. As I slung my backpack over my shoulder, I realized I was feeling a lot better.

Up in my room, I flexed my arms, working the soreness out, stretching for the walls, the ceiling. When I was a kid I

stretched my arms toward the ceiling every morning, never doubting I'd be able to reach it some day. What a letdown when my growth ended with my fingertips barely touching the curtain rod.

Nicki took a shower while I unpacked. When she came back wrapped in a couple of towels, I grabbed my old flannel robe and headed for the bathroom. I hadn't even finished adjusting the water when she jumped in with me and started lathering my body, front and back, rubbing the hot water into all my tight muscles. As each released its tension, I sighed, and my breathing deepened. After rubbing me from head to toe, she put her arms around me and held me against her in the needle-sharp spray. I didn't feel it coming, but suddenly I was sobbing against her shoulder. When I looked up to apologize, I saw that she was crying too. We clung to each other while the water went from hot to lukewarm, then downright chilly.

We toweled down, and she led me back to the bedroom. I tried to remember how long ago I'd changed the sheets, but Nicki bypassed the bed and pushed my bare butt down on the desk chair. Then she knelt and kissed me everywhere, slowly and with great interest, as if she'd never seen or tasted a body before. "Oooh!" she said as she licked the underside of my knee, and "Mmm" while leisurely sucking my big toe. By the time she hit my quick, I was good and ready. The chair wheels squealed as my reflexes took over and I pushed again and again against her tongue. My last rational thought was *This chair could sure use some WD-40.*

I stood and eased Nicki onto the bed, where I returned the favor threefold. If the sheets hadn't needed changing before we started, they sure did after that. And noisy? Nicki amazed and delighted me with her vocal acrobatics. As her final "Oh, baby, baby!" was fading, I heard a faint "Jo?" from downstairs. I scram-

bled into my robe and went out on the landing. "Hey, Mom," I said, looking over the railing. "What are you doing home?"

"Mr. Wing called me at work. He said your motor home is sticking out into his driveway."

"Why didn't he call me?"

"He tried."

"Oh," I said, remembering a ringing phone we'd ignored about 30 minutes ago.

"Anyway, dear," she said, "I wanted to see you. Did you find Weezie's friend?"

"Sort of. I'll tell you about it after I get dressed."

"Good. I'll go make a pot of tea." She started for the kitchen, then turned back. "Is...is everything all right?" Then she stared past me and said "Oh," as if that explained everything.

Nicki joined me at the rail, dressed in a pair of my cutoffs and my purple muscle shirt. "Hi," she said to my mom. "I'm Nicki." I performed the rest of the introductions, and Nicki went down to have a cup of tea while I got myself together and went out to move Dan'l.

The following Sunday was Mother's Day. I got up early and wrote out a nice-size check to the New Scotia Women's Shelter, which boosted my self-esteem several notches. Then I went to the kitchen to make cinnamon toast, the breakfast-in-bed Mom had asked for every Mother's Day since I was 10 and tried to make waffles.

It was Mom's year to eat with Rose's family, so I got the job of ferrying Great-aunt Concetta to Mother's Day Dinner at my cousin Lorena's over near Rochester, a journey of close to 60 miles. I was glad I hadn't taken Dan'l out to hibernate at Uncle Greg's yet; I figured Great-aunt Concetta could sit in cushy comfort on the sofa bed, and even take a nap if the urge came

over her. But no such luck—she insisted on riding in the front with me.

When we left Buffalo, the sky was an ominous gray, and the wind was tossing plastic bags and pieces of paper all over the place. Every time a bag scudded across the road in front of us, Great-aunt Concetta screeched and grabbed my arm. It was a *long* 60 miles.

The wind was so fierce by the time we pulled in Lorena's driveway, Nicki and I had to hold on to Great-aunt Concetta to keep her upright.

We were in the middle of an excellent fried-chicken dinner when Lorena's next-door neighbor phoned to ask if we were aware there'd been a tornado warning issued for the immediate area.

Tornado! Forgetting what I'd read about staying away from windows, I got to one just in time to see a giant tree limb fall on Dan'l's windshield, shattering it and seriously denting the hood. My cousin Kimmy wasn't at all happy to have to drive Great-aunt Concetta home.

Nicki and I rode back to Buffalo in the tow truck, and I called Weezie to come pick us up at the garage. I'd been putting off telling her about Honey Lou, and I figured this was as good a time as ever. I was glad I had Nicki along to cheer her up, and, wow, she cheer her up. I'd never seen two people hit it off so well so fast. They chatted about New Scotia and Lake Eudora, and a lot of other places I'd never heard of. They made plans to get together to cook up some chicken-fried steak and okra, and, almost as an afterthought, invited me. Weezie even offered Nicki a job waiting tables at Marlo's Diner, and Nicki accepted with pleasure.

So it was no big surprise a couple of weeks later when Nicki gently asked if I would be really hurt if she moved over to

Weezie's place. I told her, "No, of course not. Go ahead," but I *was* hurt. Later, I realized it was more of a hurt ego than a hurt heart. I was fond of Nicki, of course, but to tell the truth, I found her a bit irritating. In any case, it was nice regaining control of my bedroom.

To her credit, Weezie later apologized to me, saying, "I couldn't help it, Jo. She's, you know, an Oklahoma girl."

I kept my lip zipped. If Nicki hadn't told Weezie she was an Ohio girl, I sure wasn't going to.

On Tuesday, I went to Bellefleur's Music and bought a guitar.

ABOUT THE AUTHOR

Anne Seale is the author of *Packing Mrs. Phipps: A Jo Jacuzzo Mystery*. A creator of lesbian songs and stories, she has performed on many gay stages, including the Lesbian National Conference, where she sang tunes from her tape *Sex for Breakfast*. Her stories have appeared in many anthologies and journals, including *Set in Stone*, *Dykes With Baggage*, *Wilma Loves Betty*, *Harrington Lesbian Fiction Quarterly*, and *Best Lesbian Love Stories 2003*, *2004*, and *2005*. She winters at an RV resort in Arizona and spends her summers in New York State.